Scions of the Aegean C
Descent into the Wilds

Book 1 of
the Scions of the Aegean C series

by Terry L. Craig

Wild Flower Press, Inc.
Leland, NC

Scions of the Aegean C
Published by Wild Flower Press, Inc.
P O Box 2532
Leland, NC 28451
www.wildflowerpress.biz

Paperback Version:
ISBN: 978-0-9909616-8-0

Dedication

To sisters everywhere, but particularly
to my precious sister, Jo Ann

To my beloved Bill
To my precious Lord

Have you ever felt truly ODD?

(A note from the author)

When I was a teen, adults would say to me, "These are the best years of your life!" and I would wonder (given the unhappiness of my daily existence) what horrors might await me in adulthood.

The good news is that my younger years were NOT the best years of my life (nor are they usually the best years of ANYbody's life). But back then, I had no way of knowing this. I lacked the ability to see that most people my own age were as lonely and felt as out of place as I did, and that FEW teens and young adults have the gift of being truly comfortable in their own skin. Most of us tip-toe, blunder, blindly plunge, bully, or fake our way through the maze that takes us from childhood to maturity.

As a girl, I knew the daily pain of feeling like I didn't belong anywhere . . . but lacked the desire to compromise my eccentric sense of "me" in order to fit in. I had little in the way of friendship or fellowship, no sense of community, and no long-term experience to draw upon, so I just crashed along in a continuing "now" with only my sense of "me" and the (limited) knowledge of what I wanted as guides. No life is without tragedies, but if I could have seen the road ahead from a higher vantage point, mine might have unfolded with fewer of them. Hence this story.

Although there is theological content in this series, it's primarily about the relationships that help to determine who we will become.

I will tell you that some of the more painful aspects of this series are reflections of situations in my own life—but so are some of the eventual triumphs. Although some of the plot lines weave around worldly deeds and hard realities, the ultimate themes of the series are unapologetically from God's redemptive perspective.

So . . . if you are truly odd, or one who is called to befriend odd people, I hope you will join me in the journey of this story and the series as it unfolds.

Terry L. Craig

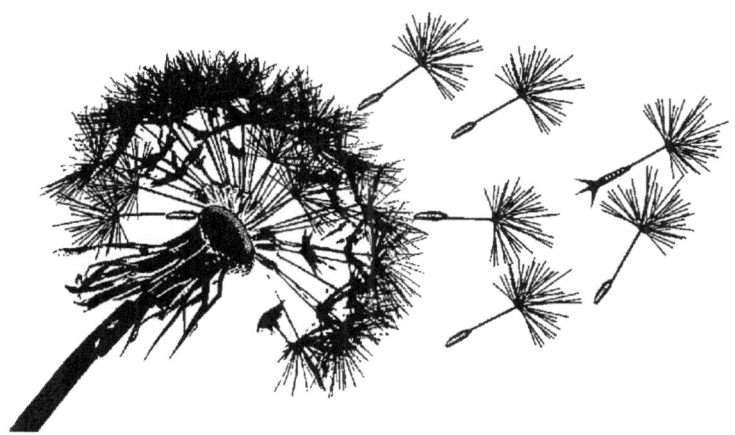

CHAPTER 1
Descent into the Wilds

"Humanity is sometimes like seeds, carried by the wind or in the belly of a bird to a faraway place. Yet God can still send the sun to shine upon them and waters to give them life, and some will survive to bear fruit."—*Joel of the family of Pel, a Firstlander and one of His people*

August 19, 2044, 15:15 Eastern Daylight Time

"Mayday mayday mayday! This is Bravo X-ray Nine declaring an emergency. We've been hit and we are about to re-enter the atmosphere. Mayday mayday mayday. Again I say this is Bravo X-ray Niner and we have catastrophic failures. We currently have pressurization and oxygen. Instruments are down and we have no power to engines. We did not achieve transfer—that is negative on transfer—and we are re-entering the atmosphere with 1,903 souls onboard."

As co-pilot, Major John Dench, continues to send the distress call out on the radio, the pilot-in-command Major Nathan Rice struggles to maneuver the craft, using only its speed to control movement and descent. Other than looking out the small windows in the cockpit, they have no means of seeing anything else in the sky. Even now, whoever unleashed the slice of light that pulsed through the craft and disabled it might be closing in on them. They are defenseless.

"Mayday mayday mayday. This is Bravo X-ray Niner and we are attempting re-entry with no instruments and a dead stick. . . . Transponder squawk 7700 . . ."

Along with sirens and automated warnings sounding in the cabin, the voice of Major Rice can be heard in the background of the last transmission saying, "attempting to maintain forty degrees." The craft's engineer is saying, ". . . no other visual contact . . . attempting to adjust my point of orientation . . . [unintelligible words] . . . points of reference are gone. . . ."

August 19, 2044, just before sunset, location unknown

A soldier in uniform is standing near a group of boulders at the foot of a tall peak. These large rocks undoubtedly slid down the steep slope behind him at some point in time. Under other circumstances, he might think it unwise to consider them a refuge, but greater dangers than a possible landslide face all the survivors huddled nearby.

The soldier's eyes continually scan the sky overhead and the open ground between where he stands and a line of large trees several hundred yards away. Behind the hardwoods, a column of black smoke is rising in the diminishing light.

He places his index finger on a spot where his right ear and jaw come together and applies pressure so he can both record and broadcast his words to anyone with a radio on his designated frequency. "This is Captain Arthur Penway, an officer on the spacecraft Bravo X-ray nine, which is also called the Aegean C. We have no idea if anyone can hear our distress calls, and the battery on the emergency radio will die soon."

He sees more civilians running from the trees toward the rocks. Nearly everyone including Penway, momentarily drops to the ground when they hear a *pop* followed by a loud *boom* and he watches in horror as a ball of flame rolls upward through the column of smoke like a bulge working its way through a hose.

"We're still hearing explosions . . . and that was a loud one," he says between rapid breaths, "but it looks . . . like all the smoke is still coming from the same section of the craft that broke off."

He stops speaking and waves his arms until the people leaving the woods see him and correct their course toward him. Penway and two other soldiers run out across the expanse of grass, carrying weapons to protect the oncoming civilians from any potential threat. Two of them help a large man with an injured knee close the distance across the open terrain to where the others are waiting.

Two hours later, in the dark of night, his initial rush of adrenalin is slowing and he continues his message in a calmer voice. He moves a few feet from people who are sitting on the ground, wanting some privacy while he communicates his thoughts. "It looks like we will have to hole up here tonight. Hal Dobbin, one of the passengers, will attempt to return to the wreckage of the craft with some soldiers tomorrow in order to scavenge the parts for a solar array that we can use to operate some of our tech. Hopefully our emergency beacon is sending out a signal, but the section of the craft where it was located isn't with the rest of the wreckage, so we don't know for sure."

August 20, 2044, midday

"We lost more than two hundred in the crash, mostly passengers but soldiers including our pilots Majors Rice and Dench as well. At least a hundred more people are injured—many of them critically, so the death toll is going to rise. We have two doctors who survived, but little in the way of medicine to sustain the injured more than a day or so unless we can get back into the wreckage and locate the medical supplies. We can only hope we'll be rescued soon.

"Our first hours after the crash were spent getting people and then livestock out of the wreckage along with any weapons we could carry and then finding places to take cover in case we were attacked . . . but so far, we've been lucky. Major Rice did a good job, I'll give him that. He managed to get us down on a large shelf that sticks out from the side of a mountain. The shelf is much longer than it is wide and looks like it's more than a couple of miles wide. Most of the wreckage skidded to a stop on the northeastern end. We think the craft was intact until the first impact and bounce . . . probably about a klick from here.

"It's been nearly twenty hours now and although we're grateful we've not seen any hostile forces . . . we're not sure why we've had no contact with anyone and we've seen no signs of rescue. Even though we're obviously in remote terrain it's weird that we haven't seen *any* signs of other human life. No signs of roads or trails. We saw no smoke where other craft similarly damaged might have crashed. . . . There are no contrails in the sky, and now as it's getting dark, we see no lights or fires in the distance to indicate habitation. We don't know what to make of all this but, like I said earlier, hopefully Hal and some of the others can scrounge up some tech so we can make better attempts to contact the outside world tomorrow and see what's happened.

"My buddy Pete says there is a jungle a mile or so below this plateau. He says it extends all along the base of the mountains and spreads out as far as the eye can see . . . but we won't send any recon down to look at it. We're trying to stay up here near the wreckage in case help comes. We have no idea what threats might be nearby.

"We had a full load. Our mission was to relocate that group of people—the Genon, the terraformers—along with their livestock and belongings. We also had the Second Jump Battalion onboard and a "scaffold crew" of a few hundred scientists and techs who would help the Genon with the initial setup at New Hope. Three of our translators were killed in the crash, so communicating with the Genon poses some difficulties since a good number of them don't speak Command Dialect . . . and it seems a lot of the way we think doesn't directly translate, either. They're kinda rough and primitive, like Special Forces, so they can survive anyplace where human life is possible . . . but they aren't savvy about tech at all and they don't operate with a chain-of-command structure, so we're having some difficulties with them.

"All I keep telling myself is that this will all make for a great series of entries on the ComNet newsfeed when we get home." The officer pauses for several moments before continuing. "Or, at least if someone hears this later, they'll know what happened."

August 24, 2044

"We had a memorial service today for all the people who have died so far. We buried them in a common grave before the bodies became a health hazard. Right now, there isn't enough time, manpower, or equipment to bury them separately, or with the honor they deserve. The gravesite is east of the wreckage of Bravo X-ray Niner, near the eastern end of the plateau. A group of men dragged a chunk of the nose of the craft where the name, Aegean C, was painted to serve as a kind of memorial or headstone at one end of the gravesite."

August 25, 2044

"It's been six days now . . . another forty-three people have died, among them five small children. It's so weird how people were either VERY injured or had only scratches and bruises. We still don't know exactly what it was that hit us, or why no one—neither friendlies nor hostiles—has found us. If extremists hit us with some sort of new weapon, maybe that one pulse was the only shot they had . . . but then why hasn't any rescue been attempted? None of our satellite communicators or radios are picking up anything. *Nothing* on the com. Not in any language, not on any frequency, and . . . well, we're really spooked about it.

"Gus Tremont and six others—scientists and techs on the mission to New Hope—are starting to speculate about our circumstances here. Several think we may have somehow slipstreamed to another planet. Others say it may not be a case of *where* we are, but *when* we are. None of us recognizes the constellations in the sky . . . that could be due to spatial or temporal displacement. Whatever the case, the commander of the Jump Squadron, Major Roland is trying to keep energies focused on survival—both short and long term—as we wait for rescue. Although no one has attacked us here, he's ordered everyone not on recon to stay near the crash site.

"We've had continuing problems with the Genon. They seem to operate more on instinct and they're used to being autonomous . . . but we know our key to survival is in unified effort directed through the command of the senior officer, Major Roland.

"In the way of positive news, one of the Genon did find a ready supply of water nearby on the second day we were here. It's a natural spring and it should supply all that we need. Much of the cargo, tools, agricultural equipment, and livestock the Genon would have used at New Hope was salvaged, too. And the climate is moderate so far. The soldiers that have traveled to the edge of the shelf, about a mile from here, see a dense jungle below, so we believe we're in a tropical zone. We can also see snow and ice high up on the peaks behind us. Man, those peaks are jagged, and they look like they nearly extend out beyond the atmosphere. I've never seen mountains so tall before. . . . But we're on this shelf, this plateau that's maybe a mile above the jungle, and it's like we're suspended between eternal winter above and eternal summer below. It is probably about 50 degrees during the night, but it warms up during the day. I don't know what we would have done if we hadn't found water or if we were forced to contend with extreme cold or heat. . . . Wherever we are, we're all just hoping to leave soon.

"Major Roland is in charge of all our efforts to survive until we're rescued. A number of professionals among the civilian crew have been a big help. Hal and his daughter Janna helped us make a small power station using solar collectors we pulled out of the wreckage. It won't run much but we'll take what we can get. At least we'll be able to use a few things like lights and signaling.

"We sent ten men out to recon more of the plateau today. They're supposed to be back within a week."

August 27th

"We've heard some strange sounds the past two nights. We're not sure if it's human or some sort of nocturnal animal—but I'm telling you, it would make your blood turn to ice to hear the sound this thing makes. It sounds like a woman's scream, only louder . . . and different somehow.

"Major Roland sent out four of our special ops guys today to see what it is and to find out if our recon unit is okay."

CHAPTER 2
A Century Later

"**W**e chased them into the Poison Forest and did not let them return. We chased all of those who would strike down the order of our civilization—and therefore life itself. We chased them without pity, and their names will not be found in the record of the Second Generation."—*Captain Martin Jared, a keeper of the history of Aegea in the Second Generation*

The mingled scent of spiced tubers and hot bread drifts beneath her door and the room fills with scents of the morning's meal. The young woman abruptly awakens when she realizes bread dough takes more than an hour to prepare and rise before baking. She should have been up long ago!

She sits up in bed, but before her feet are out from under her small blanket a piece of a dream floats through the back of her mind, like a single bright flower petal drifting away on a current of water. She closes her eyes and focuses all her will upon it.

Much of the dream has already slipped away to wherever it is that dreams go, but she intently lifts that one small piece back into view. A hint of a smile comes to her lips as she replays it. Yes. It's mother's melodious voice. And for a moment she can see the long, flowing hair, so black it shines blue in the sun. The words her mother speaks are in their ancient Genon, a language forbidden since the rebellion of His people in the second generation.

Mother's strong, slender hands unwrap a moist roll of cloth and she places the items side by side in front of her. "Here is the root . . . this is the bark, and these are the leaves, Shaye." A pungent odor unlike anything on the plateau fills her sinuses. "Smell it?" Mother asks. "This is the scent of the forest. See the color of the wood within the root? The first generation of His people said these trees smelled like something called 'cedar'." She lifts the small branch with a cluster of leaves. "We have gathered these since the first generation—and now we do it in secret. We boil them or we crush them—not from the root or the bark—and we mix the juice with water, just a few drops at a time . . . so we are strong in the Great Forest—the land of cloud and leaf." The voice of her mother fades and disappears with the rest of the dream.

At times, Shaye fears she might forget her mother's voice. She thinks about the spot where the small bundle is hidden, but as tempting as it might be to retrieve it and unwind the coarse string wrapped around it, the escalating noise from the kitchen demands attention.

Although there is no window here, the narrow shaft of light coming beneath her door illuminates the compact space where she has slept for the past four years. Still wearing the slip she slept in, Shaye rises and quickly realizes she's standing on salt granules scattered about the floor. She'd brushed them out of her bed last night.

"Ohhhhh, *lah*," she says in an exasperated sigh. "That stupid girl."

It was so late when she crept into her room last night, she'd forgotten to check her bed before getting into it. As soon as she fully reclined beneath the cover, however, she noted with disgust that her bed had been sprinkled with salt. She'd picked up the mattress cover and sent the salt cascading onto the stone floor, too tired to clean it up.

There's no time to sweep it up now, either.

She grabs one of two dresses hanging on pegs near her bed, steps into it, pulls it up over her tall, slender frame, then buttons it. With several swift movements, she gathers her long, black hair at the back of her head, winds it into a large knot, then weaves two slender wooden rods through the knot to pin it in place. She opens the door and rubs the bottom of each foot against the top of the other to remove the salt, then steps through the door. Padding down the hall in her bare feet, she passes by the doorway to a small room where soap, water and basins for personal hygiene are kept. Next, she passes a storage room for supplies and utensils.

By the time Shaye reaches the arched entrance to the kitchen, loud noises are no longer reverberating through the downstairs rooms of the house. She scrunches her whole face into a squint and comes to a complete halt. The tall shutters along two walls of the kitchen, facing east and north, are flung wide open and full daylight is pouring through them. Despite a cool morning breeze just outside, she feels warmth radiating from the brick oven where Mosha has already cooked the day's bread and a morning meal.

Once her eyes adjust, she focuses on the figure of a woman on the other side of the room. It's Mosha, and she is energetically tending to a dish in the basin located in front of the center window. Watching the old woman's silver bun bobbling about with the cleaning effort, Shaye wonders, *Is she ever still?*

Mosha and Shaye are the only servants who sleep in the great house. Mosha has served in Colonel Jubal McClaren's family her whole life. The colonel was wise to take Mosha in and give her the honor of a room in this house when his father died. Over the years, as her reputation for producing the most extraordinarily delectable cuisine grew, she could have had any number of opportunities to work elsewhere. The fact that she is treated nearly like family (with her own room in the great house) helps ensure her continued service here. It was Mosha who insisted, Shaye be allowed to move from the servant's quarters into the bottom floor of the house when the girl was orphaned at the age of ten.

Shaye watches the old woman and her expression softens.

Mosha creates a nearly constant flow of food and dirty dishes. As a testament to her life in the kitchen, her clothes carry the permanent scent of spices and freshly ground banji beans. Her weathered face and hands are evidence she's worked with great intensity for many seasons. The ample proportions on her short frame (and the deep laugh lines around her eyes and mouth) show that she enjoys her work.

This morning, however, even the air around Mosha bristles. Sensing Shaye's presence, she stops scrubbing for a moment and speaks without turning around.

"Oh. Did I *wake* you? . . ."

Shaye knows better than to respond. It will be over much sooner if she lets Mosha express her dismay. The old woman's anger is like a bubble in a boiling pot: Once it pops, it's gone. So Shaye quietly waits while the old woman airs her grievances. Openness is now a rarity among the Genon, who have learned that transparency with emotions means vulnerability. Shaye assumes Mosha's willingness to be frank is the result of her long tenure in the house. The lecture is building to its peak.

". . . and I would thank you to *not* spend all hours of the night on the roof, staring at the stars. I don't know why I let you do this to me." She lowers her voice and mutters to herself in Genon while zealously scraping the dish. She need not mutter—it's not as if anyone from the grand house above them would visit the kitchen at this hour and overhear snippets of taboo language. Although the Colonel's wife, "the ishi" keeps a firm command of all the domestic doings in the house, the kitchen has been exclusively Mosha's domain for more than two decades.

But the lowered volume sends a signal. Shaye crosses the space between them, and the old woman stops talking. Has the bubble popped yet? Mosha keeps scrubbing, so Shaye slides her arms around the old woman's generous waistline and leans down to rest her chin on the shoulder where she's received so much comfort in the years since her mother died. It was Mosha who emptied out a storage room and said it was "Shaye's room."

The old woman's posture relaxes somewhat, and the fury of the cleaning in the basin slows before she says, "Well girl, you'd better eat something quick and get moving. It will be a long day for us."

Shaye gives her a squeeze and speaks with a softness that acknowledges the bond between them. "I'm only *a* girl and not *your* girl? I am sorry I slept late."

Mosha turns and gazes into Shaye's golden eyes—once a distinct characteristic of the Genon people, now a feature fewer of them possess. She has known Shaye since the girl was hardly more than a toddler holding onto her mother's skirts, but those eyes still give her a bit of a jolt every time she looks into them. Shaye may be an inch or two taller than most Genon women, but there is no doubt of her heritage.

"Of all mornings to be lazing about in your bed!" the old woman scolds. "The colonel arrived late last night to help make the final plans for Jariel's day. It's less than two weeks away and there is much to do!"

A hint of something momentarily smolders in Shaye's eyes before Mosha tilts her head to one side and declares, "And don't think old Mosha's head has gone all stupidy. I know there's some kind of skirmish going on between you and Miss Jariel lately. I might not know who threw the first clout, but I know the signs of a struggle when I see one. You and that girl have been in the business of getting even on and off since you were six. I don't know what broke the truce again, but one day the ishi is going to decide to take notice of it and I can tell you—the only thing Jariel stands to lose is pride points for caring about what you think or do. On the other hand, Miss Shaye," she stops and lowers her voice, "you stand to lose a good deal more."

Mosha sees she's not making much progress, so she tries a different line of reasoning. "You know the colonel is in the middle of preparations for the games and the draft, yet he came back to help the ishi settle all the final details of his only daughter's planning day. Tomorrow, all manner of soldiers and service people will be here getting their assignments and schedules for the big day and *everything* will be in a skitter. Belina will be coming across the road tomorrow to help plan menus, we still need to make out the list of supplies we'll need, and I just know she'll take every opportunity to snoop in my spice jars!" Mosha stops talking and takes a deep breath before she throws herself into a tizzy. "Do you want to make me look bad? *All* of us will suffer if the colonel and the ishi feel the slightest embarrassment! Should we all have to drink a bitter cup for *you*?"

Shaye looks directly at her. "No, Mum," she says, hoping that the endearment of the word "Mum" will further soothe Mosha's ire. "I'm sorry I didn't wake up sooner."

With fingers still dripping from the basin, Mosha reaches out and grasps Shaye's hands. "You need to stop stretching for things beyond your grasp. It will only bring you sorrow.

You're seventeen now and there is no more time for imagining. There are some things—like those stars above—that will never be yours."

Because she prides herself in her ability to hide her innermost thoughts, it annoys Shaye that Mosha can see right through her sometimes. She ignores the remark and slips out of Mosha's wet grasp. After patting her hands on her dress she pulls a warm roll from a basket on a large wooden tray. She bites into the bread and pushes the soft morsel into her cheek with her tongue before saying. "I'll get to washing the rest of the dishes then. It's probably time to serve breakfast upstairs, isn't it?"

With a scolding look, the old woman dries her own hands on her apron before plucking another roll from a bin, and placing it in the basket. "Don't think this conversation is over, my girl," she says while stacking more food on the tray. "Let me tell you—"

A sound emanating from the rooms above them interrupts the conversation.

Mosha makes the Genon sign for a vow by touching two straightened fingers to her lips, then pointing upward. "We will speak of this—at great length—the next time you're late," she says in a stern voice, then hefts the tray up to her shoulder.

Shaye darts forward and puts a hand on the rim of the wooden tray. "Where is Lem?" She asks. "Here, let me carry that for you."

"Lemon found an excuse to run off with some of the field workers for the day. I'm sure they'll be at the *meechi* again," the old woman says before muttering, "That man is a jot in want of a good shaking! He'll probably appear long after our work is done and skulk off to his bed. His head is a *corsha*. I hope it pounds for a week!" She turns toward the stairs and composes herself before adding, "And, no, I don't need your help. I've been carrying trays up stairs since . . ."

Shaye makes a conscious effort to keep from mouthing the next words along with Mosha as she says them.

". . . before you were born. Since this house was built."

The old woman makes her way up the stairway before Shaye hurriedly eats the roll in her hand, then one more from the bin, smearing it with the paste made of sweet and spicy mashed tubers. While she chews, her mind wanders and the fingers of her left hand glide back and forth along the smooth stone top of the counter next to her. Carved from the mountain, the dark blue-gray slab is worn to a soft shine by the preparation of meals by four generations of servants in Colonel McClaren's family. These counters were carefully installed the first year that Shaye and her mother came to live here—just after the colonel's uncle died. A family member of lesser rank moved into the shell of the uncle's house after all the valuable furnishings and these stones were removed. Although a nice home in its day, the uncle's house in the best section of Oldtown wouldn't compare with this one. Even a new home in Midtown wouldn't compare to this.

Shaye stops moving her fingers, closes her eyes, and allows her hand to rest on the surface of the cool stone for a moment. It represents more than wealth or beauty. It is a tangible connection with generations gone that will exist in future generations. No words or symbols are carved here but it represents a history of lives none-the-less, and the spices, oils, and labor of Mosha and others are worked into the very surface of the rock.

She gives one final pat to the counter before she swallows the last bite of her breakfast and finds one of Mosha's old aprons to wear. It's threadbare in several spots but softer than anything Shaye has ever owned. It wraps all the way around her—and the tie goes around her twice before she makes a loose bow in it. She leans across the counter to open the lid of a wooden bin containing coarse-ground grain and puts a small spoonful in her pocket, then moves about the large kitchen gathering the last of the dishes. The butcher will arrive soon and the kitchen should be ready to begin the preparations for a fine dinner tomorrow night.

As the dishes are scraped, rinsed and dried, each one is carefully stacked with others of its kind—gourd, wood, stone, or clay. The serving and eating utensils, some of which are real metal, will be used tomorrow and then counted before they are put away.

After blocking open the servant's door at the back of the house with a wedge of wood, Shaye lifts the large basin off the flat wooden ring on which it normally rests. She steadies it between her arms, and exits, being careful not to slosh any water on the floor. Just outside the back of the house is a stone courtyard surrounded by a short wall and a gate that is always open. Beyond the courtyard is a large, rectangular open space. The left side of the rectangle is closed in by the single-story servant's quarters where most of her peers, two dozen men and women and four children, all servants of the colonel, sleep. Although nicer than the quarters of many servants on the plateau, it is unpainted, utilitarian, and sometimes cold at night.

On the far side of the rectangle, facing the back of the house, stands a covered kitchen and dining area where servant's meals are cooked and served. At this time of the day no one is there except Palma, a round little woman with brown hair, who is cleaning off the tables.

To the right of the open space are clothes lines where laundry is hung, and beyond them is a large herb and vegetable garden. Keya, a dark-haired woman in her thirties, is hanging clothes and sheets on a line.

Shaye declares a swift "Good morning!" to Keya as she glides toward the garden with the bowl of water.

"Good morning," Keya calls back. The woman's two-year-old-daughter pushes by a sheet wafting in the morning sun to grab her mother's leg.

Once she's out of the home's shadow, Shaye relishes every step of sun-warmed soil between her toes. At the farthest end of the garden she pours the water from the basin on several plants. For the rest of the day, each time dishes are cleaned, she will water plants closer and closer to the house. By the end of the day, all of the plants in this row will have been watered. Fresh water from springs has been bountiful elsewhere on the plateau, but here in Westland water had to be stored in cisterns or pumped by hand from wells and carried where it was needed. Now, through the newly completed aqueduct supplying the area, the house has access to a constant supply of fresh water, but old habits still rule its use. Not a drop is wasted—at least not by servants.

Shading her eyes, Shaye turns to gaze at the main house. Freshly plastered and stained a golden yellow hue from top to bottom only a month ago, the large, stone structure rises from the ground like a fortress made of sunlight itself.

She walks past a tall row of plants and sees a man, Old Menoh, at the far end, harvesting some of the *corsha* gourds off the vines. He'll carefully cut the round gourds of different sizes in half and scoop out the slimy substance inside them onto a pile. The hard outer shell of the *corsha* will be dried and used for a variety of purposes (such as spoons, ladles, cups, bowls, and the basin she now holds). The goop inside the *corsha*, occasionally used as a source of seeds for more vines, is pretty much useless.

Old Menoh is the only Genon working for the colonel who is allowed to keep his beard (which is long and white). He and his wife live in a small hut over by one of the ponds nearby—not because the colonel makes them live there, but because Menoh wanted to live there. Everyone knows the colonel respects Menoh. Didn't he take heed last year when the old man warned of a terrible storm on the way? Indeed the colonel's household, his livestock, and much of his crop were saved because of it.

It would be disrespectful not to greet an elder so she calls to him. "Good morning!"

A man of few words, Menoh looks up and nods in response before turning back to his work.

Shaye pauses again when she reaches the edge of the garden. Retrieving the grain in her pocket, she places most of it on a flat rock. Within seconds, a several tiny finches flit onto the rock and start pecking at the grain. They have dark wings and black throats, but their beaks and bellies are the color of fresh cream.

She gets one last pinch of grain out of her pocket and places it in the palm of her left hand. One of the birds flits up to her hand and lights on her thumb.

"I know I shouldn't let you be so tame . . . but you will be my only exception. We are friends, are we not?"

The little bird gets the last speck of grain before he flits back down to the rock where his kin are feeding.

"Enjoy your breakfast," she says softly to them all, then resumes her journey back toward the house, dangling the empty basin from a handhold carved into the rim.

The shrill call of a large bird echoes through the air and it's an irresistible invitation to take a quick detour around the side of the home. Moving past the clothes lines and turning left as she reaches the back corner of the house, she strides through the cool air under the wide brim of a shade tree. When she reaches the thick hedge guarding the garden at the front of the house, Shaye sets down the basin and pushes her hands and arms through the wall of green as if she were diving into a sea of foliage—parting it just enough to make a small window into what lies beyond—a garden, being prepared for a grand event the likes of which the Westland has never seen before. Elegant birds from the Great Forest are preening and squawking in sheltered cages stationed near giant ferns and thorn prickled trees. At the garden's center is a deep pool where rare plants hover in the dark water. The large, floating leaves of these plants are as round and flat as the trays used to carry food upstairs, and between these giant green platters, a host of spikey white, blue, and lavender blossoms stretch toward the morning sky. Flying insects hover over the pool, taking turns landing on the leaves and drinking from drops of water that sparkle in the morning sun.

Three workers tend to the birds, plants, and water in the garden on a continuing basis . . . and Shaye can't imagine that any home in all of Aegea could have a garden that would rival the beauty of this one.

She cannot see it from her vantage point, but beyond the garden, another, thicker hedge six spans in height marks the southern boundary of the colonel's compound, sheltering his grounds from the eyes of those passing by on a road that leads through the main gate for the post and all the way to the original settlement of Oldtown. By now, the road is busy with men in the military, workers on their way to a day in the fields, and tradesmen carrying their tools or their wares. Across the road are barracks and a mess hall for young soldiers and individual homes for officers stationed here in the Westland.

Beyond the barracks, Shaye envisions the fence that surrounds the post, and—as if she were a bird flying free—she imagines what lies on the other side of the fence: the last miles of the plateau stretching out with farmlands and orchards, filled with the most valuable foods in Aegea, tended by Genon workers. Beyond all that, at the farthest end of the cultivated land is a towering stone wall—the last rampart between the Aegean Plateau and the rest of the world. Still considered "new," this final wall was finished when Shaye's grandfather was a gatherer in the Great Forest, and her mother was a young woman learning all he knew. All of this comprises Westland of Aegea and all of it is under the colonel's command. On the other side of the stone wall is the edge of a steep six thousand foot drop down to the misty tropical forest, *the land of cloud and leaf,* below.

The scrape of a man raking a bed of pebbles near the pond brings Shaye back to the here and now, and she realizes she has no more time for idling about. She reluctantly heads back to the kitchen, picking up the corsha basin and drying it with the corner of her apron. When she is mere steps from the courtyard at the rear of the home, she hears a tradesman calling from the direction of the back gate.

"Meat here! Meat here!"

The voice is different from the one she expects, so she stands on her toes to see who it is. Instead of the butcher or one of his helpers, it's the butcher's son, Korel, striding up the walk with an arched wooden yoke slung over his left shoulder. His muscular arm is stretched forward and his hand is resting upon the yoke to steady the load. At the front end, more than a dozen headless sooshi hens sway, bound together by a thick string. At the other end, a sizable portion of red meat wrapped in an oilcloth and tied with another cord swings back and forth in rhythm with his stride.

As soon as she recognizes the young man, Shaye lets out a disgusted moan and hurries to the kitchen, leaving the back entrance of the house open. She gathers a stack of large wooden trays and places them on the counter at the center of the kitchen. Within moments Korel arrives and the sweat rag on his head is as fully drenched as his clothing. He slows then stops just outside the doorway, flexing his arm to steady the load on his shoulder.

Without a word, Shaye motions for him to enter and Korel squeezes through the doorway before stepping to the counter. He grabs the string holding the hens and hefts the large mound onto the counter before sliding the string off the yoke. Shaye slides several of the trays closer so she can divide the large pile of birds between them. While she is doing so, Korel swivels around and sets the wrapped meat on another tray before resting the yoke at the end of the counter.

Although Korel hoped to see Shaye this morning, being alone with her in the kitchen is an unexpected opportunity. Pulling the rag off his head, he mops his face with it and then frowns while he pauses to formulate some sort of statement.

Shaye notes that his usual smirk is gone and, hoping he'll simply leave, she moves away from the counter in the center of the kitchen. Not daring to turn her back on him completely, she leans her hip against the cabinet near the wash basin and gazes out the window while keeping him in her peripheral vision. He doesn't depart. After a few moments of silence, she begins tapping a fingernail on the stone countertop, the peck peck peck of it signaling her desire to get to her work.

"We killed all this for colonel just this morning so it's fresh," he says. His tone is polite, but he's still frowning. "And I made sure to bring it first thing."

He's waiting.

Rather than look at him, Shaye moves back to where the trays of sooshi hens are stationed and occupies herself untying the string from their feet.

He's rocking from one foot to the other, impatient for some sort of response. As he waits, his breathing speeds up.

When she can't stand his intensity any longer, she says, "I'm sure the ishi and colonel will appreciate it."

He makes another effort at wiping up trickles of sweat off his face and arms with the rag before he blurts out, "I was hoping to see you."

She keeps working at the string. The call of a bird out in the garden only amplifies the complete silence in the kitchen.

The son of a tradesman who provides his skilled labor to households of high rank, Korel is accustomed to courteous treatment from servants who are beneath his station in life. He places both hands on the counter and slowly leans toward her. "There was a misunderstanding last week. I saw you under the trees watching the festival and I just wanted to talk to you. That's all. You misunderstood me. I didn't mean to startle you and I only took hold of you because I feared you would run away and say I tried to harm you."

Without wanting to, she recalls the delighted look on his face while she struggled to free herself. His crushing grasp bruised her arms before she managed to wrench herself free and run away. There is no doubt in her mind that, without an ounce of remorse, he would have gladly stolen her virtue and left her bruised and shamed in a clump of bushes. He knows she has no father or brothers who could exact revenge.

"Well?" he finally asks. "Do you understand?"

She slowly blinks, then turns her full gaze upon him, making no attempt to hide her complete contempt. She doesn't care if it makes him angry—or so she thinks until he slaps his large hands further onto the counter and moves as if he might leap across it. She recoils to stay out of reach.

"You're nothing to me!" he nearly shouts. Then, becoming mindful of their location, he leans a little farther across the counter, lowers his voice, and speaks with all the venom he can muster. "Why would I want someone like you? Certainly, no one else would. You may sleep in this house, but don't think you can act so high above—"

At the sound of Mosha descending the stairs, he stops talking and straightens to his full height.

The old woman enters the kitchen with an empty tray, her clear eyes taking in the whole scene. "Good morning, Korel. I expected your father today. Is he well?"

His hands fall to his sides and he takes a step back before addressing Mosha. "Yes. He is in good health but he is busy. I'm doing the deliveries this morning—and these are fresh."

"You honor the colonel," Mosha responds.

Korel nods before he says, "Please excuse me. I must be leaving." He slides the yoke and oilcloth off the counter before giving one last look at Shaye. "You can have the string. . . . I have more."

Without waiting for Shaye to respond, Mosha smiles politely at the young man and says, "Why thank you. Please take the ishi's thanks and my greetings to your father."

Once the kitchen door closes behind him, Mosha turns her attention to Shaye. "At the market the other day Ruby told me he beat up her son. Has he bothered you? Do you want me to complain to the colonel?"

Shaye rubs the memory of the hurt on her left forearm. "I'm fine," she answers, not sure Mosha would actually do such a thing . . . or what might happen if she did. "Hopefully, his father will keep him busy and we won't see him that often."

The old woman nods and then changes the subject. "The colonel is the only one who has eaten breakfast. Help me get this meat into cold storage and then you'll need to go upstairs. Beth is already up there with Jariel, but the ishi says she needs extra help this morning. Be back as soon as you can, though. I need you down here, too. Like I said, Belina, the new cook from the officer's mess, will be here tomorrow with a couple of helpers."

In the second generation of Aegea, the Genon learned that the only way to be necessary to society was to have some craft or skill that wasn't common knowledge. A family with a specialized craft fared much better than a family of common laborers.

Mosha gives Shaye a knowing wink. "I'll not be giving her any of *my* secrets. We'll be combining the spices and mixes for the meal today."

CHAPTER 3
Knowing One's Place

"**B**eware of the one who cannot appreciate beauty, for beauty reflects a part of the One who created all things."—*an ancient proverb of His people*

Earlier on that very same morning . . .

Shaye is yet dreaming of her mother and Mosha is just starting the dough for the day's bread as the sky brightens along the eastern rim of the earth. The population on the entire plateau will soon be rising for another day.

The settlement on the plateau of Aegea has grown. It was built first with gathered pieces of wreckage and mud, then with stone, wood, thatch, and brick. The people of Aegea are the descendants of survivors from the craft that fell from the sky more than a century ago. Those who first boarded the large airship christened the *Aegean C* were all from free societies. Now they are divided by class and rank, each group maintaining much of its knowledge and distinctions, all of them participating, one way or another, in the ebb and flow of making a life here. The only things they *all* have in common are the Universal Command Dialect and the fact they all live here on the Aegean Plateau.

Unlike their ancestors, those alive today give no thought to rescue—nor do they struggle each day to stay alive in an unfamiliar environment. Over the course of five generations, the people of Aegea have learned how to live where they are with what they have. Few of them think beyond their day to day needs or consider what lies outside the wall that now encompasses the entirety of the twenty-eight-mile-long by four-mile-wide shelf of land nestled on the side of a towering mountain range. With a wall to keep out the many dangers of the Poison Forest below and sheer ice-capped mountains behind them, many are content to dwell safely in the year-round moderate climate of Aegea.

On this particular day, two men, a soldier on the wall and the last worker to exit the Northeastern Gate both see the sun rising on a horizon below the plateau, much the same way that workers and soldiers have watched the scene unfold for a hundred years. The soldier watches from his post. The worker, on his way to the charcoal pits far below, stands just outside the wall. It is the dry season on the plateau so there is a clear view of the sun's first rays illuminating a feathered patch of alto cirrus clouds far above them, shimmering in the morning light like an iridescent wing on a wild bird. A sight of equal glory is unfolding at the bottom of the steep path that snakes back and forth down the sheer mountainside. The sun's orange and gold hues seem to ignite the undulating mist blanketing the vast expanse of the Poison Forest. Both the soldier and the worker pause to view the grand spectacle as the sun crests over the edge of the horizon. Within moments the display dissipates and the men return to their tasks.

###

Out in Westland of the plateau, Duana the ishi, the matron of the great house, rises to start her day. Within minutes several dresses, unsuitable for one reason or another, are strewn about the room before a servant girl finally arrives. Almost the exact age of the ishi's own daughter, the servant rarely speaks and usually does what she is told, but as far as Duana is concerned, the girl's black hair and gold eyes draw entirely too much attention for someone who should spend her life in the background.

"Come and finish the bed quickly," she tells Shaye while tying a sash around her own waist. "And I need some help here before you do the rest of the cleaning."

The girl straightens the covers on the bed and places the pillows in the customary locations. Once she pulls the last wrinkle out of the cover on the bed, she stands near the head of the bed, anticipating a correction.

"Move that large pillow just to the left," Duana says before turning to inspect her own reflection in a mirror made of highly polished metal then seating herself on a cushioned stool. "Now come here and help me put on my necklace. This one," she says, pointing to a strand of beads on the top of her dressing table.

###

Just down the hall from Duana's room, her daughter, Jariel, is preparing to go down for a late breakfast. The ishi's daughter is a skinny girl with pale skin and dull brown hair. She's already in a foul mood about a certain dress: She doesn't like it at all.

"Here are your shoes, miss." Beth says, placing them on the floor. In her late twenties, Beth is the wife of one of the other servants, John, and is expecting their second child in several months. Her growing belly combined with her small stature makes her a little less agile, but she'll be expected to work until the day the baby is born, and return to moderate tasks with a baby on her back within three weeks of the birth. If the baby is sickly or cries a lot, she'll be assigned jobs outside the great house.

Jariel takes the shoes from her and says, "That's all I want for now." She sits down and slips on shoes before turning to face the dressing table, all the while silently rehearsing what she will say to her mother.

Before Beth can leave the room, Jariel suddenly lets out a short shriek and tries to push herself away from the table. The legs of her chair push against the rug, scrunching it up in great folds. When her seat can slide no further it tips over backward with a flailing Jariel still onboard. As soon as the back of the chair hits the rumpled rug she quickly rolls off of it and scrambles away from the dressing table, leaving one of her shoes behind in the commotion.

The servant's first reaction is to jump back, but then she quickly offers a hand to Jariel and helps her to the safety of the corner.

"There's something in the drawer!" Jariel says in a panicked voice.

It takes a few seconds for Beth to work up her courage, but then she lets go of Jariel, snatches up the loose shoe and creeps back toward to the dressing table. She stands on tip toes so she can see into the drawer without getting any closer. Is it a giant poisonous spider? A scorpion?

A little green head pokes out of the drawer, then disappears again.

"Oh miss," Beth says, exhaling loudly and dropping the shoe. "It's just a little lizard. He won't hurt you." She takes another step and reaches into the drawer. "I'll get him for you."

Jariel pushes herself further into the corner. "No, no, just kill it."

"But miss, he is good. He will eat many bugs for you—especially the kind that can bring sickness."

Closing her eyes, Jariel says, "Fine. Then just take it away!"

"I will, I will. Just wait a moment. . . . As soon as he feels how warm my hand is, he'll be my friend." She bumps her hand around in the drawer a few times, then says, "Got him!" When she pulls her hand from the drawer, the small creature is in her loosely clenched fingers, his tail protruding at one end. "He's quite a lovely color, miss," Beth says. "Want to see him?"

Jariel shrinks further into the corner. "No! Just get it out of here!"

###

Down the hall, Shaye has fastened the hook on Duana's necklace before they hear a loud yip coming from down the hall. Then they hear a big thump followed by some bumping, a few short exclamations, and then silence. Duana and Shaye both head for Jariel's room, but before Duana can push the latch on the door, Beth opens it.

"Just a lizard, madam. Miss Jariel met him in a drawer and he gave her a start." Beth says covering the hand holding the lizard. "I don't suppose you want to see him, either."

Duana backs up to give Beth plenty of space to exit. "No. You can just take it to the garden."

Shaye raises her chin as if she'd like to get a look at the creature as it rides by.

Beth moves past them both. "Yes, madam."

"Are you alright?" Duana asks her daughter.

Still standing at a safe distance from her dressing table, Jariel carefully leans over to peer down into the drawer. There are lizard droppings all over the contents. She slides it shut before turning toward the door and briefly narrowing her eyes at the face peeking over her mother's shoulder. "I'm just fine."

"Then I'm going back to my room to finish getting dressed," Duana says, turning to go back down the hall with Shaye in tow.

Within a minute, Jariel enters her mother's room and makes no attempt at working up to the subject. "Are you sure I should wear the blue dress on my planning day?"

"Yes," Duana says while she eyes herself one last time in the long mirror. Suddenly sensing her selection is in jeopardy, she faces her daughter. "Blue is such a rare color for cloth . . . and this is *your* planning day, my dear. The best families with eligible sons will be here. Shouldn't you shine like a rare jewel?" she asks before her attention returns to her own reflection. She sweeps the graying brown hair off her shoulder and studies the necklace.

Once she's certain that Shaye can see her, Jariel flips the cover across her mother's bed, toppling several pillows onto the floor. "Well I think I like the green dress better," she says before sitting on the bed.

Giving no indication that she's noticed the provocation, Shaye walks to a corner of the room and pulls down a small cobweb dangling from the corner of a tapestry.

The ishi glances from her own reflection in the mirror to that of her daughter and suppresses a sigh. Neither the cut nor the color of the green dress will improve her daughter's appearance but Duana knows the desirability of it will only increase if she forbids Jariel to wear it. "Fine. Then wear the green," she responds casually. She leans closer to the mirror pretending to inspect a wrinkle near her left eye before saying, "But it's such a common color for a special event, don't you think? The whole world is green." She lifts a brush from the table in front of her and starts pulling it through her hair.

Both mother and daughter turn when they hear the *thud* of something falling to the rug. It's a small stone carving the colonel gave the ishi when they were newly married. In an attempt to get a cobweb away from it, Shaye knocked it off a small shelf. She immediately picks it up and shows it to Duana, who inspects it thoroughly before handing the undamaged object back to Shaye with a scolding look.

While Shaye is placing the carving back where it belongs, Jariel stares at her and wrinkles up her nose. "You *are* going to make her cover her hair for my planning day aren't you? She looks like we just plucked her out of the forest!"

Rather than stand there like a piece of furniture being sanded, Shaye turns her attention to flowers floating in a bowl right beneath the souvenir shelf. She gently spins one of them in the water.

The ishi folds her arms and takes a moment to do something she almost never does. She openly looks at Shaye from head to foot.

Under the scrutiny of Duana's glare, Shaye is reminded afresh of her own poverty, a hunger that gnaws at the soul.

Taking in the whole picture, the ishi realizes several things. First of all, the dress (of the "standard" kind that all female servants are given—tent-like and brown or gray) is beyond shabby. Second, the girl is no longer "developing a figure,"—she has one. Lastly, the dress, (which should be loose and have a hem that falls at least to mid-calf) is quite snug at the bust line, and is almost up to the girl's knee.

"Oh dear." Duana says. "You have something else to wear when you go to town, don't you?"

"My other dress," Shaye responds without looking up. "The gray one."

The ishi is horrified. "We can't have people thinking that this is how our servants look. What about that darkish sort of dress I gave you to wear when we go somewhere?"

"Do you not remember ma'am? . . . You gave it to the servant of the colonel's sister when they returned Jariel here last year. She tore her own dress on a piece of furniture and you gave her my dress."

The pained expression on Duana's face says she remembers.

Shaye knows it would be improper to turn away while the ishi is talking to her, so she stands still and folds her hands together while she awaits further queries or directions.

Even though she's still looking in Shaye's direction, Duana is no longer looking *at* her. She crosses her arms and squints as she concentrates, then shakes her head and begins to pace, speaking again, but to herself. "Well, I can't have her buying Mosha's supplies from merchants in town wearing *that* thing. . . . Maybe we could send Beth or one of the other girls to town." She waves both hands in front of herself as if she's erasing the idea. She knows that Mosha would be livid at the thought of giving her secret list of herbs and spices to anyone who might reveal the information. Duana stops pacing and looks at Shaye once again. "Mosha's dresses would be much too wide. . . . And too short."

Of a truth, the ishi has avoided replacing any of the girl's clothing. Why invest in clothes when the servant's time of service is nearly up? . . . Until just this moment she has never considered the reflection this would cast on the family. How could she have missed such an important detail? It's an uncharacteristic oversight. She motions for her daughter to come closer, and the two of them walk to the corner at the other end of the room before Duana says in a whisper, "She'll need a dress and scarf of yours to wear."

Jariel is indignant, but keeps her voice down. "Why should *she* be allowed to wear one of *my* dresses?"

Her mother ignores the question. "What about that dark brown dress of yours? It's very plain without the embroidered sash, so it would be suitable for her."

The brown dress is ugly, but that's not the point. "It's my dress! I won't do it!"

Making a conscious effort to avoid looking at her daughter's bony figure, Duana searches for the right words. "That dress . . . wasn't cut correctly. It's an ugly dress—more like a sack than a dress, really. And Shaye is about your height. . . ."

"But—" her daughter sputters.

Duana leans in and lowers her voice. "Would you rather that she wore some old rag from the kitchen while she did our shopping in town? Would you like people to see her in that as she served them on your planning day? I'm sorry I didn't think of it before now, but I've just had too much to do."

Now staring at the servant, Jariel resigns the argument. "Fine. She can wear the dress and I'll find a scarf for her to wear over her hair."

Her mother tilts her head in momentary satisfaction and says, "Very well. It's settled," before striding back to her mirror for a few last touches on her hair.

Taking advantage of a possible segue to her current obsession, Jariel says, "Now what about *my* dress for the planning day?"

Duana slowly turns to look at her daughter and speaks in a deliberately calm voice. "Jariel. I've spent the last six months preparing for this day. I even have a woman coming from Midtown with special powders and perfumes for you. Few girls in the entire history of Aegea would be able to say they had a planning day that would rival yours—so change your tone or go back to your room. You know very well that the blue dress is the best choice. I had it specially made for you! The General's niece wanted some of that cloth so I paid for the entire length of it to ensure only you would have it. . . . But if you don't want to wear it, then by all means, wear that green dress."

Jariel looks up at the ceiling and bobbles her head around as if she's listening to an old tune. She's heard the saga of the blue cloth too many times to care. And besides, is it that she would look good in the blue, or that the cloth itself would look impressive? She begins pleading her case again. "But you didn't ask me about the cloth. You never let me go to Midtown."

The root of the problem has been exposed. Jariel hasn't been allowed to travel to Midtown since the disastrous trip last year when she stayed with Jubal's sister—who purchased a number of hideously bright dresses for the girl and gave her the liberty to make a total fool of herself by wearing them in public.

"I feel like a prisoner here," the girl pleads. "I'm seventeen and I don't get to go anywhere—or even pick out my own dresses!"

This is not the day for a battle of wills. Duana moves and sits on the bed near her daughter. "You'd look just as well in either dress, Jari. But we have a busy day ahead and I don't want to argue." She looks around before finding her shoes and pulling them on. "Is your brother up? I haven't seen him this morning."

Jariel reclines on the bed and pulls the remaining pillows under her head before answering. "He was out late again last night. I think he's trying to sleep in longer every day—before he's trapped in the life of a man in the military." She stifles a laugh before adding, "My brother, a soldier. That will be so funny."

"Did you come in here to upset me or did you have some other purpose?"

Ready to renew the previous topic, Jariel sits up. "I wanted to talk about my dress."

Duana stands up and covers her face with her hands before letting them drop to her sides with an exasperated plop. "Please don't do this," she begs. "Not today." She quickly strides out of the room and down the stairs with Jariel only a few steps behind her.

Shaye watches the empty doorway for a moment then looks back at the bed. She replaces the covers and pillows before she walks around the large room, collecting four dresses and several pairs of shoes then placing them in a cabinet. With another tour of the space she gathers scarves of varying color, draping each one over her arm before placing them on a post by the mirror. She stops for a moment and her eyes sweep across the dressing table. After a quick glance back at the doorway, Shaye carefully lifts a golden earring and holds it up by her ear in front of the mirror, studying her own face, then gazing at her shabby dress. She places the earring back with its mate on the table.

Remembering that Mosha needs her in the kitchen, she leaves the room and is halfway down the first flight of stairs when she hears a male voice behind her.

"Good morning, Shaye."

All of the commotion must have awakened him. She turns and looks up at Jariel's brother, Tyrone. He's wearing clothing typical of young gentry: a soft, long-sleeved shirt, long pants, and leather boots. All the wrinkles in his clothing reveal he must have slept in them—and on his right side—for the hair on that side of his head is flattened and jutting up at the top. Before she can say anything, she notices his gaze drifting over to someone standing on the landing below her, then back to her. He clears his throat before adding, "I suppose all of you are really busy," in a casual tone. "What with the event preparations . . ."

She turns away from him and continues to move down the stairs before answering. "Yes, it's a busy day." She has already greeted the colonel this morning so she only nods as she passes him.

The colonel allows her to walk by and waits until the door to the kitchen at the bottom of the stairs has closed. "We need to talk."

With the exception of a few spindly hairs jutting out from his jawline and chin, Tyrone is a younger reflection of his father in every outward way. Ty straightens his posture, and then begins moving down the stairs. "Well, I haven't had breakfast yet. Should I look for you when I'm done?"

There is an unmistakable resoluteness in the older man's voice. "No. Now. Come to the ready room with me."

When his father turns to lead the way, Ty's shoulders heave with a silent sigh before he follows. The two men pass through the living quarters, the large great room where they entertain guests, then into a passage which leads to the tower on the northeast corner of the house. After climbing two flights of stairs to the highest room of the tower, father and son enter the large, airy space. It contains none of the tapestries or frills that decorate so much of the home. The windows have views in all directions, and from this room the colonel can see light signals from other towers on the plateau. It's here, away from the eyes and ears of the servants, he has private conversations with other officers and intelligence operatives. As a boy, Tyrone longed to be invited to this secret sanctum where his father would go all hours of the night and day. Now . . . he wishes he could be elsewhere.

"Sit down," Jubal says as he moves to his desk and sits behind it. Every object on the desk has a purpose and sits in exactly the spot where it should be. There are no useless items here.

Ty knows better than to dawdle. He takes a seat across the desk from his father without a word.

Jubal gazes upon his son and it takes nearly all of his endurance to keep from leaning across the desk, grabbing at least one of the inch-long straggly hairs on his son's face, and yanking it clean out. Instead, he locks eyes with Tyrone. "I hope you're getting all of this out of your system. When you're at the academy, you will be the essence of a young officer, anxious to prove his worth. . . . Won't you." It isn't a question.

No longer wanting to hold his father's gaze, the young man looks down at the hazy reflection of the man in the surface of the dark wood on the desk before answering quietly. "Yes. Yes sir."

The colonel leans back in his seat. "I understand. Really I do. I was young once and I wanted to pursue a folly or two. I wanted to go out carousing with the other boys my age. . . ." He purposely lowers his voice. "I wanted to spend time with young ladies. But I was smart enough to realize that I didn't want to end up with a mediocre life. I listened to my father and I gave some real thought to the future. And nearly everything I've done," he says with a sweeping gesture, "I've done with the future in mind. Our future, your future, and—mark my words," he says, leaning forward and poking a finger on his desk for emphasis, "the future of all Aegea will be steered from this very place. If you will listen to me, there will be no limits to what you can do. But you have to get hold of yourself now, son. You may have been born into this family, but that will only get you so far. The last part of the climb is up to you. When the general dies, this plateau will see a shakeup. Don't let future opportunities be lost because you threw away your energy on foolishness today."

Ty's thoughts drift to a seemingly random memory of sneaking off to be in the garden with Shaye and her mother when he was about six or seven. While her mother was speaking to one of the gardeners, he looked at Shaye—a skinny little stick of a girl at the time—and asked what she was doing.

"I'm checking the plants."
"Checking?"

She sticks her fingers in the soil at the base of a fluffy fern. "Yes," she says with a sober little face. "He wants water."

He's skeptical and asks, "The plant is a 'he'? It looks like a frilly, girlish sort of plant to me."

Shaye looks annoyed. "Well, these," she says, running her hand over the tops of several ferns, "are like the soldiers of the garden."

He laughs. "Why? What makes them soldiers?"

"They will overtake everything else in the garden if you let them . . . so I think they are soldiers."

That was probably the beginning of his fascination with plants, trees, land, and water.

Ty shifts around in his chair and says, "Why is it that whatever I may want—as long as it's not what you want—is foolish? What if the future I want is simply different from what you've planned? . . . What if things shake out differently than you wanted?" His words aren't spoken in anger, but they aren't well received.

"You have no idea," Jubal says before he realizes how harsh his tone sounds. He pauses, then continues in a softer voice. "You have no idea what we might be facing in the near future. . . . Like so many other young people, you think you can sit around and have 'deep conversations' and things will change for the better simply because you want them to. But if you want things to change, then prepare yourself to get to the top and make those things happen. The weak minded and poor will always have their lives dictated to them. The vast majority of young men entering the military will choose to live somewhere in the middle of the pack. They will waste lots of time sitting around with their friends and whining about how much better it could be—but honestly, in the end they will be content to change nothing and to live under someone else's command. . . . If you *really* want to change the way things are, then *this*, right now, is your opportunity to start your rise to the top. Get up there and *then* decide what you might do to make your world better."

Until six months ago, Tyrone worked hard on various parts of Westland, learning different aspects of farming, water management, and construction. He would go out for long days and nights with workers in the fields or the orchards. He'd even labored on the aqueduct and then on the mill his father was having built near the great falls. Working the land was the life Ty wanted . . . but it *wasn't* what his father wanted.

According to Jubal McClaren, while learning all the aspects of agriculture were important as far as "general oversight" would require, these things were just pieces in a much larger puzzle. In order to have control of the whole puzzle, one had to be able to navigate the political, economic, and social realms—and these realms could only be navigated within the military. It was likely that Ty's father would be the next General, and in Jubal's mind, the only thing that could surpass this would be for his son to build upon his legacy in the future.

It is now certain to Ty that going to the academy and becoming a soldier are unavoidable, and he's simply given up trying to win his father's approval in other ways. Will Jubal ever understand the things that matter to him?

He looks at his father and says, "I'll do my utmost, sir."

Those words encourage the colonel. For a moment the tension leaves the room and his demeanor is more like he's conversing with a comrade over a cup of steaming banji. He looks at his son and says, "It's not as easy or as simple as it looks. A society of thousands of people doesn't turn like a little cart behind a horse. Believe me, no matter what you change, no matter how simple, fair, or noble you think it is, you will face resistance. Even small changes to the system ripple out in unexpected ways. You have to be willing to just chip away at goals for a lifetime." Jubal pauses to look out the nearest window, but his focus goes far beyond anything he could see there. "I've made it a point to educate myself well beyond what the Academy requires. I've studied history and I've learned two things." He faces Tyrone again. "The first is that power can change hands relatively easily as long as daily living remains tolerable for most people. The second is that enormous changes in daily living are only accomplished *quickly* when there is chaos and blood, and the memory—the scar of it—lasts for many generations.

"I'd be the first to admit that our society is far from perfect but it *works*. There is no starvation here, and everyone has something to do. No matter what the system, there are some people who will find ways to exploit it and others who end up with little or nothing. When you are in the Academy, you'll have some access to the files. Study what happened in the Second Generation. Miscalculations were made on *both* sides—and it was nearly the end of *everyone*. There were many lean and bitter years for everyone after it was all said and done."

Jubal suddenly realizes he's strayed from the purpose of the meeting. He straightens up in his chair and looks at his son again. "Ty, right now is your opportunity to start your rise to the top. Get up there and *then* decide what you might do to make your world better. Of all the young men in your generation, you have the best chance to have it all. Don't throw it away."

An hour later, Jariel is searching for Shaye. She has the brown dress and a drab brown scarf set aside in her room and she needs to be sure Shaye has them. She makes her way down the stairs to the kitchen and opens the door at the bottom of the stairs. Although she played in this room nearly every day as a small child, it's a place she rarely goes now.

Mosha and Shaye, are standing with their backs to the stairway, unaware of Jariel's presence. The two women are preparing vegetables for the evening meal.

It's been a very tense day so far and Shaye feels the need for a little fun. She bumps her hip against Mosha's and says, "I bet I can finish mine before you finish yours."

The old woman ignores her at first . . . but as Shaye speeds up she can't resist the competition. After a few moments of frantic action with knives, they both laugh.

As Jariel watches them, she's transported to a scene that took place when she was only three or four. She and Shaye were sitting on the large counter in the center of the kitchen.

Mosha had made something gooey and sweet and they all had their hands in it. . . .

> *"Okay. You give a bite to Jariel. That's right. Now, Jariel, give a bite to Shaye."*
>
> *A small hand comes from below the level of the countertop and steals a pinch of dough.*
>
> *"Oh look!" Mosha says in pretended horror. "It's a great horrible beast from the forest and he's going to eat all the dough!"*
>
> *A growl is heard before a strawberry blond head appears over the edge of the counter, then a set of blue eyes.*
>
> *Mosha covers her face. "Oh, no! Maybe he will eat all of us!"*
>
> *The two girls squeal in delighted terror as Ty snatches more of the dough and runs from the room.*

Jariel blinks away the memory and once again she's watching Mosha and Shaye chop vegetables.

Mosha says, "Okay, you could win, my girl. But mine look better so let me finish the rest."

"Yes, Mum."

Jariel clears her throat.

Both of them turn, both are smiling but when Shaye sees Jariel, her smile disappears.

"I need Shaye to go get her dress," Jariel says to Mosha. When she came down to the kitchen, Jariel intended to tell Shaye to go and get the dress herself . . . but, perhaps she doesn't want Shaye to have an excuse to be alone in her room. "She needs to come with me right now to get it."

Shaye wipes her hands on her apron before removing it, then follows Jariel back upstairs.

Once they are in her room, Jariel points to the garments draped over a chair.   "Take them. Make sure you wear the scarf."

When Shaye walks over to gather them up, Jariel closes the door so that she can speak privately. "I know you put that creature in my dressing table drawer."

"I did not."

"Liar."

Under her breath, Shaye groans, "Oh laaaaaaah," before she says, "You think that one of the *thousands* of lizards outside couldn't have come in through your window and crawled into an open drawer?"

The ishi's daughter stares into the face of her childhood ally-turned-enemy. "Say what you want." She juts her jaw forward and bobbles her head back and forth as she speaks. "It won't do you any good. I know you sneak in here and do things that look like no one did them. You put that creature in the drawer and I should ask Mother to make you work off the value of the things that it ruined."

Shaye knows it could happen and there is little point in counter-accusing Jariel of putting salt in her bed. Besides, why give her the satisfaction of knowing the salt was noticed? Shaye looks down at the garments. "Am I to return the dress and scarf?"

"I wouldn't wear them after you had them on."

Shaye walks toward the door. "So I am to keep them?"

"As far as I'm concerned," Jariel responds, "you can take them when we put you out of the house."

Shaye's hand misses the latch on the door but she catches it with a second attempt. Jariel hopes it's because she's finally unnerved someone who *should* know her place in life.

There is nothing Shaye can say in response to this so she makes no attempt at it. *Any* words at this point would stir up a conflict she cannot win. She opens the door and exits the room.

Jariel watches till Shaye is about to descend the stairs then adds, "Soon, Mosha won't be able to save you anymore."

It's time for the midday meal. Shaye is running late, so she hurries through the courtyard and the open space behind the great house, toward the outdoor kitchen where most of the servants' meals are cooked and eaten. Although she eats breakfast in the great house with Mosha, she's expected to eat her lunch and supper out here.

Ana, the adolescent daughter of Clement and Geena, runs out to greet her. "Good afternoon, Miss Shaye! Guess what?"

Shaye puts on a serious face. "Don't say it. I want to guess."

Since Shaye turned seventeen, she is no longer considered a child and that makes Ana, at the age of eleven, the oldest child living here. While there is a large gap in maturity between them, Ana is closer in age to Shaye than any of the other servants.

"Okay," Ana says. She stretches her arms out and twirls around once so the hem of her gray dress floats out, wraps around her, then unwinds.

"You got married."

Ana laughs. "No! That's silly." She takes a few steps to keep up with Shaye, then twirls again.

"You found a golden egg in the hen's nests."

Ana shakes her head. "No!" She twirls in the opposite direction.

"A tree grew out of your ear last night and your mother had to pull it out."

Ana stops twirling and laughs again. "NO! It's about the kitchen in the great house."

"*Hmmmmmmm.* Let's see."

Ana can't wait for any more guesses. She grabs Shaye's hand and pulls her into the dining area. "It's about ME in the kitchen. Mosha says I can help in the kitchen for planning day!"

"That was going to be my next guess."

"No it wasn't."

Shaye smiles. "You're right. But it will be so good to have your help on planning day. You're not excited about it, are you?"

Ana hops up and down. "Yes."

"I would never have guessed that."

Ana's mother calls to her so the girl leans over and says "I have to go now, but I wanted to tell you."

The rooms in the servant's quarters have small hearths, but nearly all the cooking for workers is done here. Although high ranking families think of private meals as a privilege, most Genon consider common meals taken together part of community life. Since many of the people here work long hours at solitary tasks, this is where the social order is established, friendships form, and common problems are discussed. To them, community itself is a living organism whose health and welfare often depend upon the loyalties and relationships forged here.

There are eight large tables under the roof of the kitchen/dining area and though there are no rules about where people must sit, tradition puts unmarried women and men at separate tables. Families often sit together for the evening meal, but the midday meal is generally divided by sex, with the women sitting close together so they can feed children and share the latest news, giving the men a little time for problem-solving concerning the day's jobs or the freedom to be silent. Young single men generally sit at the table farthest from the kitchen so they can watch all the women and make the occasional coarse joke without being overheard. If they become too much of a nuisance, one of the older women will scold them for being disrespectful.

Because she sleeps in the "great house," Shaye is somewhat at a disadvantage in the community. She learned years ago that her words about the colonel's family or her life inside the house could be interpreted to say she thought she was on a higher level than others in the group. To this day, some fear she might share the community's internal information with the colonel's family for her own advantage. Because of these things, she spends most of her mealtimes with the other women who work in the house and avoids discussions on topics that might throw her loyalties into question.

Several people greet Shaye and she waves as she walks to where the food is served. Two women are standing in the kitchen; one of them, Monique, is Old Menoh's daughter-in-law and the other is the round figured woman Shaye saw cleaning the tables earlier.

"Good day Palma."

"Good afternoon, Shaye," Palma says with a round-faced grin. "Do you want everything?"

She scans the counter behind Palma. There are fruits, chunks of cheese made from goat's milk, and some bread. At the hearth, Monique is stirring a pot of thick bean soup seasoned with spices, onion, and garlic.

Shaye nods. "Yes please."

She's given a small bowl of the soup with the flatbread on top and the other items stacked on the flatbread. She walks to the table where she normally sits.

The dining area is still crowded due to an influx of workers who are constructing a new building behind the dining hall. The colonel had hoped to have the building finished before Jariel's planning day, but a few engineering problems and bad weather have delayed progress several times. Of course, there has been great speculation about the future occupants of the new building. Rumors have floated around for weeks. Some say it's for an increase of farm hands now that the land is producing so well. Others say it's for the workers with the longest tenure with the colonel, and that the new workers will get the old living quarters. And, with all those rooms, will Menoh and his wife move into the building? No answers have been forthcoming.

At the back of the hall, several of the construction guys sit with the single men watching all the goings on, making funny remarks and laughing regularly. They grow quiet for a few moments when Shaye enters the hall, then they resume their conversation.

Shaye takes a seat between Beth (who works as a personal maid to Jariel and the ishi) and Chessie, a newly acquired worker who helps with food prep in the outdoor kitchen, washing clothes, or in the great house if needed. Because Chessie is new and comes from a family of gleaners (considered the lowest class of people in all of Aegea), she hasn't been fully accepted into the community of workers here and she has slowly gravitated to the table where Shaye and Beth usually sit.

"Good day, ladies," Shaye says to them, then hands a bit of cheese to Beth's toddler. "And good day to you Mister Eli. How is everyone today?"

"I twisted my ankle this morning, on the way to the kitchen with the eggs." Chessie says. "Three of them flew out of the basket and broke so Monique is mad at me."

Almost as if she could hear the comments, Monique looks up from the back of the kitchen, eyes Chessie, then shakes her head.

"Sorry," Shaye offers.

Young Ana skips over to the table and slides in next to Eli and Beth.

Beth puts down her food and holds her stomach. "The baby is really kicking today," she says. "This one is so much more active than Eli was. I so hope it's a girl."

"Me too!" Ana chimes in.

Chessie leans forward so she can see Beth on the other side of Shaye. "*Eh eh*. Fiona says it's a boy. She's always right."

Old Menoh's wife, Fiona, has attended the birth of more than a hundred babies in her lifetime, and all the births of servant children in Westland—with the exception of Marta's baby who was born suddenly in the pear orchard eight years ago. Now that Fiona and Menoh are old, the colonel lets them live in a little place over by a pond and Fiona isn't expected to do a lot, but she still gets out and about, keeping track of the expectant mothers. Her accuracy of predicting the sex of babies is legendary.

"Well," Beth sighs, "I hope she's wrong. I want a girl to help me the way Ana helps her mama."

Ana beams.

The whole room falls eerily silent, so they look up from their conversation to see a young man standing in front of their table. Shaye surmises that he's one of the men working on the new building since she doesn't remember ever seeing him before. His clothes are stained and the only clean skin on him is on his face and hands because he washed them before lunch. He's short with dark hair and dark eyes . . . and he's staring at her.

When she makes eye contact with him, he momentarily freezes, then looks back at his compatriots for encouragement. All the young men at the table laugh and wave him on, so he reaches into his shirt and produces a single, white flower—the symbol of interest in a new relationship—and places it on the table in front of Shaye.

Her face burns as all the young men and nearly everyone else in the room begins to say "*Woooooooooo*," or laugh.

She doesn't touch the flower and after a few moments of her *non*-response, most of the people quiet down and look away.

Beth stands up and hoists Eli onto her hip. "I need to go now," she says before looking at Ana. "I think I heard your mother calling you again."

Ana is captivated by the whole idea of a young man presenting Shaye with a flower. "No. I didn't hear her."

"But *I* did," Beth says quickly. "Come right now."

The girl reluctantly gets up.

The other woman at the table, Chessie, has no intention of leaving.

"Did your friends at the table put you up to this?" Shaye asks the man. "Did all of you need some sort of new mischief?"

He looks wounded. "No, Miss. I've watched you every day for several weeks since someone told me you were of age and that you would like to receive the flower from me."

Chessie puts an elbow on the table and rests her chin on her hand so she can watch the whole scene unfold in comfort.

Shaye knows that the entire conversation will be repeated for everyone later so she just gets on with it. "Well I certainly hope that in exchange for this bit of information that 'someone' didn't have you do him a big favor—or pay him with *meechi* juice." She sees that her remark has struck a chord.

"What is your name?" she asks.

"Rio."

She doesn't want to be unkind . . . but she *does* want to bring an end to the public humiliation for both of them.

"So . . . Rio. I mean no scorn toward you, but I don't even *know* you. I'm sorry that someone spoke an untruth to you, but there it is. I wouldn't want to give you any sort of false idea by accepting this," she says, indicating the flower by pointing her chin at it. "I thank you for the compliment, but I cannot accept it."

"Just so your friends don't tease you, though," Chessie suddenly chimes in, "why don't you sit down for a moment and talk to us?"

Shaye's eyebrows shoot up as she looks at her friend.

Chessie smiles and says, "Well, I'm closer to his age than you are."

Rio is shocked as well but he sits down.

Another buzz goes through the dining room and the young men in the back look impressed.

"So how much longer do you think you'll be working on the building?" Chessie asks.

His face takes on a hopeful/happy look. "At least two weeks."

Within minutes, Shaye excuses herself and walks back to the house. Chessie and Rio continue talking until their lunch break is over.

CHAPTER 4
Jariel—View from the Window

"Only the One who made our hearts knows all that is in them."—
From the Tell of His people

Jariel runs her hands across the different skeins of yarn, looking for just the right color. Deep red. She thinks for a moment before pulling the skein out and carrying it over to the loom. She holds it up next to the red on a completed portion of the piece of the work and compares them.

"Yes. You will do," she says to the skein.

Next, she sets about winding the yarn onto a bobbin that will fit into a shuttle she uses to weave the yarn into the tapestry.

Working on a loom is one of the few traditional crafts that a young lady in a high-ranking family can freely pursue. While smaller looms are used by servants and tradesmen in lower classes, what Jariel produces is considered "art" and therefore it's an acceptable use of her time. Anyone viewing one of Jariel's tapestries would say that she has elevated the craft to an art. She creates scenes and patterns that are a wonder to her parents, and they ask themselves, *How could so much creativity abide in such a mousy girl?*

Later tonight, she'll be expected to attend a dinner and a meeting where her parents will lay out strategies for the finishing touches on her upcoming "planning day," but she won't think about it right now. She'd much rather be up here working her loom than preparing for the day when she will be surrounded by people who are nearly strangers to her, yet their main purpose is to pry into her life and discuss who she should or should not marry. Scarier still is the very thought that she will be expected to court and marry a man when she's probably never had more than two sentences of conversation with someone who isn't a relative or a servant.

She hears a sound outside and looks out the window.

Household servants, Shaye and Beth, are carrying baskets of clean, wet laundry to the area where the items will be hung. The two women are striding along nearly in unison with the wide hems of their dresses flowing out in the current of a breeze. Beth's three-year-old son is following along, more or less, when he isn't looking at rocks or other objects he finds along the way. Shaye points at something in the sky and they all stop to look at it, shading their eyes from the midday sun. Jariel cannot see whatever it is unless she leans out the window and reveals her presence, so she opts to stay in the privacy of the shadows. Perhaps they're looking at a bird or a cloud. Soon they resume walking toward where laundry is hung, now separating to move to different ends of the lines. Each woman drapes wet clothing or bedding on a line, occasionally reaching over to feel items hung earlier to determine if they are dry.

Beth starts humming a song, and before long she and Shaye are both singing it as they work. It's a child's song about a rivalry between a bird and a mouse. The little boy begins to clap and bounce to the tune.

Jariel hovers just inside the window with the song now spilling into her mind before each part is sung, and she's amazed that something she's not heard since she was small has lingered in some crevice of memory, waiting to be set free again. She smiles a couple of times while the song winds around a silly plot and the melody stops and starts at catchy points. It's as if she can hear Mosha warbling the tune along with them the way she did so many years ago.

The bearded old servant, Menoh, walks by and the two women stop singing to greet him. He nods and keeps trudging along.

Shaye and Beth return to hanging clothes. Jariel waits, but they don't resume the song and soon they are done with the task. They walk their separate ways and Jariel watches them until they are out of view. Even after they are gone, she stares out the window at the empty courtyard behind the house and a memory comes to life in her mind.

When Jariel and Ty were old enough to be left in full-time care of servants, Mother and Father went on several extended trips to town. It was a wonder-filled time when Jariel roamed gardens, played hide and seek with Ty and Shaye, ran up and down the stairs to the kitchen, hid in cupboards, and even traveled in a wagon with Shaye's mother, bumping along amongst the potted plants. She can see a bit of that last day as clearly as if she shot back through time and was allowed to watch it.

> *Someone took a soft, white stone and made markings all over the courtyard. She and Shaye are singing and playing a game that involves hopping and tossing small rocks into the different boxes marked in the courtyard. She is right in the middle of a successful turn when Mother, arriving home from a trip, comes out the back door of the house, and swoops down on her like a large bird of prey upon a small creature.*
>
> *In one motion Duana sweeps her off her feet and spins back around toward the house. Once she realizes Mother is not playing the game, she begins to cry and struggle against being hauled into the house. When they are on the upper floor of the house, Mother plops her down so roughly it hurts her bottom.*
>
> *"Look at you!" Mother says loudly. "You're covered with dirt. You have no business playing outside, much less with that girl. Don't you ever let me catch you out there again . . ."*

Jariel continues to stare out the window for a few moments before returning to her loom. While she works, she begins to hum the tune.

Hours later, Beth and Shaye are at lunch in the dining area. Beth's three-year-old Eli and Young Ana's toddler brother are busy mashing peas onto the table as the two women watch with amusement. Fellow worker Chessie joins them at the table.

"It's a pretty day, isn't it?" Chessie asks.

They nod in agreement.

"A good day if you must work outside."

They nod again.

"Where are all the men today?"

Beth is scraping a few of the mashed peas up with a leaf—giving a new activity to the toddlers—when she looks up and says, "John told me that many of the men are out to haul more lumber and some bricks for the new building."

"Have they gone far?"

"They should be back before dark as far as I know."

Shaye has nothing to add to the conversation so she sits quietly and eats the last bit of her lunch.

"Do you think they'll be finished with the building soon?" Chessie asks.

Beth shrugs. "We see they are making progress . . . but that's all I know about it. John mostly works with the livestock, so he's not generally aware of other things."

Young Ana, who often helps watch the toddlers while their mothers are working, comes to collect the boys. When Ana is out of earshot, Chessie looks at Beth and asks, "When did you know for sure that you were pregnant?"

Beth glances at Shaye before she says, "Well, you know. The usual way. I didn't have my period for a couple of months. When I missed three, I knew."

"So if you only missed one you wouldn't be worried."

Beth's eyes open a little wider. Sex isn't often an open topic of discussion. "Well . . . I wouldn't be worried about it in any case. John and I are blessed to work here. The colonel treats us well. We want children."

"I've missed periods before," Chessie says. "Never more than one, though," she quickly adds.

While she's very curious about the topic, Shaye is also very uncomfortable with such a conversation in a public place. She wants to listen . . . yet doesn't want to seem overly interested. She looks toward the back of the great house and is almost grateful to see Mosha waving to her. "There's Mosha. I need to go. See you later."

Once Shaye leaves the table, Beth turns back to Chessie. Not certain what the real purpose for starting the conversation might be, Beth says, "But if you're not having physical relations with a man . . . you can't be pregnant."

Chessie nods. "I know that."

CHAPTER 5
Stargazer Shaye

"Our Great Father formed the hands of man and woman. He placed
   in the hands of His own people the ability to tame plant, animal
   and earth, to shape stone and wood, but we shall not be satisfied
   until we are gathered together with Him beyond the stars. For
   who can be satisfied with a shadow of the true substance? Who
   can be content with less than the full glory to which we are
   called?"—*Part of The Tell, given to Kesh in the beginning of sojourning,
   long before the First Generation of Aegea, to be remembered by all of His
   people*

A long day's work is done and Shaye stands alone near
the waist-high wall that surrounds the flat rooftop. She ties a
knot in the front of the old shawl to keep it over her shoulders
and breathes in the night-cooled air. A half moon is in the
sky, but she stands with her back to it, gazing up at the stars.
She raises a hand as if she might touch one of them before a
voice behind her makes her jump.

"If you manage to catch it, are you going to keep it in your
pocket?" Ty asks. It's a question he's probably asked
thousands of times since they were children.

She regains her composure. "Oh no. I never keep them.
It would be a shame if I did that. And what would people
think if all the stars began to disappear? Panic on the
plateau."

"I dare say, there would be havoc in the streets. And if
they discovered it was you who'd stolen all those stars, you
might be set before a tribunal."

She keeps watching the sky. "It's been so long since I've
seen you up here I'm surprised you care about the stars
anymore."

"I still care about the stars. But tonight I came up because I heard somewhere that you're headed to town tomorrow and you'll be gone a whole week. I wanted to make sure I said goodbye."

She rests her hands on the top of the chiseled stone wall as her eyes sweep the heavens. "Goodbye."

He stands next to her and mirrors her pose, facing the wall with his hands upon it. His right hand is nearly touching her left. "Don't say it like that," he chides. "You make me feel as if we will never see each other again, or like you don't care that you're leaving."

"You will be going away soon—for a long time," she counters. "And it seems as if it has been cause for endless celebrations on your part. As for me," she says with an unintended sigh, "my time of service here will be paid off this year. Perhaps, while I am in town I will get the offer of a trade . . . but," she shrugs, "I'm not sure what I will do."

"I wasn't 'celebrating,' I was trying not to think about where I must go and the things I must do. But soon, you'll be sort of free. I envy that."

She glances at him. "*Sort* of free. Do you hear yourself? 'Sort of free'? Free to do what? Attach myself to another household and do their bidding? Free to go hungry? Free to live in Oldtown? I'm a servant and what I want doesn't matter. How could you envy such things?"

He looks out at the view, takes a deep breath and then exhales slowly. "I'm sorry. That was a stupid thing to say."

"Do you know when you will be leaving?" she asks.

"I'll be leaving on the second morning after Jariel's day. Leaving this house, my family, and the life I've lived until now—I will leave the crops and trees and waters of Westland. I will miss them." He doesn't dare look at her. "I will miss you, Shaye."

"And I you," she says in a barely audible voice. "You were nearly my only friend for many years."

They are both quiet as each of them ponders the confession of the other.

"You know, if you lived in town . . ." he says in an offhand manner, "the Academy is near Oldtown. Perhaps we could meet sometimes and just talk the way we used to."

She turns to face him and he can make out her features in the moonlight. There's a look of such sorrow on her countenance. "We have different paths set before us," she says, "and those paths lead in different directions. A continued friendship between us won't be possible."

"I cannot accept that," he says, drawing close to her. "Stargazer Shaye . . . what a perplexity you are. You long to walk in heavenly realms . . . yet you choose this moment to insist on practicality." He leans forward so that his mouth is only an inch from her ear. "Who is to say what changes we might see in this world? Don't say you won't see me anymore. I couldn't bear the thought."

"You have been gone so much this past year it seems as if I've barely seen you," she says. "Why do you care now?"

Ty steps back and searches her eyes. "Today, it occurred to me that all the time I spent doing anything that would keep me from thinking about my departure from Westland was such a waste. I've *always* cared, Shaye."

"Have you?"

He realizes he doesn't have the nerve to say all he'd like to say, but he cannot allow her to think she means nothing to him. "I still remember the very first time I ever saw you."

"Is that so?"

As if they are children again, he reaches over and pulls the short sticks from her hair and it tumbles down over her shoulders.

"Instead of being all twisted up in back," he says, "your hair was down. You turned and looked at me with those eyes," he takes her hand and places it on his chest, "and it made something in my heart jump."

He hasn't held her hand since they were small. Shaye lets her palm rest on his chest for a few moments before taking it away.

Her brow furrows as she tries to recall something, then her whole face relaxes as it comes to her. "The first thing I remember about you . . . was when I was four or five . . . you had a cut on your forehead," she touches her own face to mirror the spot his was hurt, "and you told me you had been doing battle with a large beast. I asked you where it was and you said you'd made it disappear when you struck it with a sword."

He laughs softly. "Did you believe me?"

"I wasn't sure. But mother said you were a good little soldier."

A light from the tower suddenly spills out onto the roof on the far side of the house. It's from the window of the colonel's ready room. A moment later the sound of the colonel's voice begins to waft out of the tower as well.

"We'd better go." She whispers.

With a reluctant nod, he answers, "You go first and I'll leave after you've gone."

She looks intently at him and says, "I will be back three days before Jariel's planning day," before walking away.

He watches until she is gone.

CHAPTER 6
Shaye—Journey to Oldtown

"Home is where welcome voices, sights, smells, and tastes call you to
come and rest."—A proverb of His people

For an entire afternoon, the aging brown horse pulled the
wagon with three passengers across the entire western half of
the Aegean plateau, plodding past fields, groves, and rocky
outcroppings, occasionally passing workers plowing for new
crops or tending to fruit trees. Now that they've reached a
stopping point, the animal is anxious to be unharnessed,
watered, and fed. He turns his head to eye the passenger now
idly standing near the wagon. He snorts at her.

Shaye waits in the fading light while Lemon and a field
worker by the name of Ski secure their lodging. The horse
keeps looking at her, so she's pretty certain he wants her
attention. She hasn't had much experience with horses but
she knows they are capable of some pretty powerful kicks so
she approaches him cautiously, leaving plenty of open space
around his hind legs. She makes sure he's looking right at her
before she slowly stretches out a hand to gently scratch his
head the way she saw Ski do it earlier. The animal moves his
chin closer to her so she rubs his muzzle and is surprised at

how soft it is. While she pets him, she keeps shifting her stance from one foot to the other because her feet are so uncomfortable. Although most of the peasants and servants on the plateau wear wooden clogs, the colonel hates the *clack clack* of them on his floors so he gives his house workers leather sandals or allows them to walk in bare feet. Shaye has had these sandals for a couple of years, but since she rarely uses footwear of any kind, her feet don't like them. She imagines that the horse must feel the same way about the bit in his mouth.

"I've seen you before," she confides to the horse. "In case you don't remember me, I'm Shaye. I don't remember your name either, but you seem like a fine horse."

He wiggles his lips around and shows her his teeth. Smiling, she responds, "You agree, eh?"

While she pets him, she lets her eyes sweep around the area. After all, a trip to this side of Aegea is a rare treat for servants who live in Westland. It's been a year since Shaye last passed through this little outpost, consisting of an inn and the shops of several tradesmen. She wants to take in every detail around her.

Someone nearby is splitting wood and the slow rhythm of a large hammer pounding against a wedge is punctuated by silence when a log splits, then is replaced with another log. Even if she were blindfolded, she'd know the sounds and smells of this place. The odors of hay and manure from the barns and pens are mingled with scent burning wood and spicy ethnic food cooking inside the house. These are pungent smells that speak of hard work and simple pleasures. Not many have managed to make a go of small enterprises, but with rugged determination and much sweat, the six families living here have gained a toehold in a world run almost entirely by the military and people of high status. It's an unsteady endeavor at best since these families here aren't permitted to "own" any of the land. Despite their low standing, however, they've thus far been allowed to live in quasi-independence out here. They provide needed services in an isolated area—allowing the military to use resources elsewhere—but there are no guarantees the situation will be permanent. Thus far, both sides have chosen to ignore the lingering questions of what belongs to whom as long as the existence of the tradesmen here is mutually beneficial. Had her father lived longer, Shaye's family might have attempted to join these pioneers.

The inn itself is the curious mixture that results when people keep what they have and just add onto it as needs arise. From this distance, she can see the overall picture of what that looks like. The oldest part of the building is the original house of the family—rough stones held together with a little mortar. The wood of the shutters is gray and faded, the window openings are small. Branching out from the right side of the home is a newer addition. Cut stones, larger windows to accommodate the flow of air, and larger rooms where visitors can sit and eat. Atop this section is the newest part of the inn, containing three small guest rooms where officers and people of eminence can rest out of sight. Now that the road extending to Westland is fully paved with stones, who knows how this little outpost might grow?

A huddle of small buildings surrounding the inn are the homes and shops of the other families who live here—people skilled at working leather and wood, and one old man who can even work with metal. Soldiers and workers can come to this small settlement for repairs to tools and equipment, or if they are weary from a long day, they can come, eat, and rest.

Her view of the sunset is blocked by the second story of the barn, but Shaye knows it's only minutes before night descends upon the outpost. Their late departure from the colonel's house has kept them from making it all the way to Midtown before dark. They must stop now because the road ahead isn't lit and the horse might get injured or the equipment might fail, leaving them stranded in the dark. Besides, there are reports about occasional robberies on lonely stretches of the road at night.

Although she didn't plan on staying the night, it's a welcome bonus for Shaye and she is glad to have a respite from her fellow traveler, Lemon—who, as far as she is concerned, will never find a mate. He's lazy and ill tempered, and has spent most of the ride thus far complaining about the unfairness of his life and the waste of his many talents.

Lemon and their other traveling companion, Ski, will sleep in the wagon in the same shelter where the horse will be kept. Because she is a distant relative to the family who owns the inn (through the household of Zim—a Firstlander, an ancestor of her mother), Shaye will undoubtedly be invited to sleep on a cot inside the family's quarters.

The small bag slung over her shoulder contains her brush, a slip she can sleep in, a few toiletries, and a small bundle of cloth hidden at the bottom of her bag.

Quinn, the oldest son of the innkeeper, exits the house. About twenty years old, he is of medium height, slim, and muscular. He has dark hair, and like many of the people here, he is of mixed lineage. Because they want to stay in the good graces of the military force, Quinn and most of the men here (like the Genon men who work for the colonel) are clean shaven.

Shaye calls to him and waves. He says a quick hello before disappearing back into the home. A few moments later, he emerges with one of his sisters by the name of Joy. She has her mother's brown hair and hazel eyes, but she is taller than the other girls in the family. Her dress is modest, but the dyed yarns from which it is made and the style of the dress look well on her slender frame. Her apron and moccasins are made from leather—traditional garb which is both functional and protective for someone who works inside, outside, and around fires.

Joy's brother leads Lem and Ski to the barn where they will unharness the horse and get him set up for the night.

Joy rushes over to give Shaye a warm hug. "We didn't know you were coming! Welcome!"

"It's good to be here."

"That is nice," Joy says, feeling Shaye's sleeve. "Is this a new dress?"

"The ishi gave it to me yesterday."

The two turn and walk toward the house, both exceedingly happy for the company of a peer.

"Will you be in town long or are you just headed to market for a day?"

"I'll be there for a week. I'm going there to order Mosha's supplies for Jariel's planning day. Mostly fresh herbs and spices."

"Where will you stay?"

"With my great aunt. She moved to Oldtown this past year."

"Pearl?"

Shaye nods. There are so many things to say, so many questions to ask. It's quite likely that the two of them will talk long into the night. She leans over and whispers, "Does your sister know that Ski is here? I wouldn't be at all surprised if our delay in getting away today had something to do with the possibility of stopping here."

"Mother sent Kenny to go and tell her," Joy whispers back. "I'm sure she'll hurry back here as soon as she finishes her chores."

They share a delighted shrug and a smile. Both of them realize that people of low status often must marry for practicality. Love is a luxury few can pursue, so anything that has the slightest appearance of a genuine romance is significant to them.

"You'll have to give me all the news from Westland," Joy says. She's never traveled the twelve miles between her house and the farthest wall of Aegea.

Shaye shifts the bag on her shoulder. "Last year, they finished the aqueduct, so more of the land could be farmed. They are already increasing the fields and orchards. More soldiers and workers seem to be coming in all the time. . . . We had a harvest festival a few weeks ago."

Joy nods. "I know. The road was fairly clogged with people in fancy carts and soldiers on horseback. Some of them stopped here."

"The ishi had the great house painted," Shaye tells her. "Golden yellow."

Joy nods. A wonder like this wouldn't have stayed a secret. "I know that too. Golden yellow. It sounds like a dream or something."

Shaye nods. "You can see it from far away. And they painted the big hall inside the house a softer shade of the same color."

This is new information. "*Ohhhhh*, my," Joy says in a dreamy voice, then she falls silent for a few moments as she tries to think of anything to share that would be of equal importance. Then it comes to her. "I heard the General painted his house, too. But he painted his white and his people have to be dabbing it up all the time since it doesn't want to stay white."

Shaye tries to picture a house the color of clouds and mountain tops. "Judging by how hard it is to keep cloth white, I can only guess how hard it would be to keep a whole house white."

They enter the home and Joy's mother greets their guest warmly. Lilly is a graceful woman, but she looks older than her years. Many days of hard work plus raising four sons and three daughters has aged her, and her crinkled skin seems to hang a bit on her face.

"Shaye! What a nice surprise!" she exclaims. "Is that a new dress?"

"She just got it yesterday," Joy says. "From the ishi at the great house."

"Well who needs a mouth when Joy is here, eh?" Lilly asks with a smile. "How nice it is to see you, Shaye . . . and turning into a woman now I see!" Lilly shakes her head. "To think of the little girl who used to come here with her mother, bringing me shoots and roots when we were first starting out. You had skinny little legs that looked like two snakes falling out of the hem of your dress!" Lilly sighs. "What a special woman your mother was. . . . ." She focuses on Shaye. "And now you look like a full grown woman yourself." She touches two fingers to her lips, then points upward. "And I'd give an oath, you look just like her now."

Shaye blushes before a hint of a smile lights her face.

Lilly turns and starts walking down a hall through the center of the house. "Come and set your things down and then we can get you something to eat while you tell us all the news from Westland."

Joy follows her mother and their guest. "The men who came with Shaye are sleeping in the barn."

"I knew that," her mother says over her shoulder. The sound of her voice is softer now. It must be the fine wool rugs, added since her last visit.

"Yes," Joy answers her mother, "But did you know that the colonel painted his house?"

Lilly stops near a doorway and steps aside to let the girls enter. "*Hmmm*. I knew that, but I forgot about it."

"Golden yellow!" her daughter announces proudly. "Even inside the great hall of the house!"

"Now that I don't think I heard. Golden yellow . . . inside the house. Imagine that. What an extravagance, yes?"

Joy and her sister, Lu, share a room, but both of them have nicer beds than Shaye does. She notices they've hung a small tapestry on one wall since her last visit and she stops to admire it for a moment before placing her bag on the floor. It's not as lovely as the tapestries that Jariel makes, but it's pretty nonetheless.

"Lu can move whatever she needs into Abby's room later." Lilly tells her. "Come get something to eat."

Mother and daughter take her back through the hallway and to the kitchen hearth the family uses, and Joy gives her a seat by the fire. Lilly places four pieces of flat bread on the stone shelf inside the hearth to warm them for a few moments, then ladles up several large wooden plates of thick stew.

Shaye glances around the room. Although it isn't grand like the colonel's home, she likes this cozy space. The simple furniture, the carved posts supporting the beams, and the pegs that hold the posts and beams together are like a large wooden puzzle.

Lilly looks up from her task. "So, how is Mosha? Is she well?"

"Yes. Very well. She did put me in mind of a wet bird yesterday though." Shaye splays out her fingers. "It was like her feathers were all standing up. We are making preparations for Jariel's planning day and I think all the extra 'help' is more upsetting to her than the extra work . . . but once the kitchen is back in order and the colonel and the ishi give their compliments, she'll be right again."

Lilly nods. "I miss her. I haven't seen her in so long. . . . And what is happening with you? What brings the three of you this way?"

Before she can answer, they hear the voice of Quinn speaking to the men coming into the dining room on the other side of the inn.

"Do you want to eat in here by the fire or out at the table with your friends?" Lilly asks.

"Here is good. I'd be glad to sit with you and Joy by the fire. It's a cool evening."

Lilly gives one of the plates and a spoon to Shaye before handing the two plates to her daughter. "Please take this out to the men. Tell them we have bread—I'm just warming it up a little."

Joy leaves the room while her mother places a cloth napkin on a small table near Shaye's chair, and asks, "So what brings you to this side of the plateau?"

"Lemon and Ski will do business for the colonel in Midtown. I will go to Oldtown," she says, referring to the area inside the First Wall where many of the homes of the First Generation still stand. The wall, built to keep out the creatures and dangers that so terrified the Firstlanders, is no longer maintained, but the remnants of it still mark the border to Oldtown. "My Great Aunt Pearl has moved there and I'll stay with her."

Lilly is thinking aloud. "Oldtown. *Hmmmmm.*" She knows as well as anyone that Pearl must have fallen on hard times to be living in Oldtown. "She must be very old by now."

Shaye nods. "Yes, she is seventy."

"Is she still a chaplain?"

"As far as I know, yes. I haven't seen her in a year."

"My. It must feel good to be able to spend time with someone in your family."

"Yes. It will be especially wonderful this visit because Aunt Pearl has a small place of her own now. I can stay with her and have her all to myself."

"It must be extra special," Lilly says, "to spend time with someone who was connected with the Ruins and the records. Someone who is able to see our connection to our past, to know it."

Shay remembers the time she was allowed to walk with her aunt among the "ruins" of the airship called Aegean C.

She's only nine and she has to promise to be quiet and to not touch anything. Actually, there is very little that could be seen unless it's pointed out and explained by Aunt Pearl. Most of the craft was cut up and used by survivors in their efforts to stay alive. Pearl takes her to an earthen shelter where two old "seats" and a number of other objects are kept. Shaye is permitted to walk very close to one of the seats but not to touch it. The thing has an odd sort of upright shape, and it's upholstered with a type of material she's not seen before.

As they walk away from the shelter, Pearl points out the long gash in the surface of the plateau where the craft skidded to a stop. Given more than one hundred years to heal, the gash has eroded into a shallow valley covered with grasses, trees, and vines. Her aunt points to a giant arc in the distance, emerging from the ground, taller than eight spans, and wide enough for a cart to pass through. She says it's a partially buried "engine casing." Shaye has no idea what an engine casing might be but it certainly looks like nothing else in Aegea. Even seeing a few bits of wreckage for herself, it's hard for Shaye to imagine what the craft might have looked like. And she certainly can't picture something large enough to take nearly two thousand people flying through the air.

Indeed, some people in Aegea claim that it never happened. But in her youth, Pearl knew people who had actually flown up above the tall mountains, into the sky itself, beyond the clouds. When Shaye repeats the doubts others voice, her aunt says, "How do those people think we got here? Did we spring up from the grass? Creating these objects took a skill beyond what anyone here possesses." She leans down and holds Shaye's chin in her hand. "People will always try to find ways to disown the truth, but truth will eventually catch up with everybody no matter how far they wander from it . . ."

"Want butter on that?" Lilly asks.

Shaye refocuses her attention on her hostess and accepts the offer. "I would like it very much."

Lilly retrieves a knife and a small crock with butter while she continues to talk. "And the colonel and the ishi, are they well?"

Shaye nods and swallows a bite. "They are well."

"I hear he's made a proper farm out of Westland since they finished the aqueduct and the new road. It's said that inside the gates of the post, it's bustling with soldiers and workers alike. And I know there was a harvest festival for some of the soldiers out there a few weeks ago. We got some good trades out of that—a few soldiers and their families stopped by on the way back as well." She pauses a moment before observing, "Must be lonely to be all the way out there most of the time, though."

Perhaps it's the connection she feels with Lilly and this family, but Shaye surprises herself with words that come straight from her heart and reveal an inner part of her soul. "Oh, but the gardens, fields, and groves are beautiful. Like it must have appeared in the first garden."

Lilly nods. "I guess there is something of earth and plants in our blood, eh?"

Joy returns from the other room and it's obvious that she is anxious to share something. She pulls a chair close to Shaye and looks as if she might burst if she doesn't say whatever it is.

Shaye studies her friend's face. "*What*?"

That one word is all the encouragement Joy needs. "I saw the colonel's son, Tyrone a couple of weeks ago. He came this far with Major Cam's family the day after the festival, before heading back to Westland on his horse. He said he was going to be entering the Academy soon."

"Seems like yesterday," Lilly interjects, "when Shaye and Tyrone and Jariel were chasing each other around the bushes in my garden. I can still hear the three of you laughing." She looks at Shaye. "To think all of you are grown makes me feel so old!" she says. "But life goes on, doesn't it? I suppose Tyrone will be out of the Academy and wedded to someone like Major Cam's daughter Linsey before I know it."

"*She's* sure counting on it," Joy says.

Shaye stops chewing. She and Lilly both look at Joy.

Joy shrugs. "After he left, I heard her saying so when she and her friend were waiting to use the privy. She said he spent most of his time talking to her while she was there, and she thought it meant something that he escorted them this far."

Joy and Lilly both turn to Shaye for confirmation.

"Is it true?" Joy asks.

Shaye slowly swallows her food. "I didn't get to go to the festival." She frowns and starts stirring the stew around on her plate before she realizes they are staring at her. She looks over at Lilly and asks, "Did I hear that your son Pete is raising some cows now?"

"Why yes. He started with two last year but now he's got three. We get cream, milk, cheese, butter . . . and of course fertilizer—all of which we can use or trade. He's even had contact from the butcher who lives out near you about the possibility of trading with him next year."

Shaye coughs and Joy gets her a cup of water.

"You know the butcher, don't you?" Lilly asks.

Shaye nods.

Lilly frowns. "I'm judging by your silence you don't think highly of him."

"No. That's not so. The colonel does business with him and he sells fine meats. . . . It's just that I know little of how he runs his business."

Lilly nods. "I see. You're right."

###

Out in the dining area, Shaye's traveling companions, Lem and Ski eat their meal and talk to Lilly's oldest son, Quinn. Two oil lamps on the long wooden table give soft light to the room. Half a dozen empty chairs are against the far wall beneath shelves holding dishes, folded napkins, a variety of clay jars, and several more unused lamps. Quinn's father is at a neighbor's shop working on a project with one of his brothers so Quinn sits at the head of the table, nibbling now and again on a piece of bread. On his left is an empty seat. Next to it is Lemon who has finished his meal and pushed his chair around so he can face Quinn. Beyond Lem, Ski is popping a last bit of carrot into his mouth and scraping the plate with his last bite of bread.

"It's terrible in Westland for anyone who isn't in the military forces," Lem says. "We're out there away from friends and family and no one cares. They just think they can work us all the harder since there's nothing else to do—and they get all the benefit of our labor." Lemon pulls the empty chair out to place his feet on it, then makes a sweeping gesture with his arm. "You are so lucky to have this place, freedom to be yourselves, freedom to enjoy life. We toil away for nothing. We spend weeks getting the grand house ready for one skinny girl to parade around like a broomstick in a blue dress. Days and days of 'Move that couch upstairs,' or, 'Get me tea and biscuits,' late at night without so much as a 'thank you.'" He momentarily takes his feet off the chair and leans toward Quinn to ask, "Do we get so much as an hour off to make merry with our friends at the festival? Of course not. And then: 'The festival is over, go clean it up.' And now here we are on the way to town to do the colonel's business and we're sleeping in the barn with the horse!"

"Couldn't you find someone who'd offer the colonel a trade?" Quinn asks. "There have to be lots of people in town with workers who'd gladly take your place to work in the colonel's house."

Lem swats the air with his hand. "*Hmph*! He knows he can't trade *me*." Leaning his scrawny body back in his chair he taps a finger on his right temple. "I know too much. It would take years to train someone to do all the things I do 'round there. . . . And I know other things that they wouldn't want me imparting to anyone in town," he says with a wicked smile. "No they won't let me go. They want to keep me near at hand."

Quinn looks skeptical and is about to ask another question when another of his sisters, Lu, comes into the room.

Until now, Lem's fellow worker, Ski, has barely offered two words of conversation, looking bored while Lemon regaled their host with his complaints. But as soon as he sees Lu, he sits up in his chair. His eyes don't leave her while she puts several items away. He smiles when she reaches across the table for one of the plates and asks if either of them wants any more food before the pot is taken away from the fire for the night.

Much to everyone's surprise, Lemon quickly rises to his feet and takes the girl's hand. She jolts at his touch but before she can pull back, he nervously plunks his other hand on top of hers, trapping it in his grasp. "Thanks Miss Lu, I've had my fill. It's good of you to have us into your home and give us such a nice meal." He keeps talking while his head bobbles up and down with little bowing gestures, oblivious to the look of horror on Lu's face. "You're a fine cook—and I should know—I work in the great house in Westland. My compliments to you, Miss Lu."

He finally lets go of her hand and sits down again. She steps back from the table and recovers her manners before saying a quick, "Thank you." She turns to his traveling companion. "And you, Ski? Would you want more?"

"No. Thank you, Miss Lu, I'm full, too. But . . ." he says before pulling a small goat skin bottle from his coat, ". . . may I fill this with water from one of your jars before I turn in for the night?"

She nods. "Certainly. Come with me."

Lemon pops up again and jams a hand inside his vest. "I have a skin, too." When he pulls it out, however, everyone can see it's nearly full. He does a double-take at it before he says, "I'd love to be able to empty this out and fill it here. We have the aqueduct in Westland, but the water's just not the same as cool water fresh from a spring."

Everyone is silent, so Lem stands a little taller, puts the hand with the water bottle to his chest and adds, "It was my ancestor who first found the spring at Oldtown, you know."

Ski leans over and snatches the bottle out of Lem's hand. "Here. You were just saying how overworked you've been in recent days. I'll go and fill it for you."

Seeing the pleading look in his sister's eyes, Quinn clears his throat and asks, "So, Lemon, how long do you plan on being in town?"

Lem shoots a sour look at Ski before seating himself. "We'll be heading back this way in a week. Of course we'll have long days ahead getting the colonel's business done. . . ."

# # #

Later that night, when all the tasks are done and the house is closed up for the night, Shaye settles onto the cot in Joy's room. Joy blows out the lamp and opens the shutters before crawling into her own bed. They both gather their thoughts while the glow of the moon and thousands of stars outside the window gently illuminate the room.

"What's wrong Shaye? You've seemed a bit sad since dinner," Joy observes.

Shaye doesn't answer the question but asks one of her own. "Do you ever wonder if some of our people survived the exile? Do you ever wonder what would it be like to live in the Great Forest among His own . . . to be free? Living . . . as He intended, standing shoulder to shoulder as upright people . . . able to speak in our own tongue."

Joy has heard the stories too. All of the Genon have. The tales of sightings may only reflect a dim hope, but it's one shared around the fires of Genon people late at night.

A breeze brushes by the curtains and Shaye pulls her covers up against the night air. The knotted ropes holding up the mattress in an old wooden frame creak as she turns to face her friend. "Do you ever think," she asks, "that the Exiles might really have survived? I know we used to make up stories about it and pretend when we were little, but do you think that their children and grandchildren might really be out there in the Great Forest, living on their own, taming the land and the animals, like our ancestors did in the time before?"

Joy turns to face Shaye. "Sometimes. But then . . . I wonder why no one has ever seen them, or how they could live in such a dangerous place."

"I'll tell you something," Shaye whispers, "but you have to promise to keep it a secret."

Joy leans forward so she won't miss a word. "I promise."

"I mean it Joy. You cannot tell anyone."

On the very edge of her bed now, she touches two fingers to her lips and points up. "I promise. Truly I do."

"My mother told me that grandfather saw one once. And my mother said that in her last year as a gatherer, she saw one, as well. Two years before I was born."

"What did they look like? Did they see a man or a woman or both? Or do you think they saw the same person?"

"Both of them saw a man. My grandfather told my mother about a time when he and other gatherers fell sick while exploring the Great Forest . . . a man came and gave him a bush to boil and told him to drink the tea from it, and it made them better. This was many years before mother also encountered a man in the forest. She didn't think it was the same man since the one she saw was tall, and Grandfather didn't say the man he saw was tall. She thought he would have noted that."

Joy doesn't think she's ever heard anything so frightening or so exciting before. "Did the man say anything?" she whispers. "How did she know he was from the Exiles?"

"She said that he was dressed in animal skins that were not from here and he was carrying a bow of wood she didn't recognize. Grandfather told her if she ever saw an exile, she was to make the sign vowing not to tell because they would kill soldiers or anyone they thought would tell soldiers. When she saw the man, he didn't speak to her and she didn't dare speak to him but she made the sign like Grandfather told her and he didn't harm her. He pointed to her, repeated the sign for the vow, and then he ran away."

"Oh my." Joy says in hushed astonishment.

"I think of this sometimes," Shaye says. "I don't want to be a servant for the rest of my life. Sometimes, I want with all my heart to see the Exiles."

Joy shrugs. "Well it's not likely you'll ever see the Great Forest since they forbid women to be gatherers now. . . . Oh Shaye," Joy suddenly gasps. "Do you think that those women gatherers who disappeared before that went to be with the Exiles? That would be so much nicer than thinking they got eaten by animals or died of a terrible sickness."

Shaye has already considered the same thing. She whispers, "All I know is that I was made to be free, Joy, and I'm not sure I can spend my life living like I was nothing, like I don't really belong anywhere. It would be good to find a place to have the freedom to speak truth, to walk as a free and upright woman before I die."

Joy sighs, "Don't say things like that. It sounds as if you want to die or something. Even here, we aren't completely free to do as we wish . . . we are free to work very hard and starve if we don't. And after all our work, my family could still have everything taken away from us. But when we are all gathered to God we will all be free even if it doesn't happen now. Please don't despair, Shaye. We don't know the future, but we do know the One who holds it in His hands. I know He can help you find a better situation soon. Let's pray for that."

CHAPTER 7
Great Aunt Pearl—Living Link

"**W**hy waste time on myths about where we came from or how we got here? What does it matter? The point is that we are here right now and that is all any man need concern himself with."— *Kyle Dorchester, a General of Aegea for six years in the Fourth Generation*

Despite the hubbub of activity in the marketplace bustling all around the fountain, the young people seated around the old woman have listened intently to her words. She is sitting on the short wall that wraps around a small pool in the center of the square, stirring the water with hand.

"I can say that God is everywhere, but He is not always evident. Sometimes, you must remove from your view those things that so easily take up your attention . . . and you must allow *Him* to take the honored place in your heart.

"Then, when you come to a time of great hardship, you will see God stirring the waters, and know that He is visiting your soul, changing your very image to reflect His. Then you can see Him in your hardship, and you can say, 'God gives grace.'

"When you come out of hardship, you can say 'God has shown mercy.'

"When you feel abandoned, you can know it is a test. You can know He is waiting to hear your heart singing to His in the midst of the darkness, as one would sing to a beloved in the night.

"When your enemy seeks to do you harm, you can say, 'God is greater.'

"When you can love your enemy, you can say, 'God has prevailed.'

"When praise comes of your talents, you can say, 'God has worked through me.'

"When wisdom speaks through others, you can say, 'God bears witness.'

"When kindness is given to you, you can say, 'God has blessed.'"

She smiles at all of them. "It should be just so, and when it is," she says touching her heart, then pointing up, "He smiles."

Not far from the fountain, Shaye squeezes down the street toward the old marketplace, hoping her Great Aunt Pearl has lingered there for her. This is the day of the week when many laborers are free to attend to their own needs, so the streets are crowded. Women are dressed in traditional Genon garb, some of them with babies in slings over one shoulder standing beside carts laden with goods. Some mothers of toddlers have used the corner leg of a cart to hold down the long tail of the child's garment—allowing the child perhaps to stand and reach for things, but not to get far from her. Men with long beards stand in close proximity to one another and argue over trades of goods or services.

An old woman sprinkles water on the cobblestones in front of her cart and makes an effort at sweeping some of the dirt away, using a broom with bristles as old and bent as she is.

The man at a neighboring cart says, "Eh, eh. *New* brooms sweep clean!"

The old woman gives him a toothless smile, and pokes the bristles of the broom under her cart before she replies, "Ah yes, but the *old* broom knows the corners."

On this bright day, many have come to squeeze fruit, run their hands along new cloth, and wrangle for the best possible trade. It's a tradition that goes back to the beginning. One person has something the other one wants. What will he trade for it? How much of it? How about some of this in exchange for a little of that? Both will claim they were cheated until they are alone with friends and family—then they'll say they got a bargain.

Shaye presses by the women selling garlic and strong-smelling herbs, a man with skeins of spun wool, and a number of people haggling over sooshi hens and other meats. Here and there, she can hear snippets of conversations in Genon. Since this market is used almost exclusively by Genon, they have little fear of trouble over it.   One man has stacks of various sizes of bowls, carved from corsha gourds. He's telling a potential customer that the decorative border he carved into the rim will add a touch of elegance to her life. A woman has baskets of flowers and dried bugs that can be crushed to make dyes for wool thread.

A man wearing an apron is stirring a large pot and shouting, "Goat stew! Goat stew!"

Two men are standing near the pot of stew, each with a corsha bowl. They've stopped eating and they're arguing.

The first man leans forward and insists, "The draft is the worst thing that ever happened! They're stealing our best and brightest sons and making them abandon their heritage!"

The second man gets right back in the face of the first. "Well said by someone who wants to be *poor* all his life! I say if a man has a chance to make something of himself, why shouldn't he take it?"

"I suppose you think Sergeant Shocky is setting a good example eh?" the first man sneers.

"He's a fine man.   A great Genon!" the second man shouts.

The first one starts waving his arms so much, his stew is slopping onto the ground. "He's a false symbol! Worse than that, he's a traitor!"

Every Genon in Aegea knows who Sergeant Shocky is. "Shocky" was a nickname given to him, but it stuck, so now *everyone* knows him by that name. He was part of the first draft eight years ago and has worked his way up to being a sergeant—the first Genon to ever do so.   He's the most admired *and* hated Genon in the world.

Shaye stays out of spilling range of the two men arguing and keeps walking.

A dozen doorways down from where the men are still having their lively conversation, Shaye passes by a shadowed doorway, and a movement catches her eye. She stops and peers down a short hall where a young woman stands, leaning against one side of the passage. The woman's dark hair is piled atop her head with looping curls hanging down. She's wearing a long robe, tied at the waist but open far enough above and below the tie to leave little to the imagination. For one moment, their eyes meet and Shaye has a sudden revelation of the woman's occupation. She's heard of such things, but never actually *known* a woman who permitted herself to be such a scandal. She is startled by the thought that someone would sell access to their very soul . . . and she quickly averts her eyes. The woman in the hallway laughs. Not a joyful laugh, but the loud mocking laughter of one who needs to feel something other than their pain.

Shaye speeds up in an effort to put distance between herself and the embarrassment she feels. She's rushing by carts, playing toddlers, and marketers. *How could a woman ever choose to live in such disgrace?*

Finally making it through to the center square of the marketplace, Shaye sees the pool where people come to quench their thirst or to sit and chat about life. The natural spring here was the original source of water for the settlement and five generations of Aegea have tasted the water here. In the First Generation, a small barrier was built around the spring to form a pool. Over the next generation, the area surrounding the pool was paved with stones and became a market. It is the oldest gathering place in Aegea.

Once she emerges from the crowd into the fountain area, Shaye spots a group of young people gathered around an old woman seated on the short wall around the wellspring. The woman is wearing the dark garb of a chaplain and people are listening intently to her words.

Although clerics known as "chaplains" are still part of Aegean society, their numbers have dwindled to scant few. In the beginning, even though the chaplains had rank as officers in the military, they were allowed to mingle within the many layers of society and associate with anyone. During the uprising of the Second Generation however, many of the chaplains sided with those of the lowest status who (according to the military version of the story) sought to overturn the orderly society that was keeping the people of Aegea alive. After the uprising, religion was increasingly portrayed as an irrational attachment, something not in keeping with reasoned, orderly, military life. Fearing the loss of benefits of high social standing, a few of the chaplains forsook their profession and sought other positions within the military, leaving the complications of any sort of "spiritual belief" behind.

By the Fourth Generation, high ranking officers began to challenge the belief that a god (or any being) from another time or another place could have any relevance at all in daily life. By the Fifth Generation, some began to question if *people* had ever existed in a "time before" or in a place other than Aegea. Perhaps the Firstlanders were only pilgrims on foot who simply migrated to the plateau.

Most of the remaining clerics were old but for some reason, they were becoming quite popular with the younger population on the plateau. Much to the dismay of the military, a growing number of the Fifth Generation were questioning the idea that rank and power should be inherited or that life consisted solely of the physical here and now. Thus far, little has been done to impede the conversation, but those in authority are keeping an increasingly wary eye on such things.

Shaye walks to the edge of the small crowd and finds a place to sit on the ground not far from the chaplain—her Great Aunt Pearl. The old woman gives her a broad smile, but before she can speak, a commotion coming from one of the lanes that leads to the fountain draws everyone's attention. Merchants and customers jostle out of the way before two men appear, one on a gray horse, the other on a sorrel. They trot counter-clockwise around the fountain until they come to the group gathered around Aunt Pearl.

Nearly everyone in the square stops what they are doing to watch them. Since those of high rank began to abandon Oldtown for the larger, newer homes of Midtown, the exodus of the military has continued. No ranking families live here now—certainly not officers who can ride horses. This is a curiosity.

The men don't speak at first, but they don't move away, either.

"You honor us," Pearl says in a calm voice. "May I assist you?"

"No," the man on the gray horse says.

Saddle leather creaks as both men shift around trying to keep their beasts stationary. One of the horses backs up a few steps before his rider nudges him forward again with a tap of his heel. "We heard someone was telling fairy tales by the fountain, and I see by the number of children you've gathered here," he says, nodding to the crowd seated around her, "that it must be true. I like a good story as well as anyone. Go ahead."

A girl seated on the ground scoots sideways to avoid being near the animals' hooves and several people stand, but only one person leaves the group.

"Oh," Pearl says, "then you'll have to come earlier next time. I was about to go home."

The man grins. "What? No stories about an imaginary world in another time? No encouragements to listen to . . . how is it you hear from that god of yours?"

Pearl leans on a slender cane to stand. "If you know how to read, you can request to see some of the records for yourself and learn of the time before. Even if you can't read, there are many relics from that world which I doubt you could explain away. I spent many years working inside the archives. In addition, I've heard the eyewitness accounts of many others who were Firstlanders. My grandfather, Arthur Penway, was both an officer and the *first* keeper of records in Aegea. I have no reason to doubt."

Now the man laughs. "Unexplained objects. Stories of old people. I had an old uncle who thought the spider in his closet could speak to him."

The old woman shrugs. "I have no wish to dispute the past with you. . . . If you want to know about faith, however, you may come next week and see if I am here. Or, if such a gathering as this would hinder you from actually listening, you can set a time and I would meet with you."

It is a game of intimidation that Pearl has declined to play.

The horseman grins again and nods to her before he pulls back on the reins of his horse. The animal retreats a few steps then turns. He prods it again and the horse trots back toward the lane where it first entered the square. His companion follows him and the crowds in the lane part once more before the men ride out of sight. Within moments, the distraction is over and the people in the market resume their haggling.

The young men and women rise from where they are seated and draw close to Pearl, who says, "I must go home now, but perhaps I will see some of you again soon. Until then, bless you."

Before they've all spoken good-byes and departed, Great Aunt Pearl opens her arms to Shaye and then locks her in a tight embrace. Shaye isn't accustomed to such affection in public, but she's glad enough to see her aunt to hug her back. It is good to feel so welcome.

"Oh my dear Shaye, I was hoping your plans hadn't changed again. I have missed you so much. A year is far too long to wait to see you."

"I've missed you, too."

When the hug is over, Pearl says her last goodbyes to those lingering nearby, then takes Shaye's hand and says, "Come now! Let me show you to my new home. It's not very grand, but it's every inch a blessing to me. We can have tea and dried fruit . . . and we can talk as long as we want with nobody to complain." The woman starts out toward the lane directly in front of them and keeps talking as she guides her niece along. "Did you come by wagon? How long can you stay?"

"Yes, we came by wagon and we'll be here nearly a week. We began the trip yesterday, but we got a late start so we had to spend the night at the outpost with Lilly and Joy's family. You should see it. The outpost looks like a little village now and Joy's house has a second floor for officers to stay in."

"Is that so?"

"Yes. They look as if they are doing very well and I was happy to see them again. We'll probably make a quick stop there on the way back, so if you want, I can take your greetings to them."

"Oh, I'd like that very much. Lilly was always a fine woman. Her father and my youngest brother Benjamin were friends when they were young. I know her situation out there was hard for many years, but my heart rejoices to hear they are doing so well now. Is everyone still alive? Have any of the children moved away?"

"They are all still there. The eldest son, Quinn, will surely stay on there with them. Their oldest daughter I think would like to marry a certain man . . . but as you know, situations have to be worked out first. The man will have to work off his term or see if some sort of trade can be arranged."

They amble down the street, then turn on a narrow alleyway. Shaye knows it's like walking back in time. The older the homes, the narrower the paths through them—and the smaller the dwellings become.

"How is the colonel? How is his family?"

"They are well."

"How is Jariel? Is she excited about her planning day?"

Before Shaye can respond, they stop walking and Pearl points to a doorway. "Here we are."

Shaye's eyes grow wide as she takes in the scene and figures it out. At some point a little alley that ran between two houses was enclosed to make an "apartment." The door sits squarely in the middle of the front wall . . . and the windows on either side of the door are hardly more than slits with single shutters.

The old woman takes the two steps up to the door one at a time and opens it with a bit of effort. Shaye keeps her hand near her aunt's elbow in case the woman gets unsteady, but once the door is open she steps inside with no effort. She hangs her cloak on a peg a few feet from the door and looks back at Shaye. "You can hang your shawl here or on the wall by my bed." She groans with the effort of lifting a board off the latch for the window shutter, then swings it open to let in light and air. Watch your step," she warns. "It's dark until I get the other shutter open. Don't leave your bag within reach of the window. You're in town now, and people are more likely to give into easy temptations."

They walk, single file, down a short, narrow hallway to a tiny sitting room that smells a bit like damp cloth . . . and leather . . . and other things Shaye can't quite identify. She can see light shooting in around the shutter for the living room window. "Here," she offers, "let me get that open for you."

Once the shutter swings open, the room floods with light and Shaye turns to look around the room. The walls are a sloppy combination of wood, stone, and mud bricks. Rough wood shelves line the room, looking like they are also shoring up the walls and holding up the roof.

Pearl points to a sagging brown chair and footstool in the center of the room and says, "This is where I sleep most often. I prefer it to the bed in the little nook just beyond that doorway leading to the back part of the house. This was the residence of my brother Carl's oldest child—you remember hearing about Charles, don't you? The one who stuffed those vegetables up his nose when he was little and nearly died?"

Shaye remembers. She pulls in her lips to avoid smiling and nods.

"Well this was where he lived after he finished at the academy—he didn't get on well with his father and didn't get any offers of promotion . . . but when Carl died last year, he made captain and got the house. He wanted me to vacate my room there . . . so he gave me this."

Despite all the ridicule heaped upon Pearl, Shaye is convinced that her old aunt is quite sane. And while her current situation is very humble in comparison to her days of status, she notes that Pearl seems very grateful for a place to live among people whom she loves. Although not Genon by birth, if there is such a thing as being a Genon in the heart, that would describe Pearl.

The woman is a living part of history and a witness to the childhood and life of Shaye's father. Much of the space around Shaye is cluttered with bits and pieces that serve as mementos of her aunt's life. Few of the items would be valuable to a scavenger or a robber, but each little thing is connected to a remembrance. If she could, Shaye would hear the tale of each thing as often as it took to put it to memory.

Once Pearl is seated, Shaye offers to start a fire in the small hearth and make tea.

"Oh my yes. That would be nice. The tea is on the shelf to the left of the hearth. We won't waste the heat—go ahead and warm a couple pieces of the bread there. I have some fine cheese and a couple of pears I got just for us. We'll have them now to celebrate your arrival."

Within minutes, Shaye has cleaned off the little table near Pearl's chair and placed two mugs of tea and their little feast there. She finds a stool in the corner, but looks at Pearl for directions. "What should I do with the things stacked here?"

"Just put them on the floor."

Pearl watches her niece and feels a fresh pang of an old sorrow. Once Shaye is seated Pearl reaches across the table and takes the girl's hand.

Shaye assumes that Pearl is about to pray over the meal, so she bows her head.

But her aunt doesn't pray. The old woman says something that has weighed on her conscience for a long time. "I'm so sorry, child, that I didn't find a way to pay your service off and take you in. You are as dear to me as anyone in this whole world, and you should *always* have been able to stay with me. I know it is not much . . . but I want to offer what I have here to you. I know your time of service will be up this year and I want you to know you could live here with me and have the bed."

Shaye knows that her aunt is the only one in her father's family who would openly acknowledge her. And she knows that before now, even if her old aunt had found a way to pay off the years of Shaye's service, she had no place where Shaye could have stayed—not while she lived with her brother Carl. Pearl would most likely have been pitched into the streets if she'd attempted to take in a Genon niece. But now. Now that she has her own place and is offering to share it with Shaye . . . well, this is something altogether different.

A flood of ideas rush into Shaye's mind and a small shaft of light shines on a secret hope. *Perhaps Auntie can help me find a job in an officer's kitchen . . . or tending a garden near a home . . . or even as a personal servant if need be.* But she doesn't want to rush to conclusions. "Of a truth," Shaye responds, "I did have the hope of finding a lead to a position while I was here in town, but I have no idea how it would work out."

"So you *would* like to leave Westland?"

"Yes."

Pearl nods. "I suppose you'd greatly miss dear Mosha and the people there, though."

"I would. But, more than anything," Shaye says, "I should like the opportunity of a new beginning here."

Pearl raises her hands with joy. "Oh I like that! Just so!" She leans forward and excitedly whispers, "And I'm not without connections, you know. If you have your own place to live, they have to give you higher compensation. I know it is small and shabby, but you and I could do well in this little place here."

Peering into Pearl's bright eyes, she realizes that this may be a good solution for both of them . . . and that a door may have opened for more than just a change of scenery. "Can you teach me to read and write?"

The old woman takes both of Shaye's hands. "Oh yes I can!" The old woman pulls in a big breath as she considers all the possibilities, then she smiles. "Well then! We'll have to plan out a strategy tonight and I will start out first thing tomorrow to see what can be done."

CHAPTER 8
Jubal McClaren's New Project

"Survival requires a constant eye on the big picture. Quality of life requires an eye on all the little details."—*Hal Dobbins, a Firstlander*

Colonel Jubal strides along the building-in-progress, listening to the man in charge of the workers.

"I have men working on the beams for the roof."

"Good. And when will the building be habitable?"

The man swallows hard. "Well, I hate to make any promises. A lot of it depends on the weather and the number of men I have."

"You'll have the men you need," the colonel says, "and Menoh thinks the weather will hold for the next few days. So how long?"

"Two weeks. Maybe three."

"Good. Let me know if you require anything else." Jubal heads for the house. Rather than walk around the side, he moves through the small courtyard behind the house and enters through the kitchen.

Mosha is just pulling something from the oven. A stray lock of hair is in her face and she makes an attempt at blowing it out of the way.

"Good morning," he says to her.

She sets the pan down on the counter and looks around. "Oh! Good morning." It's been more than a year since she's seen him in the kitchen. "Would you like something?"

He shakes his head and points to the door leading to the stairs. "No. Just thought I'd take a short-cut through the kitchen and say hello. That was a fine breakfast this morning. You seem to be faring okay without your assistant."

She sighs. "Well, yes. But I miss her."

"I know. I know," he says. "She'll be back soon, though, and then there will be all manner of frantic activity, won't there?"

"Yes sir. There will. We'll do our best for you. . . . And if I might say so, she's of great value to me. Not just because she's my girl, but also she's a big help to me."

The colonel smiles at her and moves to the stairway. "I know."

CHAPTER 9
Shaye, Pearl, & Shell Bones

"**W**hat is faith? Our forefathers believed they could soar above the sky in complete safety. Were they fools? Faith is choosing to trust the One who sees the beginning and the end of the journey."—*A saying of Kya, a Firstlander*

After a day jostling around in the marketplace and lugging items back to Pearl's house, Shaye was bone-tired, but she still wanted to come to the meeting. Now, she is ever so glad she did. She can only compare the evening to the sweetness of a lullaby in the ears of a child just falling asleep on her mother's breast. She would linger here for hours if she could.

It's time for everyone to go home, but Eli waits. He is much older than Great Aunt Pearl, and at the unbelievable age of eighty three, he is nearly the oldest person on the plateau. (Only his sister, at eighty four, is older.) Small of stature but still able to stand erect and speak in a clear voice, Eli has been a keeper of the history of His people for more than four decades. Since it is a beautiful night, he will end the evening with a small portion of a particular favorite of many Genon children: The story of the stars.

He asks everyone gathered on the rooftop to blow out the flame on their lamps and as they do so, gray smoldering ribbons of smoke, twirl skyward into the still night air. Glowing wicks fade to black and the people sit in customary silence while their eyes adjust to the darkness. Like everyone else gathered on the rooftop, Shaye has heard the story of the stars many times, but she always wants to hear it again.

Eli clears his throat and slowly lifts his hands upward.

"Before years or days or time were counted, before the first seed or root was planted in moist soil. Before a bird flew across the heavens or the first of our people drew breath, the Maker of all things existed. His voice rang out and light shined forth. . . ."

Although Shaye loves the earth, the plants, and creatures of the world with an abiding love, she never feels closer to the Maker than when she looks up and sees the sky. She is stirred beyond her ability to speak when she is among His people and considers the vastness of all He has made. Eli's voice is as close as if he's standing right next to her.

"The Maker separated the day and the night and He set the stars in the heavens—so when the cloak of darkness is pulled across the sky each night," Eli says as he slowly sweeps one arm in an arc over his head, "there are yet lights that sing of His nature and power. . . . So all will be reminded—even when there is darkness—that He is over all things and His glory never dims. We can look up and know that He is yet present and listening to those who seek Him." Eli bows his head and ends with, "It shall always be remembered thus."

Those who have gathered here on the rooftop respond, "May we always remember it. Just so."

"Oh Ruler of the day and the night," Eli says softly, "may all who have come tonight be blessed. May they be stirred by your revelation, led by Your hand, protected under Your wing. Let us leave this place filled with the rich Spirit of peace You have bestowed upon all who trust in You."

And they all answer, "May it be just so."

The meeting is over but there is a lingering quiet as people move around and gather their things. Some re-light their lamps in preparation to walk home. Shaye looks over at her Aunt, whose head is bowed, so she remains still.

Several people rise and leave before Pearl looks over at her great niece and says, "I always love coming together like this. It makes me think about what it will be like in the final gathering, the one that will never end. . . . Do you ever think about that? All the generations of all time standing together in the open presence of the Maker. . . . It will be a joy we can scarcely imagine from this distant place."

People stand and begin to trickle out of the meeting and the damp night air closes in around them, so Pearl buttons up her cloak. Shaye pulls the warm red shawl her aunt gave her up onto her shoulders.

With a sigh in her voice, the old woman says, "I suppose we should be going home now. Go ahead and light the lamp."

Like most of the lamps brought to the meeting, the small lamp Shaye holds is made of dark, red-brown clay and filled with olive oil which burns slowly and poses little danger if spilled. The lamps in the colonel's home are larger and have multiple wicks so that they can sit on a table or a shelf and help light a whole room. But this little lamp reminds Shaye of a pointed shoe with a bead holding the wick at the toe end and a small handle for two fingers at the heel. She lights the lamp on the flame of another one held by a woman seated next to her. She rises before offering her free hand to her aunt, who grasps it and pulls herself up. Like everyone else in the meeting, the two of them move to the far end of the rooftop toward the wooden stairs that will take them around the side of the building and out into the street below.

When they are nearly down the stairs, Shaye sees someone familiar in the crowd milling around below. It's her fellow servant, Lemon, and he approaches them as soon as they're off the stairs.

"I thought you'd be here," he says without any greeting. "We will finish the colonel's business by late tomorrow evening. We'll be leaving an hour after first light the day after tomorrow."

"Is this one of the men you traveled with?" Aunt Pearl asks.

Shaye nods and gestures toward him. "Yes, this is Lemon. Lemon, this is my Great Aunt Pearl."

He bows his head slightly toward Pearl and mumbles, "Yes'm," before turning back to Shaye. "Meet us in the small market, in the corner by the place where they make the wooden utensils. An hour after first light. Day after tomorrow."

His breath reeks of alcohol. She can only imagine the shape—and the mood—he'll be in the first hour after sunrise day after tomorrow. "I will be there," she answers.

Lemon nods once. "Fine." He starts to walk away before he remembers his manners and turns again. "And a good evening to you ma'am."

Aunt Pearl nods. "A good one to you as well."

Her words are no sooner spoken before Lemon pushes unsteadily into the crowd and is gone.

The two women begin walking along slowly, threading their way through laborers and their families who are out and about for one last stroll before bedtime.

The old woman chuckles to herself. "Lemon, eh?"

Shaye looks at her aunt. Many years of Pearl's life were spent deciphering the writings left by those who first came to Aegea. "Does it mean something funny?"

"Well . . . the Firstlanders said that in the time before . . . a lemon was a fruit. It was yellow and about the size of your fist . . . and it was *very* sour."

When her aunt says this, something rare happens: Shaye laughs out loud and declares, "Oh, it's like a *prophecy* over the man!" She thinks a moment, then asks, "But why would you name your child after something very sour?"

Pearl shrugs. "As you know, once they realized that they would never make it back to the time before, and they saw that the records on the airship would all be lost, the survivors of the crash began an account of all the things they could remember about the time before. Some of them missed those days greatly. And, since the beginning of all time, people have often named their children for what they treasure or things of beauty, so it only seemed natural to some of the Firstlanders to name their children for the things they missed the most. The practice wasn't widely accepted and it fell out of favor with some, but with others it became tradition. Of course, most people have lost the knowing of what the names mean," she smiles, "but obviously, someone in his ancestry missed a yellow fruit called a lemon. I've read that it could make a good drink if you added something sweet to the juice. *Lem-ahh-day* I think they called it."

"It seems as if the only thing that ever gets added to this Lemon," Shaye declares, "is *meechi*."

They are at the door of the apartment now and Pearl slowly ascends the two steps, then gets the door open before she says a little breathlessly, "Well, it's a hard world for those who live disconnected from their Maker. They are separated from the One who gives meaning to life. What can we expect?"

The two women travel down the narrow hallway and Pearl moves to her chair. "I'm glad the topic of names has come up this evening, though because it reminds me I have something for you." She turns and slowly reaches back with her right hand to grasp the armrest on her chair. Once she's certain she has a firm hold, she lowers herself down and sighs. "*Ahhhhh*. That's my chair. It's like my old friend." She looks over at her niece. "Make yourself comfortable. . . . Now what was I saying? Oh yes. Names. Give me a moment to rest and think . . . I have something for you and I need to recall where I stored it."

Shaye uses the little lamp to light a bigger one on a table, then lights a lamp next to Pearl before extinguishing the flame of the portable one and placing it on a shelf.

The old woman leans back and slowly tilts her face upward, as if she is about to gaze beyond the ceiling at a star in the night sky . . . but she is remembering. She closes her eyes, searching through the piled scrolls of words and ideas stored up . . . up somewhere in a warehouse of ideas and the narrative history of her life—all the things she's heard, seen, felt, and learned.

In the Second Generation, women were no longer accepted in the military, and jobs such as archivist and chaplain, while still considered "professional" (high status) occupations, were de-militarized. But in the Third Generation (sixty years after the crash),the reigning officers wanted a "history" that would depict the military as a permanent, omnipotent force that had always ruled the world and they began reassigning workers at the Archives who didn't care to 'interpret' the records in a way that would support this view. The military wanted to limit access to information (written by the ancestors of every person in Aegea) to officers in the military. The problem was, however, that few people in the military knew how to read the great wealth of wisdom that the Genon had recorded on agriculture, animal husbandry, survival skills, and even simple things like weather prediction.

And even for those who could read Genon, there was yet another barrier: Contained within the language of these people was a culture with nuances of thought and belief that were rarely grasped by military men who were educated to see things in a rigid, empirical light. To the Genon, faith and life were completely intertwined, the visible was a reflection of the invisible.

Pearl's interpretations, correlations, and analysis of Genon language and culture were so helpful that she was one of the last civilians to be removed in a purging process that officially retired all civilian archivists nearly twenty years ago. She had already taken vows as a chaplain by then (driven mad, they said, by her constant exposure to Genon ideas) and she was content to leave the Archives. While the military still occasionally consulted her in efforts to locate or clarify information, it was only when all other options failed. Since the job of chaplain no longer had status, Pearl was reduced to near poverty. Her brother, an officer in good standing, took her in.

A slow smile lights Pearl's face and she opens her eyes. Since she's looking up, most of the lines in her face have faded out of view—almost as if she has returned to being the young woman who first began the study of Aegea and the record of its people.

Shaye looks at her and thinks about what Pearl must have looked like in her youth. There are no images that record what she looked like (such as a person in the family of a high-ranking officer might have), but Shaye sees an ember of sweet vitality still burning. She can't help but ask, "Why did you never remarry?"

Pearl cocks her head to the side and glances at Shaye, then closes her eyes again. "Peter and I were barely wed a month before a fever from the Poison Forest took him."

This is new information for Shaye, but, since she's spent very little time with anyone from her father's family, how would she know? There were no children from the marriage and it happened so long ago. . . Shaye could see how it had faded from the list of conversational material.

"I know the Genon call it the Great Forest," Pearl continues, "but it took my husband away, and I cannot think of it as 'great' in any measure. . . . I didn't have the heart to even look at another man for a long time."

A silence engulfs them. Not an uncomfortable sort of silence, but the kind of silence that's like a soft shawl that can be shared by two people who know each other well enough to huddle together.

Pearl's eyes are closed again, but when she is ready, she opens them. "I was in love once after that." She momentarily points upward. "Secretly mind you. I was still a young woman of twenty-four seasons and he was fifteen years older than I . . . and his name was Snow. He got into a fight with a drunken soldier and was killed. After that I just never found anyone who suited me I suppose. And then I was busy with my work." She stops talking and her eyes wander around the room. This is an uncharacteristically short answer for an old woman who loves to tell stories.

A multitude of questions have popped into Shaye's head. *This man named Snow wasn't a soldier? Was he in a profession . . . a tradesman . . . a Genon? Would you have married him?*

But before Shaye can ask any of these things, the old woman says "Ah!" and strains to rise out of her chair. "Now I remember where I put it. Come." Once she's upright, she picks up the lamp and heads out of the room. She keeps talking as she walks along. "I lost them for many years, but found them again this year when I moved here. I was so glad to think I could pass them on to you, my dear."

Pearl takes up the lamp and Shaye follows her down another narrow hallway past the small nook where her cot is, then to the left and up five steps to a tiny room packed with shelves. Pearl has Shaye hold the lamp while she slides a box from a bottom shelf halfway out, then roots around in it, grunting with the effort. She extracts a small cloth bag. "There you are." she says to the bag before she motions to Shaye. "Back up, back up. We'll have a look when we get back to the other room."

Shaye backs up slowly to allow Pearl sufficient light to see each step of the stairs, then turns and allows the old woman to place a hand on her shoulder before she walks back to the parlor. Pearl sets the bag on the small table near her chair and seats herself again. After a moment, she leans down and tugs a rolled parchment from under the table. "You'll need this. It declares that all the things I'm giving to you belong to you, and they are rightfully yours," she says, unrolling the small parchment and offering it to her niece. "It has an item history and it has my seal at the bottom . . . see it?"

Shaye takes the document from her aunt. Having never been taught to read, the only things she recognizes are her name at the top and the emblem underneath all the scratches in the middle. It is the seal of her great aunt.

"Yes. I see it," Shaye says. She has no idea what it's all about and is extremely curious to know . . . but she sits on the floor in front of the chair, sets the parchment in her lap, and waits. Great Aunt Pearl is a keeper of a vast amount of knowledge—and she will get to the point when she wishes.

The old woman gathers her thoughts before she begins. "I want to start by telling you something I learned directly from my grandfather, Arthur Penway, who was a soldier, a captain in the military on the Aegean C. He would be your great great grandfather on your father's side. What I'm about to tell you is an account of something he actually saw and touched." She pauses and frowns before looking at her niece. "I hope you will remember the things I tell you, Shaye, for when the last of my generation has passed away, the living link to those who first arrived here will be gone. If younger people don't learn it—the story of the tragedies, the endurance, the faith—the history of the Firstlanders—will be gone . . . and those who are left can lay aside truth in exchange for tales that tie people to falsehood."

Shaye solemnly listens, scooting closer to the feet of her aunt. Although some of the story Pearl is about to tell her might contain information she's heard before, now that she is older she will undoubtedly hear new details that will once again stretch the boundaries of her thinking.

"Long ago, before the time of the plateau," Pearl begins, "people lived scattered throughout a whole world. Separating people of different lands were mountains, like the ones we have next to the plateau, and great pools of water called 'oceans.'" She pauses and pronounces the word, distinctly so it will be remembered. "OH-shuns."

Shaye repeats the word. "Oceans."

"Yes," says her aunt. "Oceans. And these oceans were so big that you could stand on the edge of one of them and not be able to see to the other side. In fact, they were so big that people made giant boxes of wood and metal—bigger than the back of a wagon, some big enough to carry thousands of people—and these boxes would float on top of the water. The people would ride in the boxes for weeks before they got to the other side of an ocean. The oceans were also salty, so you couldn't drink them. . . . And you know how you can create a swell or a splash of water in a dishpan that will swish out to the edge of the pan before it subsides? The waters of these big oceans would heap up into large swells that they called waves and crash along the edges with a great roar . . . sometimes louder than the roar of the waterfall on the second mountain slope of Aegea."

The girl is trying to take it all in. It's so fantastic her heart is pounding at the very thought of it. She interrupts and asks, "Who was making the water swell?"

Pearl thinks a moment. "I think it's like the clouds in the sky. The waves moved but we are not certain why anymore."

"Oh."

Pearl goes on with her story. "And there were many creatures that lived in the Ocean. Not people like you and me but creatures with slick, shiny skins of many colors. These creatures could breathe in the water like you or I breathe the air! And just as you and I have legs and feet to move around on the ground, and birds have wings to fly through the air, some ocean creatures had things called 'fins' that looked like the leaves of a tree and wide, flat tails like a bird. I've seen drawings of these creatures and I read that there were too many different kinds of them to be remembered. They would wave their fins and their tails back and forth in the water and this would make them move forward." Pearl wags her head and moves her hands in an effort to recreate the movement of fish.

Shaye is completely puzzled and frowns with the effort of trying to imagine this. While many of those in high positions now scoff at any tales of "the time before" she believes her Aunt both read these things and spoke with people who actually lived in the time before. They told her what it was like.

"And, on the bottom of the oceans, there were creatures that had no head, no tail, and no fins. They were sort of flat and had only two bones—each one like a shallow bowl. And they wore their bones on the outside of their bodies, one on top and on the bottom. Like this," Pearl says, putting her two hands together as if she might pray, and then laying them sideways. "And the creatures who lived inside the two bones were called 'OY-sters.'" She stops to nod toward Shaye, who echoes the word.

Although Shaye believes her aunt, the thought of a creature with only two bones that were on its outside is most disturbing. "OYsters."

The old woman nods again. "Just so. Back in the time before, men and women would move around in the water, too. They would have to come to the top to breathe air, but they would wriggle around in the water and move through it almost like the fish creatures. They called this 'swimming.'"

Suddenly, Shaye can connect something she's seen with Pearl's words. "I saw someone do this once—in the pond that is near the far waterfall in Westland! He waved his arms around and kicked his feet and sometimes dove down. He was very brave and no one else would try it, lest they die."

Pearl nods. "Just so! Anyway, people would go swimming in the oceans and find oysters and bring them back on land. They would pry apart the bones to eat the creatures inside, and *sometimes* . . ." she says, opening her two hands, "when they opened up an oyster, they found a rare treasure, a gem that the creature itself made."

Shaye is awestruck. *How could this be?*

Pearl sees her niece's expression and nods in affirmation. "Yes. It was the color of cream and it was round and lustrous. It was called a 'pearl.'"

"Like your name?" Shaye asks in the loud voice of someone winning a game of wits.

"Yes! Just so, like my name."

This is as good as any mystery or riddle to Shaye.

The old woman reaches over and picks up the small bag and the objects inside rattle as they shift about. Poking a crooked finger into the neck of the bag, Pearl pulls it open. "This, my dear, is an oyster bone. It was called a 'shell' and it was given to me by my father who received it from his mother, who got it from her grandmother who found it on the edge of an ocean when she was a girl. Hold out your hand."

Shaye extends her open hand and with a complete sense of wonder and watches as the shell is placed there. The inside of the shallow bowl is white and shiny. The outside is gray and has rough ridges.

"And these," says Pearl, extracting more objects from the bag, "are other kinds of shell bones which had other creatures in them." She places the tiny shells inside the larger shell that's in Shaye's hand. "Oh to think of all the things the Maker has crafted . . . how much fun it must have been."

The girl picks up each one, marveling at the shape and color of it. Some are spiral shaped, one looks like a fancy hat, and one shell has spikes on it. "Real shell bones. From a real ocean."

"Yes, my dear. And they are part of my gift to you. Keep them and give them to your children as a reminder of the truth. I'm not sure if there are any more in all of Aegea, but these are yours."

Shaye is transfixed by the beauty of the objects. A long time ago, these bones held small creatures in a vast span of water called an ocean . . . and they were actually transported here by her ancestors.

CHAPTER 10
Shaye—the Sacred Self

"There shall be no parallel societies. There shall now be only one culture, one language and one government."—*General Lancaster, in the time leading up to the Exile in the Second Generation*

Shaye can't sleep tonight. Not tonight, not with her mind whirling like this. Her plan was to find someone who would trade for her and pay off the eight months she owes the colonel. In exchange, she would have been willing to work more than a year extra in order to pay off the debt. What she stood to gain, though, was a new place to work, a home to live in, and something of great value to her—the ability to read and write.

She runs her hand across the blanket on the bed. This could be her bed. During the day, she would work in the garden or a kitchen of an officer or a high ranking family—and when her day was over she could return to this house . . . home.

She had planned to secure all this, and then tell Mosha and the colonel what she had arranged to do. After all, wasn't she a woman of age now?

But her plan to quietly slip away from Westland—even with help from Pearl—had proven to be much more convoluted than she imagined. As it turned out, no one wanted to be the person who took her away from Colonel McClaren's home. Even at this end of the plateau, the colonel had a tremendous amount of clout and it seemed that no one wanted to risk offending him. Unless the colonel himself said he *wanted* her to have a job elsewhere, it wasn't going to happen.

She could speak with Old Menoh. He had a lot of influence with the colonel . . . but would Menoh be willing to help her? As one who lived inside the great house, she felt somewhat disconnected from the community of Genon in Westland. Menoh was always polite to her . . . but what did that mean? She'd never been in trouble with any of the elder members of the community nor had she ever specifically sought their advice on an issue as large as this.

Mosha probably had as much clout with the colonel as Old Menoh . . . but would Mosha want her to leave? No! It might be something Shaye could eventually wheedle out of Mosha . . . but she didn't want to have to wheedle her way to anything.

Her hopes aren't completely dead, but this is so much more difficult than she thought it would be. Her dream of being a woman living in her own little spot, a woman who could be fully engaged with the larger community here in Oldtown, is now little more than a remote hope. Her hope of seeing Ty on occasion is nearly gone . . . and part of her thinks that's the way it should be.

Pulling the blanket around herself, Shaye gets up and walks back out to the small parlor. The light on the table is still burning and Pearl, is sitting in her chair.

"Would you tell me, one more time, of our ancestors?" Shaye asks.

Pearl wakes from her light sleep and lets out a dramatic sigh before she smiles tenderly at her great grandniece. "Oh but you love to hear that one, don't you?"

The girl nods and sits on the floor by Pearl's knees.

The old woman begins. "The generations of . . ." and she stops. "Why am *I* telling this? You tell me the story of our generations."

Shaye pauses a moment. Can she tell it? Yes, she can. She begins: "I am Shaye of the fifth generation, and this is the line of my father:

> "Captain Arthur Ian Penway, the first Arthur, was my great great grandfather, and he married Janna, a daughter of Hal Dobbin, a man of science who was sent out with the Genon on the flight of the Aegean C—all of them were the Firstlanders. Captain Penway and Janna Dobbin had four children in the First Generation: Susan, their first child died in her first year of a sickness they got

from the forest. The sickness killed many people, and this is why many call it the 'poison forest' to this day.

The other children of Arthur and Janna were the second Arthur, Kerwin, and Trieste. Kerwin died in infancy, during another season of sickness from the forest, five years after the crash of the Aegean C. The children's mother, Janna, died shortly after giving birth to Trieste.

Their eldest son, Lieutenant Arthur Penway was my great grandfather and he married Oceanna, a daughter of Jonathan Nells, who was a doctor from the ship Aegean C."

Shaye's face lights up. "It was through *Oceanna* that the shell bones came to you? Was she named for the ocean?"

Pearl nods and answers, "Yes. Just so."

The girl continues,

"Arthur and Oceanna had three children who were part of the Second Generation born on the Aegean Plateau. Their children's names were Warren, Diane, and Bella. Against their advice, their daughter Bella joined with Kol of the gatherers and bore him one son, Pesh, and two daughters, Oceanna (who was named after Bella's mother) and Rena.

Kol was part of the rebellion, but Bella hid in the fields when Kol was captured and she renounced him at the trial prior to the Exile. Because she renounced him, she and the children were allowed to stay in Aegea but she and her son Pesh died two years later in a fire. Bella's daughters, Oceanna and Rena, went to service in different houses.

Oceanna became the second woman of a military man, Raymond Dune and bore him three sons. Her sister Rena worked for a maker of shoes.

Captain Warren Penway (my great grandfather, your father) married Carla, a daughter of Captain Clifford Sandford. Their children, born in the Third Generation, were: Carl, Peony, Pearl, and Arthur (the third Penway to be named thus).

In his later years, by a second woman, (whose name was Jaymar) Penway gave four more children to his wife Carla: They were Gerrard, Teá (who fell off the top of the first wall and died at the age of eight), Lilly, and Benjamin.

Captain Arthur Penway (Pearl's brother, my grandfather) married Faye Hale, a daughter of Massey Hale, a man of science, and they had seven children, born in the Fourth Generation: Frank, Joachim who died at the age of four, Jenny, Steven (who was five years old when he died after he was struck by lightning), Sonya, Nathan, and Othly.

Arthur's oldest son, Captain Frank Penway, married Elle, a daughter of Joash, of the family of Zim, a man of great land before the time of Aegea. Penway was decommissioned when he took Elle for his wife and they had one daughter, Shaye. He died laboring on the road project in the forest when his daughter was three years old."

Pearl interrupts her. "How did you learn this, Shaye? Who told you how your father died?"

Shaye stares down at her hands in her lap. "Mother told me when I asked her . . . but she cried so much afterword, I never spoke to her about it again." She looks up at Pearl before asking, "Why is so much of my father's life a secret? Was marrying my mother such a bad thing?"

Tears sting the old woman's eyes and she strokes Shaye's hair. "Your father was a most excellent man, my dear. He was brave and strong . . . and he loved your mother with all his heart. And he loved you. Just so.

"He saved the colonel's life in the forest during a mission to find a group of gatherers who went missing. A great snake coiled around the colonel and would have crushed him—and swallowed him whole—had your father not killed the snake. Before the mission was over, they found the gatherers they were searching for. All of them had been taken ill, but were on the mend and able to travel when they were found . . . one of the gatherers was Joash, your mother's father. . ."

Shaye's mind suddenly flashes as another piece of a mystery is put into its proper place: Gatherers . . . taken ill. *Grandfather was saved by an exile in the forest who gave him a bush to boil . . . .* Although she's excited by this, she decides to keep it to herself, and she refocuses her attention on Pearl.

". . . when they brought him back, your mother met them at the gates. Your mother was becoming a gatherer, so they ended up seeing each other often and your father fell in love with her.

"The colonel wanted to do well by your father, so he would let your father go on missions into the forest with your mother and other gatherers. I suppose he hoped your mother would settle for being Frank's woman in secret. But she wasn't having any of that." Pearl looks into Shaye's eyes. "In her mind, your mother was never 'less' than anybody, no matter what they might have thought. The Maker put the man and woman together in the first garden. There was no rank there, and no shame in their love. Elle wouldn't be a plaything, or spoken about in whispers, or have people speculating on the lineage of *her* children."

Pearl pauses to consider Shaye's age. "Did your mother ever speak to you about what happens when a man and a woman join together?"

Shaye looks right at her aunt. "A little. But I was only ten when she died. When I was fifteen, I asked Mosha and she said she'd only had one experience, and it was against her will. She said it happened before she worked for the colonel . . . and that she tries never to think about it."

"What did your mother tell you?"

"She said people aren't just 'things' to be used or consumed like food. She said we aren't like animals either. We have a soul inside us that's our true self, the part that reflects the Maker . . . and our true self is sacred. She said the only one who should have entry to our innermost self besides the Maker is the one we take vows with." Shaye looks at her hands in her lap. "When we bond together physically, we are granting someone admittance to our true self."

"Just so," Pearl says. "Some people say there is no sacred self, there is no God, and that we are just bodies with urges like animals. . . . For those who believe such things, it becomes easy to devour the beauty or goodness of others like food. Your mother knew that *real* love isn't just something that takes place on a sheet. It's not a stolen moment or a temporary flame. It's walking side by side, through everything life can throw at you. If Frank merely *wanted* her, if he didn't have the courage to *love* her, to take vows with her, then he would not have her at all."

"Do you think," Shaye asks, ". . . in the end . . . that Mother and Father regretted what they did? If they could have erased it all and begun again . . . would they have stayed apart?"

The old woman exhales deeply and falls silent. She thinks for a while before speaking again. "*Real* love is the most dangerous journey, girl. You can never be certain where love will take you. If you are afraid of the perils along the road . . . well it's best, I suppose, to let your heart stay cool and fill your life with lesser things." She nods, as if to confirm her own words, then speaks again. "Elle and your father believed that whatever they would have together—as one—was better than the lives they would lead *without* each other. Despite the disapproval of everyone in authority, despite the uproar it created in his family and hers, they took vows. Perhaps they hoped the bravery of their decision would change the way people saw it. But he lost his commission and had to become a day laborer. When you were two years old, he was offered a chance for improved provisions if he would work on the new road and he took it. He died when a great heap of stones slid down a mountainside and crushed him. . . . Your mother's heart was crushed as well and I don't think she ever got over losing him. The colonel found her several months after Frank died and took her into service. Perhaps it was his way of trying to make up for not helping Frank earlier or for allowing the circumstances that threw them together in the first place. It may not seem like enough . . . but I must confess it's more than I did for you. At least he recognized his failure and tried to help. We all tell ourselves that we are people of conviction, but that's a far bit different than *living* in that conviction despite the consequences. While I was in awe of your father and mother's conviction at the time, I was afraid. When I was no longer afraid . . . I had nothing I could offer you. My comfort by then was that you became like a daughter to Mosha and gave her a mother's joy."

Shaye searches her aunt's face and asks, "Are His own people never to be on equal footing then? Will we always be expected to walk underneath?"

Pearl frowns. "They will steadfastly deny it now . . . but when all the people loaded up into the Aegean C . . . they stepped into it as equals. Even so, people have always jostled for power. It's part of human nature. Even in the time before, there were plenty of stories like that of your parents. I believe that there was a story about two young lovers whose families were enemies. It was famous for hundreds of years in the time before. In the story, the two secretly wed, but then both of them died."

Pearl shifts around in her chair. "The Maker has always said that *every* person is worthy of respect, but even among His own you can see this is often not observed. So I cannot put all the blame upon the military. In the beginning of Aegea, life sometimes hung by a thread. Those first officers felt a huge weight of responsibility to preserve life. We are a long way from those days and now there are many people who have life, food, and shelter. We owe it, at least in part, to the preservation of those times. . . . If you could rule it all tomorrow . . . would you rule with fairness or demand revenge for what His own have suffered? When would it ever be enough? Would you then *become* the very thing you hate?" The old woman sighs as she thinks of it. "Nothing we see here is permanent, my dear. Each person in each generation must choose to accept the *real* love of the Maker and to be an example of it . . . or to be held in the clutches of a kingdom that knows only what it *wants*. Each day, the road stretches out ahead with, the same choice." She places her hand on the side of Shaye's face. "I pray you will choose the way of love."

CHAPTER 11
Highway Robbery

"**I** owned nothing when my mother gave birth to me, I will pass from this life with nothing but the treasure of the Maker's love."— *A saying from the Tell of His people*

The horse seemed slow on the way to town, but it is doubly so now. He has only one pace now: *clop clop clop*. Shaye is nearly certain she could run back to Westland faster than this animal slogging along with a full wagon. There are several stretches where tall trees on either side of the road look nearly identical to her, so perhaps they've come farther than she thinks. One could only hope. How long had they been on the road? Two hours? Three?

As if he can hear Shaye's ponderings, Ski says, "We're only about an hour away from the outpost now. This tall oak is like a marker to me."

"I sure hope so," Lemon groans. "All this rocking around is making me sick. I don't know why I feel so bad today."

Shaye is seated in the back of the wagon, atop one of the large wooden boxes that are often used to transport the colonel's supplies. She watches Ski give a sideways look to Lemon and she knows what he's thinking: *As drunk as you got last night, I'm surprised you can sit upright.* When Shaye joined them this morning, Ski was driving the wagon and Lemon was out cold in the back. It was only after they got out of town that Lemon switched places with her.

Just ahead of them, three men emerge from the trees and stand on the road.

Lemon looks at Ski, "I wonder what this is."

Ski ignores him and looks back at Shaye. "Even if I try to get the horse to run, I don't think we can get away from them unless you can manage to shove boxes off the back. Could you do that?"

She starts to ask why when she realizes that all of the men have their faces covered and they are holding machetes. The masked man in the middle holds up a hand, and shouts, "Stop and we'll do you no harm."

Lemon looks at Ski, "What do you mean, you'll make the horse run if she can shove boxes off the back? You're just going to make them angry, you are. This old horse will drop dead before you get a quarter mile and *then* what?" He pulls on the long lever that stops the wheels of the wagon. "There's nothing in here I want to die for."

Ski calls, "Whoa," to the horse and pulls on the reigns.

Several more men step out of the trees.

"Ha!" the leader says to the others. "That old horse probably isn't even good for meat." He nods to Ski. "Get down off the wagon. Keep walking down the road and I'll keep my word."

Ski and Lemon hop off the wagon and Ski offers Shaye a hand. She picks up her little bag to sling it over her shoulder.

"You'll be leaving that in the wagon," the robber says.

CHAPTER 12
Ty—Bad News

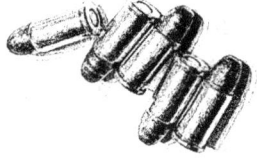

Tyrone paces the roof, watching the road leading east toward the outpost. He's had a bad feeling all day. The sun is setting and they should have been back by now.

In the fading light, he sees a signal. A message for his father. He hurries for the stairs that descend into the house. Surely, the message will tell them what has happened. *Perhaps they were just delayed.* Once inside, Ty hurries to the other end of the house. He's about to climb the stairs to the tower when he meets his father coming down, carrying a saddle bag.

Before Ty can ask where his father is going, the tower's alarm bell begins to chime. It's the signal for all the men to gather in front of the barracks on the other side of the road from the house.

"What's happened? What's wrong?" Ty asks.

"Walk with me," the colonel says as he passes Ty.

Duana rushes down the hall to meet them. "What has happened? *What has happened?*"

As he strides past her he says, "A group of robbers stopped the wagon on the way home."

She turns to watch him striding down the hall toward an exit. "Oh no!" she cries. "Our plans are ruined!"

Jubal keeps walking. "Not if I have anything to say about it."

Father and son are out the door now. Ty speeds up to walk alongside his father, "Is everyone alright? Is anyone hurt?"

"All I know right now is that they made it to the outpost on foot and that that armed men took the horse, the wagon, and all that was in it."

"What will be done?"

"We will muster some men to go hunt for them."

They reach the gate in the tall hedge and two men haul it open. The colonel gives an order to one of them. "Go find Kosh and Basil. Tell them to meet us by the barracks."

Kosh and Basil are the son and grandson of Old Menoh. Kosh has worked for the colonel since he was old enough to shoot a bow, and Basil has followed in his father's footsteps. They have worked in the Poison Forest and on the plateau as the colonel's tracker/hunters for many years.

"I'll go too," Ty says, breathlessly. "I'll get my horse."

The colonel looks at his son and there is a brief glimmer in his eye. "Here. Hold this," he says, handing Ty the saddle bag. "I can't tell you how proud I am that you volunteered to come," he says, unlatching one side of the bag and reaching into it. "But you're not a soldier yet and if anything happened to you, your mother would never get over it."

The Colonel pulls a holstered revolver out of the bag, and he straps it on. In all his years, Ty has only been close to the gun a dozen times—when his father was wearing it for important ceremonies. Although some soldiers have crude rifles that are fashioned by weapon makers, there are probably less than two dozen firearms like the one his father is now wearing. This is the first time Ty has ever seen his father wearing the revolver while in his regular uniform. He can't take his eyes off it. Now he's not just anxious about Shaye, he's worried for his father. *What does this mean? What terrible thing might happen?* He looks up at his father again. "I must come with you."

Jubal frowns. "I don't have the right to bring you, on a military op," he says, briefly clapping a hand on Ty's shoulder, "but it means the world to me that you wanted to ride with us."

His father so seldom expresses praise to him that Ty is briefly at a loss for words. When Jubal begins to move away, the young man grabs his arm and says, "Please, let me come with you."

Jubal stops and speaks quietly. "Listen, son. There have been few times in recent history when fighting was necessary, but this may be one of them."

Ty thinks his heart may stop. "I understand. I want to come."

In a rare show of affection, Jubal quickly hugs his son, then speaks to one of the soldiers nearby. "You. Jansen. You need to watch this young man when we go. Make sure he doesn't jump on his horse and ride after us. He needs to stay here. Got that?"

Jansen salutes. "Yes sir."

The colonel looks back at his son. "Hopefully we'll have this wrapped up by tomorrow, but even if it takes longer, it's something we must take care of. We can't have this— especially not with Jariel's event just days away. Since Colonel Mosely has seen fit to ignore what happens on his section of the road for too long, we'll clean it out for him. I only hope that the bandits are still hiding where we can catch them. If they've slipped back into town, it will be almost impossible to root them out."

A soldier in the distance calls out, "The men are assembled colonel."

Jubal gives a last look at their home before he says to Ty, "Promise me you'll stay here and take care your mother and sister for me."

"I'll do my utmost."

CHAPTER 13
Jubal McClaren—Search Party

Although the road is paved with stones, the darkness makes for slower travel. The men are riding along, mostly in twos with torches to illuminate the way. Two wagons, a smaller one and a larger one are at the back of the group. Soon the moon will be rising, and that will help.

Surely the robbers will have moved away from the road by now, but if they've stayed out in the countryside and not entered Midtown or Oldtown, Kosh and Basil will locate them. Up until now, there has been the occasional robbery by night—usually the victim is a lone rider—but obviously, the criminals have grown bolder. It's a mistake the colonel will make sure they soon regret.

Jubal slows his horse so he can join the first wagon. "We're nearly at the outpost now," he tells the man driving the wagon. "We'll rest the horses for a few minutes while we talk to any witnesses, then we'll split up. Half of us will push on with the trackers. We'll send word for you to bring the wagon once we've routed them so we can load up whatever we find." He reigns in his horse and lets the smaller wagon catch up with him. "Tomorrow, if all is well at the outpost, even if we haven't returned, I want you to take the servants back to Westland."

The man nods and says "Yes sir," before the colonel speeds up to rejoin those at the lead.

###

Two men have been sent ahead to scout out the outpost before they inform the residents that the rest of their group is about to arrive.

Within twenty minutes, all of the soldiers pull into the outpost and men with lamps are standing outside to meet them.

John, one of the founders of the outpost, and his son Quinn are the first to greet them and he approaches the colonel directly. "You can tie the horses over there or put them in the pen on the south side of the barn. We'll see that they get some water. And we'll have hot banji soon. It'll help take the chill out of the men's bones and keep them awake."

The colonel dismounts and hands the reigns to one of his men. "I appreciate that. Most of us will be back on the road soon, but I'd like for some of my men to stay here for a few hours. We're not thinking the bandits will swing back this way, but just in case . . ."

"We'll see they have what they need," John replies before turning to Quinn. "Go tell them to heat up some food." Quinn goes into the house and John speaks to the colonel again. "I suppose you'd like to talk to your people about what happened."

"Are all three of them okay?"

John shrugs. "I'll take you to the dining room."

CHAPTER 14
The Return

"**D**o not awaken love before its time, for sorrow shall surely follow"— *A proverb of His people from the time before*

Along with his sister, his mother, and Mosha, Ty waits for news concerning his father, Shaye, Ski, and Lemon. Of course, he's put on a brave face for the women, but with the possible exception of Mosha, he's the most worried.

Mother seemed angrier that Father left without saying goodbye than frightened for his welfare. Jariel was quieter than usual, and she looked pale. Mosha collapsed when she first heard the news. By morning, she rallied somewhat and she made everyone's breakfast.

Ty stands on the roof and stares into the distance. *It's two hours past midday and they've sent no word. Does that mean things have proceeded too quickly to stop and send a message? Does that mean things have gone well . . . or badly?*

A sound floats to him on the breeze. Is it horses? His eyes dart to where the road clears the trees. It's . . . a horse pulling a wagon. And more horses. He concentrates on the wagon. *Who is in the wagon?* He runs to the stairs and bounds down them.

"They're here! They are back!" he shouts as he runs through the middle floor of the house. He runs back and stops at the top of the kitchen stairs. "Mosha! Come out to the front of the house! They're here!"

Down in the kitchen, Mosha hears Ty and her knees nearly buckle. She pulls off her apron and rushes to get outside, shaking the whole way.

The road in front of the house is filling with the sound of horses, wagons, and jubilant soldiers fresh from a successful mission. Ty is the first one out of the gate, followed by his mother and Jariel. Mosha appears next, and she seems a bit unsteady, so Ty takes her arm as the procession stops and people start dismounting.

Captain Polk approaches them. "Excuse me, ma'am," he says to Duana with a little bow. "The colonel wishes you to know that they are all in good health, but they are taking the criminals to town. He expects to be back here no later than tomorrow evening."

Ty sees tears welling up in his mother's eyes. "Thank you, Captain," she says. "And are all the servants accounted for?"

The words are no sooner out of her mouth when the crowd of soldiers parts and two of the servants, Ski and Shaye, emerge.

The captain gestures toward them.

"Where is Lemon, the third servant?" Duana asks.

The officer's eyes widen and he shrugs. "He went with the colonel to town."

"And what of our goods? Have any of them been recovered?"

"Much of them, yes, ma'am. But some of them are spoiled and undoubtedly some are missing. The colonel says to send a swift rider to town as soon as possible with a list of anything you will need and it will be brought here speedily."

While the ishi is talking to the captain, Mosha makes a beeline for Shaye. Even though he cannot hear what they are saying, Ty watches them intently.

Mosha starts to sob as soon as she is within steps of Shaye. She pulls the girl in close. "Oh my girl. Oh my girl. . . . Are you alright?"

Shaye fights the urge to tear up as well. "Yes, Mum. I am alright."

The old woman whispers. "No one harmed you?"

Shaye knows what she means. She draws back enough for Mosha to see her face, to see she is telling the truth. "No one harmed me. I am well."

Duana looks around, and asks, "Where is Mosha?" before she realizes that the old woman is holding onto Shaye and weeping. Shaye looks haggard, but not wounded. Ski looks worn out as well. Duana grabs Ty's sleeve to get his attention. "Have one of the men drive the wagon around back and have Mosha meet us there. She'll need to help me figure out what we still need so we can make a list. We have no time to spare."

He gets the attention of one of the soldiers and asks him to bring the wagon around, then makes his way toward Shaye. He cannot take his eyes off her. She is looking back at him as well.

When he's only a step away, someone jostles him and he remembers to ask Mosha to follow the wagon around to the back. The old woman wipes her eyes and hugs Shaye one more time before hurrying away.

Ty reaches down and takes the bag from Shaye's hand. "Let me carry that in for you."

She follows him through the house to the kitchen and then takes the bag from him. She starts to walk down the hall to her room when he takes her hand, spins her back around, and embraces her tightly. "Please tell me you are okay. I don't think I've been able to breathe since I heard."

She rests her cheek on his shoulder. "I am unharmed. No one hurt me."

When she starts to move away, he pulls her back in and kisses her full on the mouth, then suddenly lets go of her and starts rambling, "I'm sorry. I know better than to take advantage of—I didn't mean to kiss . . . well, maybe I did, but I am sorry if I offended you. I was just so scared when I didn't know what happened to you and—"

She leans in and kisses him on the cheek before she rushes to her room and closes the door behind her.

Duana enters the kitchen through the courtyard door. "There you are." She stops to look around the room and is satisfied to see Shaye is not in sight . . . and that the girl's door is closed. "What a disaster all this is! And to be shorthanded on top of it. Come and help us unload the wagon."

Inside her room, Shaye leans against her door and catches her breath. *Is this a dream?* She is safe, she has her bag back . . . and Ty kissed her.

I must get my wits about me, she scolds herself. Mosha will need my help soon and I must hide my things before Jariel can come and meddle in my room. She lights her little lamp and then dumps her possessions on the cot. The first thing she grabs is the bundle of rolled cloth—the very same bundle her mother used to dip in water and roll up with small plants and roots inside. Shaye was certain she'd never see it again, but the colonel's men found her bag intact. Apparently, the first order of business for the thieves was to transport their loot to a safer locale, far from the road. Their second order of business was to feast on the food and ale. Shaye's bag had been temporarily tossed aside while they partied.

She caresses the rolled piece of cloth and smells it. *Yes, it still has the faint scent of the Great Forest.* She unties the string and carefully rolls out the cloth on her cot.

Her mother's earrings. The captain's bars from her father's uniform. One of his buttons. And the little bag of shell bones that Pearl gave to her. She wants to examine each object, but there is no time for that now. She rolls up the little bundle and ties it again before she moves her cot and locates the right spot on the floor. She uses the point of a small, sharp rock to wedge up the corner of one of the paving stones in the floor, then uses her fingers to lift it all the way off. Underneath is a small cavity that she dug out many years ago. She carefully places her bundle in the hole and replaces the stone, then puts her cot back in place before she plops down on it and takes a deep breath.

He kissed me.

CHAPTER 15
Jubal, Old Menoh, & Lemon

"The consequences of our decisions often come slowly. At times, one would have to look through generations yet unborn to judge whether a decision was right or wrong."—*Kya of the first Generation, a prophet*

It's nearly sunset on the Aegean plateau. Astride his horse, Colonel Jubal approaches the hut of Old Menoh—the unofficial patriarch of the Genon community in Westland. Sitting on a horse next to him is Lemon. After a night and a day in town, Jubal is bone tired and he's already sent the soldiers travelling with them back to the barracks. He hasn't gone home yet because he has one more thing to do.

"Inside. Inside," he calls out as the horse draws near to the hut.

The door slowly opens and the old man appears. Menoh is without his customary hat and he stops to pull on a shirt. Like his hands, the man's torso is sinew on bone, covered with loose, weathered skin.

Jubal sees the curtain to the left of the door flutter. Menoh's wife, Fiona, probably won't come out, but she's curious. *Surely he'll tell her everything later.*

Menoh steps off the rickety porch and heads for a group of stools by the large pond that the hut faces.

The colonel dismounts, looks directly at Lemon and says, "You stay here until we call you," before he takes a few quick steps to catch up with Menoh, still holding the reins of his horse.

"Back from town?" Menoh asks.

"Yes," Jubal responds.

When they reach the stools, Jubal lets go of the reins and the horse saunters over to the water where Menoh probably bathed less than an hour ago. Menoh seats himself first. Jubal takes a stool that's close enough for a quiet conversation, but distant enough to respect personal space.

To Jubal's surprise, Menoh's wife, Fiona, has left the house and is walking toward them with a rough-woven shawl over her shoulders. In one hand, she's holding a chunk of a broad, green leaf and in the other, she has a goatskin bottle. Her long white hair has been taken out of the traditional Genon knot for the evening and it is flowing in her wake.

Jubal lifts his chin to see what's on the leaf, which serves as a disposable plate, "Good evening, Miss Fi. I am honored," he says using the Genon greeting that shows respect.

She's old enough to be Jubal's mother, but Fiona's angular, lined face is still attractive. She isn't as vigorous as she once was, but her muscular little frame is still capable of delivering a baby or doing a good day's work. Fiona's normally serious demeanor is betrayed by a shine in her eyes. Jubal knows she's pleased to see him.

"It's late for you," she says. "Are you just now coming in?"

"Yes, Miss. Is that for me?" he asks hopefully.

"Well," she says, eyeing the stubble on his face, "I thought that since you were going to grow whiskers like Asher, you should have some good Genon food." Fiona is the *only* person on the plateau who calls Menoh by his first name (Asher).

Jubal rubs the scratchy growth on his face with the back of his knuckles and gives her a tired smile. When she leans down to hand him the leaf, he is delighted to see a fat *tincha*—several spoonfuls of highly spiced meat (usually goat or sooshi hen), cooked in a wrap made from cornmeal and doused with hot sauce. Although Duana forbids the cooking of such foods in or near the great house (saying, "The house will smell of it for days!") Fiona knows that the colonel loves Genon cuisine.

The colonel cradles the leaf in his hand as if it were a tiny baby or a fragile gem. "Oh thank you, Miss Fi."

She nods, then offers him the goatskin bottle which he sets on the ground, leaning against a leg of the stool. Turning to her husband, she pulls the shawl off her shoulder and drapes it across his back, saying, "It's getting cool."

A few years ago, the old man would have bristled at such a comfort, but age and love for his wife have tamed him. He grabs the shawl and holds it around his neck with one hand while he reaches over with the other to give her hip a pat.

Once Fiona has gone back to the house, Jubal feasts on the *tincha*, occasionally stopping between bites and blowing out air to cool his burning mouth, or to get a sip of *chak*, a vinegar-based drink, from the bottle. The Genon saying is, *Strong food is for strong people.* Menoh is pleased that the colonel appreciates Fiona's cooking . . . and secretly enjoys watching the man's face turn red whenever he eats it. This evening, he can even see beads of sweat forming on Jubal's brow.

The two men watch the surface of the water as day folds up its wings and the sun prepares to tuck its head down and sleep. In the fading light insects come and go, making small rings on the surface of the water that push out a few inches and subside.

As hard as it would be for some to understand it, Jubal and Menoh have abiding respect for one another. Both are men who dislike idleness, who understand the need for personal honor, enjoy the challenges of a hard task, and get up every day at dawn—not because they *have* to, but because they *want* to. They are men of similar nature and understanding.

Once Jubal has finished the *tincha* and rolled up the leaf, Menoh speaks. "You brought him home."

The colonel understands the Genon sense of community, and he is generally content to allow adjustments within the group to take place internally, under the wisdom of Menoh and others whom the workers themselves respect. "I thought I should tell you myself. Lemon may have strayed far beyond the help of anyone here. I don't believe he poses a danger to any of us . . . but he may be in serious trouble. I told him not to talk when we left town today and he was smart enough to keep his mouth shut all the way here—so he's had the whole trip home to come back to his right mind."

"Is he going to end up in the fort?"

"I don't know. When I got to the outpost, he was still in bad shape from all the carousing he did in town." Jubal wants to make it clear that Shaye and Ski didn't inform on Lemon. "The other two wouldn't speak against him, but he made a fool of himself, and I caught him in several lies. If any of the thieves name him, he'll be tried. I brought him back, but he won't be allowed in my house. We can make sure he has things to do under watchful eyes until a determination is made about his involvement in the crime. If he isn't named in the charges, perhaps I can find a trade and he can try to start fresh elsewhere."

The old man reflects with sorrow upon the loss of Lemon's kinfolk in a blood feud with another Genon clan before he says, "His father and his brother were good men, but he's been like a tooth slowly going bad since they died." Menoh thinks for a while, then nods as if he's come to some sort of internal agreement. "In this instance, the only cure may be to pull the tooth."

Jubal is relieved. The trading of Lemon away from Westland, even if it's eventually beneficial, will send ripples through the whole community. The agreement of Genon elders on the matter will carry a lot of weight.

Old Menoh slowly stands up. "We will all think about this. Leave him here tonight."

Jubal nods. "Thank you."

Jubal gives a short, low whistle and his horse saunters back to him. As the two men walk back toward the hut, Menoh calls out to Lemon. "Come. Fiona can give you some food. I'll help you find some bedding and you can stay on the porch."

Lemon dismounts the horse in silence and hands the reins to the colonel. At this point, he has no personal belongings with him, and doesn't know if his things will be given back to him. He watches the colonel ride toward the great house until he disappears in the dusk.

CHAPTER 16
Shaye—Love & Regret

"The path to 'want' is short and wide with no toll to pay today.

The path to 'love' is tight and steep, with sufferings along the way.

The path from 'want' to 'love' is strewn with the tattered remains of those pierced straight through with thorns, who perished along the way."—*An ancient song of His people*

Shaye walks out the back door of the house with the bowl of dishwater. She desperately needs to be alone, but it won't happen today or any day soon. Preparations are in full swing for Jariel's planning day—less than a day away. The entire property is abuzz with people.

She says "Good morning," as she passes her fellow house servant Beth, but she doesn't linger for conversation. She doesn't want to talk to anyone, and only hopes to be so busy that there is no time to talk . . . or to think.

She'd always known Ty cared for her, but until the moment he kissed her, she wasn't sure just how deep his affections might be. Even though she knew it was a silly dream, over the years she'd entertained the hope of continuing to see him. And then he kissed her. Despite all the warnings in her heart, despite the impossible-ness of it . . . all she could think of was that kiss.

When she went to the roof last night, he was waiting there. She knew he might be there, *hoped* he would be there, but when she saw him, something in her told her to leave, to go back into the house. She didn't. When he came close to her, she could smell alcohol on his breath. Again, she felt she should leave . . . but she was also concerned for Ty since this was not his customary behavior. She stayed.

Within moments, he told her that he'd loved her nearly all his life and held her tightly. When he hugged and kissed her the first time, it was unexpected and she didn't know what to feel. This time, she felt as if she would melt. To hear his bold acclamations of affection was more powerful than she ever could have imagined. And as they lingered together, kissing in the moonlight, all her reserve burned away and she gave herself to him.

But waves of desire very quickly gave way to sudden regret. Nearly the moment the passion ended, she felt exposed and full of sorrow. He again assured her of his undying love . . . but her inner sense of remorse and fear only grew. When they parted, she crept back to her room, feeling more panic with each step, afraid Mosha would see her . . . and know.

When she tried to go to sleep, she could hear her Aunt Pearl's voice saying, *"Real love isn't something that takes place on a sheet. It's not a stolen moment."*

All the years of aspiring to be an upright woman, to be like her mother who didn't let go of what she knew was right even if the cost was steep. All the talk of honor and right standing with her Maker . . . gone in a flash of passion. *How could I have been so stupid? Of all people, I should know this could only lead to sorrow. Even if he wanted to take vows with me, would I want him to try? What if he doesn't even offer? What will happen now?*

She hadn't simply given up her virginity in the way that some might view it. It was more than just a physical emblem that was gone. She had given up her sacred self . . . and for what? Until last night, only she and God alone had communed in her heart. Now she had allowed someone else to track across that sanctified place, someone who had no covenant right to be there, no obligation to her, someone who might very well decide to walk away and never look back.

And if I move to Oldtown, how could I ever think I could meet him there? He would certainly have expectations of . . ? He will be living at the academy for at least two years. Could I ever trust myself alone with him again? Why did I not listen to the warning in my heart and leave the roof before anything happened?

She thought again of the prostitute she'd seen the last time she was in Oldtown. What scorn she'd felt for that woman . . . but who was she to point at someone else now? She could tell herself that she loved Ty with all her heart, but how did that make her any different from the other woman? *Who knows what happened to that woman in town? Perhaps she started out as the secret passion of a man of rank and then had no other options once he tossed her off.*

CHAPTER 17
Bitter Revelations

"Old wounds are like hidden graves. You don't know what you're going to find when you expose them to the light of day."— *General Roland of the first generation*

It's nearly midnight and the air in the great house has a chill in it. Duana the ishi peers down the hall to see who is still up. Several servants are moving about, preparing the great hall for the big day tomorrow.

Duana can't remember his name. He's taking Lemon's place, but she's not used to him yet. "You," she says in a voice too tired to sound demanding. "Raymond is it? Come light a fire in here . . . and some lamps, please." She returns to her favorite chair and waits as he slowly trudges into the room.

Raymond is a bit old, but he'll have to do until they find a suitable replacement for Lemon. He lights a lamp, then the fireplace, then another lamp.

"Now go down to the kitchen and see if Mosha made any tea this evening. Maybe some biscuits as well."

Raymond nods, then disappears down the stairs to the kitchen.

Duana leans back in her chair and watches the flames while she tries to get her mind to stop whirling with all the thoughts of things she must remember to do tomorrow.

###

Shaye is wiping the last few crumbs off a counter and she looks up when Raymond enters the room, muttering under his breath. He closes the door to the stairway and looks around the kitchen.

She asks, "Do you need something?"

"The ishi wants Mosha to bring her tea and biscuits. She's upstairs in the dining room."

He doesn't wait for an acknowledgment. He shuffles through the kitchen and out the back door of the house, mumbling to himself, presumably headed for his bed in the servant's quarters.

###

Upstairs, Duana watches the burning logs. The fire is pushing back the clammy night air, melting away the final cares of the day. She allows the flickering light to burn up the mental list of things to do. If only for these few moments, her heart and mind are one—and they are floating carelessly in the warmth.

"Do you want to be alone, or may I join you for a while?" her husband asks.

She turns to see the colonel at the other end of the room, still standing tall at this late hour. His rush into danger three days ago had been both upsetting . . . and appealing. It made her realize that, despite their differences, she still cared for him.

"By all means," she says softly, "come and sit for a while."

Ignoring the matching upholstered chair six feet away from hers, he lifts a chair from the table and sets it just inches away from her. "Are things coming along the way you'd like?" he asks.

She nods once as she gazes into the fire. "Yes. It's been a long day, but I think we've done all that we can. All the remaining tasks are things that need to be done tomorrow."

He watches the light of the fire gently play across her soft skin and notices that the hand closest to him is dangling beyond the armrest of her chair. The day has been long for both of them, but the positive collaboration they shared as they pulled together the last details of their daughter's big event has eased some of the wariness between them. It's been a long time since they've had a day like this.

He gives in to an urge and gently lifts the soft palm of her hand under his. "I've always admired your ability to pull things together."

Her countenance further softens into a smile at the unexpected compliment. She turns and gazes into his eyes. "Thank you." Despite the horrific glitch of the robbery, it looks as if all her plans and her diligence are liquescing into a confidence that the event will go well.

"Do you need anything else?"

"No . . ." she says before one solitary thing manages to float to the top. "Well, there is—" she catches herself and stops talking.

His eyebrows arch upward. "There is . . . what?" Leaning toward her, he urges, "If there is something you need, please ask me."

"It's just," she says with a sigh.

For one small moment, it's as if gravity pulls him closer to her. "Please, ask me."

She studies his face. It seems ages since he's been this tender toward her. She presses her lips together in a last attempt to keep from saying it.

His eyes are almost pleading with her. She can't stop herself. "It's the girl. Shaye."

In the midst of all the tumult of preparations, this is an unanticipated topic. Jubal cocks his head to one side like he's not certain he's heard her correctly. "Shaye? What about her? Did she do something? Is there a problem?"

Duana begins to speak, then realizes this is not the right time or place for the conversation. "We're tired. We should talk about all this next week."

He's still interested in what she was going to say. He dares to squeeze her hand ever so slightly and asks, "All what, Duana?"

The combination of her exhaustion, the warmth, and his unexpected sincerity opens something deep inside her. She closes her eyes, and before she can bottle them up again the words just tumble out of her. "She shouldn't be staying in the house. At the very least, she needs to live out back with all the other servants." Once the idea has escaped, she exhales as if she's dropped a heavy burden.

Confused by the topic, he points out the error in her logic. "Mosha sleeps in the house. . . . If the girl were her daughter—"

"But she's *not* Mosha's daughter, is she?" Duana snaps. "She *never* belonged in this house."

He straightens up in his chair and his face flushes. "Did you want me to let an orphaned little girl sleep alone in the servant's house where all those men were, or to send her off to some tradesman on the other end of the plateau?"

All the softness in Duana's face disappears. "When have you ever shown half that much concern for one of the other servants' children? In any case, she's certainly not *little* anymore!"

With a great deal of effort, Jubal regains control of himself. Raised voices may already have perked the ears of servants over in the hall or elsewhere in the house. *How did things get so ugly so quickly?* He leans toward her again and speaks, almost pleadingly. "Duana, I *owe* Frank something. He saved my life."

She's unmoved. "He may have saved yours, but he chose to *crash land* his own. It's not your fault he married that gatherer. It's not your fault he ended up working on the road to the next plateau."

The colonel closes his eyes and shakes his head. "That project was a disaster from the start."

An exasperated sigh escapes her lips. "The general was in charge of the road project, not you. It's been fourteen years since then. When are we free from you *owing* Frank something?"

Truly wanting her to understand, he tries to find the right words. "They were struggling to survive when he died. I didn't help him when he lost his commission and it's still something I look at without satisfaction. I should have made sure he had other choices besides working on that road. . . . When he died it was only right that we brought his family here to be in a safe place."

Duana's hand and her whole body have drawn away from the possibility of his touch. "*Safe?* Is that what you told yourself? You were keeping his wife *safe?*"

His mouth falls open as the full implication forms in his mind. "Are you daring to act as if you could judge me? I don't know if you heard some false report or if your imagination has run amok, but you have no right to say I took advantage of Elle."

"Is that because you were only keeping her *safe* or because she said 'no'? Do you think I'm blind? You brought her here to be displayed like the carcass of that wild beast you keep on the wall. Did you want other men to think she was a conquest? A potential second woman? Was there *really* no one in either of their families who would take her in? When she died, did you have to bring her child into *my* house where my children might grow up thinking of her as some kind of equal?"

Even Duana is shocked by the extent of her outburst, but the words have rattled around like bones in the cold caldron of her soul for years. Would she take them back even if she could?

Jubal rises to his feet. "Is *this* what you've told yourself all this time?" He exhales heavily and lets his focus drift around the room before extending his arms outward saying, "All this is yours—and *nothing* you could want has been withheld from you. You're able to spend your days preening and entertaining the wives of officers that come and go at your bidding. You stand to gain the highest status any woman on the plateau could ever covet . . . yet all this is nothing when weighed against your insecurities and what you suspect I may have done."

She won't even look at him.

"Excuse me, I need some air." With several quick strides he's gone through the door toward the other side of the house.

###

On the first floor of the house, Mosha stirs out of her room and comes to the kitchen, pulling a robe over her long nightgown. She's surprised to find Shaye standing over a tray with tea and biscuits. The girl's hands are on either side of the tray, but she's just standing there, making no effort to lift it up, even though the door to the stairway is open.

"Are you taking that up to someone?"

Shaye's face is pale and she doesn't look up at the old woman. She's just staring down at the tray.

Mosha closes the door and moves back to Shaye. "What's wrong?"

"The ishi," Shaye finally manages to say. "The ishi wanted some tea . . . and biscuits. In the dining room. I thought I'd take them up there and let you rest." Her eyes roam around the tray as if it contains a puzzle she cannot solve.

"Here, I'll take it. You don't look well. Do you feel ill?" She places her hand on the back of Shaye's neck. "You don't feel feverish. I certainly hope you're not coming down with something."

"I . . . just didn't get enough sleep last night."

Mosha pats her hand. "Well, that's understandable. I just finished a nice nap and I was going to wander through the kitchen and see if there was anything else to be done, but it looks like you've got it all finished. I'll be glad to take that tray up. Go to bed, my girl."

Shaye murmurs a quick, "Yes, I will," and leaves the room.

Mosha opens the door again, gets the tray, and climbs the stairs, but once she gets there, she finds a fire is burning but no one is in the room.

She starts to leave the tray on the table when Duana calls to her from the darkness on the landing of the stairs on the third floor. "That's okay, Mosha. I'm tired. I changed my mind. You can take the tray back down to the kitchen."

"Yes'm," the old servant responds. "Have a good night."

CHAPTER 18
Planning Day—A Difficult Start

*"**M**ay the Maker hear my prayer and give ear unto my cry; for I am a stranger and a sojourner of many lands, as all my fathers were."—An ancient prayer of His own people*

On the bottom floor of the great house in Westland, Shaye awakens from a nightmare and sits up in bed. She hears Mosha in the kitchen and realizes she needs to get moving. Jariel's big day has finally arrived and Mosha will be depending upon her more than ever.

After the robbery, when the colonel arrived at the outpost, Lemon was still reeking from his binge and surly when questioned. Jubal suspected him of collusion with the thieves—or at the very least revealing too much about their travels and their cargo to unsavory people while he was busy reveling in town. For the time being, Lemon has been banished from the house and the entire compound that surrounds it. He's sleeping in a lean-to near Old Menoh's hut and day-after-tomorrow, he'll be asked to sit with some of the elders of the community when they meet to discuss his fate here.

Shaye hasn't told anyone but Ty about her hope to move away from Westland. As much as she is bursting to tell Beth and some of the others . . . she has an equal amount of dread about telling Mosha. She knows she'll have to work up her courage soon. *Perhaps when the planning day is over and all the compliments are pouring in and giving a sort of sweet glow to things, she tells herself. Or would it be cruel to ruin her victory with something that will make her sad?* Shaye sighs. *It will have to be soon.*

She pulls a dress over her head and twists her hair into the customary knot. After a quick wash up across the hall, she pads down to the kitchen. Mosha has already lit the fire and she's whisking eggs in a bowl.

"Morning, Mum," she says as she starts opening the large shutters on the kitchen windows and locking them in place. It's still dark out, but the sun will be up in less than an hour.

The old woman looks over at her and then stops what she's doing. "What's wrong?"

Shaye briefly looks away before she says, "I'm okay. Why do you ask?"

Mosha looks puzzled, but goes back to her work.

###

Before full daylight shines upon the rest of the plateau, the first rays of light pour through the open windows of the top floor of the largest house in Westland. The room grows a little brighter with every passing moment. First, the orange-colored light soaks the ceiling beams, then gradually washes down the large tapestry on the far wall. Orange brightens to gold and then to full daylight as the air in the room grows warmer. The matron of the house has been awake for quite some time, but now she opens her eyes. Today is the day. Jariel's planning day. She hears a sound at her door but she doesn't stir.

Fully dressed in his uniform, Colonel Jubal McClaren, knocks twice and hesitates before entering her sleeping quarters. Resting on her side with her back to the door, Duana is elegantly framed on the large bed by woven fabrics and soft pillows. He crosses the distance to the bed and reaches out to place a hand upon her shoulder, but thinks better of it and lets his arm fall to his side. "It's time to be up, Duana."

She turns and looks up at the golden red hair atop a tall, muscular form, silhouetted against the morning light. Tears sparkle in her eyes. He pretends not to see them and turns to leave the room.

"Jubal," she says softly.

He halts but doesn't turn in the open doorway. Looking down, he flattens the edge of a rug with the toe of his boot before speaking over his shoulder. "I could hear Mosha in the kitchen earlier, so she's probably got the morning meal ready.

The troops are due here by the eighth hour to help with placing the tables and chairs in my end of the house. After that, we can see what else you need."

"Jubal," she says again.

He stops fixing the rug and says, "I'll see you downstairs." Without another look in her direction, he disappears down the hall.

She turns to face the wall again and wonders where her life has gone. *A son of eighteen seasons . . . and now a daughter who is about to celebrate seventeen. Duana can no longer escape the reality of oncoming loss. Soon Tyrone will be whisked off to the academy . . . and that leaves a year to arrange a courtship and marriage for Jariel.* She wipes the tears from her face and sits up. *Here I am, possibly on the verge of so much that I've longed for, and I feel as if I'm dangling by a tiny thread.*

She slowly rises from her bed and makes a declaration to herself. "I will work this out. Somehow, I will make it work. I will not blink. Not when we're so close."

###

In her room down the hall, Jariel has heard her father's voice and she realizes it's time to get up. The special bath and massage oil treatments last night did nothing to relax her. She tossed and turned most of the night, thinking nervously of the day ahead and finally fell into a deep sleep just an hour or so before sunup. Now she feels like she fell from the highest tower of the house onto a pile of rocks.

She sits up and rubs the left side of her neck, then she sees feathers are stuck all over her arm. And with mounting horror, she wonders, *What is that in my mouth?* She pulls a small white feather from between her lips then sputters as she stumbles out of bed in a mad rush to the mirror on her table.

A scream is heard in the upper floors of the house and within moments Duana, the colonel, and Tyrone rush through Jariel's door. Ty is the last one in the room. When he sees the fluffy little feathers on the side of his sister's face and protruding from her hair he bursts out laughing and asks, "Did you lose a pillow fight?"

He stops laughing when both of his parents glare at him and Jariel starts to wail.

Duana plucks the feathers out of her hair and brushes them off her skin. "See? They come right off."

The colonel leans over her bed and finds a pillow with loose threads dangling from a long seam. Feathers float out every time he moves the pillow. "The thread looks very old. It must have come undone." He tosses the pillow back onto Jariel's bed and brushes a couple of feathers off of his uniform. He gives his wife a brief but cold look before he tells Jariel, "You're nearly seventeen and you need to be treated like a grown woman. This is just silly nonsense."

"Now Jubal," Duana says, "she's nervous and this was just a shock—"

The colonel interrupts her. "I'm sure Jariel can find excuses of her own. The fact remains that there is a lot to be done this morning and there is no time for hysteria over feathers from a *pillow*."

Jariel can feel her face burning with embarrassment and rage, but she looks down into her lap while her father continues.

"Nothing is seriously wrong with you, Jari, so I expect you to dry your eyes, then to go downstairs and eat some breakfast." He turns to his son. "And since you're up, you can get a quick bite and help the men with some of the furniture." He turns in the doorway to say, "I expect to see all of you at the table before breakfast is over."

Duana takes a slow breath as her husband closes the door, then forces herself to speak gently as she bends over and brushes some small feathers from her daughter's shoulder. "You'll be just fine. Put on your robe and come to breakfast before the attendant comes up to get you ready."

"I'm not hungry."

Grasping her daughter's hand, the ishi sits on the bed next to her. "Jari dear. Even if you're not hungry, you need to eat a little. Please don't make your father angry. Not today. No one is saying you have to down a whole plate of food, but have just a few bites. Okay?"

"Okay."

Duana stands and plucks a few feathers off the back of her own robe. "That's a good way to restart your day," she says.   "I'll tell Beth to pick all of this up while you're at breakfast."

Jariel waits for her mother to leave the room before she retrieves the pillow. Her eyes narrow as she inspects the thread on the seam. It may look like it was just worn out . . . but she knows better.

CHAPTER 19
Lemon

"When men have all they need, it's easy for them to be independent and resist what's necessary for the common good. Give them something fearful to remember and they are much more compliant."—*General Renwald of the Third Generation*

He leans against the wooden rake and slowly drags his sleeve across the sweat on his brow. The first day he was here, he was shaking so much, he could barely work. Even now, he tires easily. Other men in charge of the barns watched him carefully at first, but now it seems he has this barn mostly to himself. And today, with all the hubbub and visitors at the great house, he figures he might not see anyone all day.

He hears a voice behind him. "Ah. Lemon. Master of the stalls now, I see."

He's had enough of all the humor at his expense. Lemon swings around, ready to throw a punch, but when he sees who it is, he abruptly stops. "It's you. What're you doing here? What do you want?"

The short man with thinning hair spreads his hands out in an open gesture. "I wanted to see how my old friend was doing."

Lemon's face scrunches up in a scowl. "Not well." He stops talking to look around and make sure no one else is nearby. "And if your *other* friends so much as mention me, I'm finished. My whole life could be brought to ruin. It's a bitter thing when your fellow workers and those you've worked so hard for toss you off." He spits on the floor. "The great Colonel McClaren rode in like a big, red-haired hero for the whole plateau and I'm inches from a tribunal."

The man steps closer and lowers his voice. "You've had a bad turn of luck haven't you? But you kept your mouth shut. That was smart."

"*Hmph*! You mean smart if I like breathing."

The man shrugs. "If everybody keeps their mouths shut—and I believe they will—you may yet have a good turn of luck."

Lemon tilts his head to one side so he can hear better and asks, "What are you getting at?"

"Nothing for the moment. Let's just say we're sympathetic to your plight and we want to see that you're not thrown into the fort."

"So what do you want?"

"Nothing for the time being. Let's just say you can return the favor someday."

"I don't want no more trouble. I don't."

"Well good for you. All we're expecting is a beneficial deed at some point in the future."

CHAPTER 20
The Finishing Touches

"**O**pulence is one of the true signs of power."—Gen. Mayfare, the predecessor of Gen. Fairmont in the Fourth Generation

In less than five hours, around sunset, over fifty guests, a few from as far away as Oldtown will gather at the house of Colonel Jubal McClaren, the "great house" of Westland. The more important guests and their families will spend the night in extra rooms of the colonel's house rather than attempt a journey home at night. The rest of the guests will stay across the road from the house in elegant tents erected next to the officer's quarters.

Everyone expects tonight's event to be memorable. After all, Colonel Jubal is a man of great standing in Aegea—one who knows the importance of staging and drama. Only three others share his rank, and above the four colonels there is only the General. Rumor has it that if the aging General should pass, Colonel Jubal might be the next ruler of the entire plateau.

When Jubal McClaren was a newly promoted Major and this region was but a wilderness to the west of the original settlement with a large wall being built around it, he volunteered to live in the outpost from which the military could eventually oversee the orderly transformation of Aegea's farthest acquisition into tamed land where livestock could graze and crops would be grown. At the time, most of the other officers saw the move as a foolish thing. It might take generations to subdue the wild lands to the west. Wouldn't it be wiser to stay in constant connection with the General? Didn't he want to keep an eye open for opportunities hidden within the intrigues constantly playing out in the lives of the highest ranking officers?

Two decades later, however, Jubal has attained the rank of Colonel and he lives in a grand home with control over a huge portion of the plateau's resources—at a comfortable distance from much of the bitter infighting now surrounding the aging General. No one thinks he's foolish now.

For most of the evening, the men and women attending the event will be entertained separately. Keeping with tradition, the female guests will gather in the great hall where they will sit in chairs or recline on small couches, three or four women in each grouping, around small tables where food and drink will be served and regularly replenished. The women, from all the highest ranking houses of Aegea, will come with the purpose of discussing the seventeenth season of the colonel's only daughter, Jariel. They will eye each other's dresses and exchange their views on recent events before they get down to the business of suggesting potential mates for the guest of honor.

At seventeen, the girls in military families are eligible to court and become officially engaged. At eighteen they are free to marry. Tradition says that a girl younger than seventeen is too young . . . but one who is older than twenty might have waited too long for a husband.

In a separate room of the great house, the colonel will host a gathering of the men. Nothing in particular will be expected from them, but they will make use of the opportunity to eat special foods, to partake of strong drink, and to talk. They will speak of their sons, of past deeds of bravery, and current situations in need of a watchful eye. The Colonel will sit at the far end of the room in a large chair, framed by a large hide of a *chamosh*—one of his prized possessions— stretched across the entire width of the wall behind him. It's been more than fifteen years since the colonel came home with this skin. Were it not for the hide itself (and the three holes where the animal was pierced with spears) people might be tempted to forget these fierce animals still lived in the dark realms of the Poison Forest. It's a graphic reminder of the terrors the Firstlanders faced in the beginning, and one of the reasons the wall of Aegea was built. The coat of this *chamosh* is a suitable backdrop for the men's gathering.

While the ranking families of Aegea are being entertained, most of the servants of the guests will be ushered to a special tent behind the great house, where they will be fed and allowed to relax until the event is done. In light of the fact that they will be generally free to fraternize and to partake of food they didn't have a hand in preparing or serving, it's a party of sorts for them, too. Some of them will keep to themselves, others will see it as an opportunity to wheedle tidbits of information from other servants, because servants— the unnoticed people in a house—have eyes and ears, and such tidbits can be useful. Much will likely be said of Lemon, the servant who is noticeably absent from Colonel Jubal's service. Was he guilty? Was he falsely accused? To go from being a servant with the run of the great house to a stable tender mucking out the stalls of horses had to be a bitter pill.

The servants, tradesmen, and soldiers who reside in Westland will be making every effort to ensure that this is a most a memorable event, so they will most likely be unavailable for conversations.

A cart laden with the last boxes of supplies and real ice from the mountains will arrive on schedule at the colonel's home. Normally, ice is used by the wealthy for cooling stored food, but much of this ice will be chipped and brought to the table to keep delicacies cool, and some of it will float around in a special mixture of fruit juice and alcohol from an ancient recipe. (Although many of the words written so long ago were smudged, inspection of the ancient document revealed its name was probably "fruit pinch").

All around the grounds outside the house, servants are filling lamps with oil and erecting tents. Two men are tending a large barbeque pit where large portions of pork and beef are slow roasting. Inside the home, people bustle to make every last detail perfect. A gardener brings bundles of flowers into the house. In the kitchen, Mosha inspects the vegetables and rinses them as an adolescent girl (Ana, daughter of Clement and Geena) tends the flame in the hearth. Young men in uniform move up and down the stairs of the house with furniture and other objects to be placed in the rooms where people will meet. Upstairs, Shaye, Chessie, and several men are helping to put the final touches on decorations in the great hall of the house where the main event will take place. When this is done, Shaye will join Mosha in the kitchen.

The full aftermath of the robbery of Jubal's servants on the road, the manhunt, and the roundup of the criminals is yet to be felt—but a tremor or revelation has already rippled through the entirety of the plateau. By his actions, Colonel Jubal McClaren publicly shamed Colonel Mosely when he did a job that Mosley was either unwilling or unable to do. Even though any remaining criminals would think twice before robbing people on the road to Westland, Jubal has promised military escorts for all dignitaries as well as armed patrols on the road the day of and the day after the event.

The ishi enters the great hall where the women will dine on a sumptuous meal. She glides between the tables, and stops at one end to turn and view the entire space. The whole room is freshly painted with a golden wash, so it will have a warm glow in the lamplight. Rugs and pillows brought from other areas of the house will soften the sounds of women talking. Two fireplaces, one on either side of the room, will be ready to light when the evening turns cool. A high, vaulted ceiling presides over the room like an open sky over meadow and the soft aroma of scented lamp oil lightly lingers in the air. Shaye is floating the last flower in a bowl of water at the main table as a man fastens a garland over a doorway. The rest of the workers pause as the ishi's eyes take in every detail.

Along three walls of the spacious room where the women will dine, are arched doorways open to a wide hall that wraps all the way around the room. During the meal, Mosha, Shaye, and other servants will stand in the hall, out of the sight behind the large pillars, staging each segment of the meal and standing ready to be summoned at a moment's notice. All is nearly perfect. Nearly.

"Move that bowl to the right," Duana says to Shaye.

Shaye looks up at the ishi while inching the bowl over.

Duana shakes her head. "And don't look at me. Don't look directly at *anyone* tonight."

Shaye's eyes shift back to the bowl as she awaits instructions.

The ishi gestures as if she herself is moving the bowl from a distance. "Now a tiny bit to the left."

Shaye slides it back to its original position.

"Perfect," Duana utters with satisfaction before she notices a crooked garland on one table and points to it. "And straighten that garland. Yes." She looks at one of the other servants in the room. "Chessie, go upstairs to Jariel. She'll give you one more small tapestry to bring down. . . . I want to check the progress of the food, so I'll meet you back here in a few minutes." After her instructions, the ishi moves down the stairs toward the kitchen.

All the men in the room watch Chessie leave the room and as soon as she is out of sight, the three of them start elbowing each other and giving each other knowing looks. One of them leans in toward the other two and says something, then they all burst out laughing.

Shaye realizes this type of thing has been happening often lately. The beginning point was around the time that Chessie let that man sit at their table. Whether Chessie ever shared more than lunch with the fellow—*something* has happened— and now nearly all of the men have a new sort of interest in Chessie, like she became a bit of cheese they could each nibble on or a tool that they think they will borrow. Shaye might not have completely understood before . . . but now her eyes are open, and she is grieved. And if they found out about her, how differently would she be treated?

CHAPTER 21
A Memorable Event for All

"**A** party is an opportunity for the wise. It's an occasion where people routinely eat too much, drink too much . . . and talk too much."—*Major Bosworth, head of Military Intelligence in the Second Generation of Aegea*

The lamplight in the hall beckons guests to enter and enjoy a luxurious evening. Duana stands at the entrance, greeting guests before they are shown to their places at tables. She's wearing a long dress nearly the same color as the dark jewels around her neck.

Gwen, the General's oldest daughter, has arrived—no doubt with the mission of serving as an emissary for her father. When they see Gwen, those in line move to the side as she gracefully approaches the hostess. She is older than Duana, and she has never married. Her swept-back hair and deep red gown reflect the latest trends in Midtown (where most of the elite now live).

The two women clasp hands then lean forward for a quick cheek-to-cheek brush.

"Gwen, how good of you to come," Duana says. "You look like a vision in that dress! Can we hope your father's busy schedule has opened up allowing him and your mother to attend as well?"

In truth, the aging General hasn't kept his schedule in weeks and rumors say that his strength is failing or he is very ill.

The General's daughter smiles. "I'm afraid he just couldn't get away right now, and you know mother—she didn't want to travel this far without him . . . but both of them asked me to send their best wishes to your household."

"Of course. Please tell them they were missed."

Duana passes Gwen off to a servant (who will show this most-honored guest to the head table) then turns to greet the next in line. "Tea, I'm so glad you could come . . ."

A few minutes later, the line moves aside again. Novelle, Colonel Paul Kraton's wife, has arrived. Although a certain tension between their husbands exists, it's important for them to maintain the appearance of respect and cooperation, and both women are aware of their roles in this endeavor. The other guests look on and smile.

"Novelle. So glad you're here. Did you and Paul have a good journey?"

"Well, the road was long, but one endures. I see you've painted the house since we were here last time . . . was it two years ago? I bet it's lovely in the daylight."

"Why, yes, thank you for noticing. I've always thought a little splash of color can improve nearly anything."

Novelle runs her hands down the folds of the ivory lace gown covering her bulky figure. "I suppose that's true."

Duana hands her off to the servant (who knows to place Novelle on the end of the head table farthest from Gwen).

The greeting and chatting takes nearly an hour as each guest feels the need to make the rounds and greet all the other guests. Everyone knows that the wife of Colonel Wexler's oldest son was expected to give birth any day now. The Wexler's first grandchild died shortly after birth, so it was understood that they would not attend in order to remain near the family in Midtown. Of course they sent their regrets. And given the pushback Jubal gave to Colonel Mosely just days ago he isn't expected to attend either. Surely a message would arrive, expressing some reason or another for not coming.

Finally, Duana makes her way to the seat next to Jariel at the head table. She looks around the room with satisfaction. The groupings of women and their daughters are perfect . . . no one at a table alone . . . most with compatible dinner partners.

"Ladies," she says in order to quiet the room. "Let me say, once again how honored we are that you've come—from so far away—in order to share this evening with us. We hope it is a memorable night for all of you. Please enjoy the meal."

With that, the ishi gives the signal for the meal to be served. Shaye and other servants quietly bustle in and out, placing the first of the appetizers at each table. Beth moves between the tables offering water. A young man enters the room with a large jar containing the beverage for the evening. He begins serving at the head table. With one arm wrapped around the jar, he ladles out a serving to each woman.

Gwen, picks up her cup and looks at the red drink. "What is it?"

Duana leans toward her. "Jubal got the recipe from one of the records in the library and thought it would be interesting. It's called fruit pinch or fruit push or something like that."

Using a small spoon to swirl the contents around, Gwen replies. "Fruit pinch? I suppose that's in reference to the little piece of fruit that's floating around on the top. And is that ice floating in there?" She looks incredulous.

The ishi hopes that enthusiasm will win the day. "Yes! It's all part of the recipe! Apparently, people used to serve it at parties all the time." She winks. "Just give it a sip," she says, then whispers. "If you don't like it, I'll send a servant down to get you some wine."

Gwen picks up the cup and haltingly brings it to her lips. After a pause, she tips it ever so slightly.

Duana shrugs and asks, "Well?"

There is a rush of color in Gwen's face. "*Ohhhhhhhhhhhh.* This is GOOD. What's it called again? Fruit Pinch?"

Other guests who are watching the exchange now try the drink, and rounds of, "*Ohhh*," and "*Ahhhh.*" float through the room.

It's a perfect start for the evening. Appetizers are served. And pinch. And dinner. And more pinch. Then dessert with hot banji.

While the dinner guests enjoy their meal, Duana occasionally draws their attention to tapestries and beautiful cloth that Jariel herself has made. Jariel is called upon to describe her most recent creation, a truly impressive wall hanging, woven on a loom over a period of several months. Her mother is gratified by the remarks (not only about her daughter and her supreme artistry, but also about the magnificent blue dress the girl is wearing).

###

Elsewhere in the house, the officers are treated to a sumptuous dinner and superficial small talk before servants clear out the dishes and remove three large tables, allowing for the rearrangement of chairs at the far end of the room.

Jubal McClaren and Paul Kraton stand side by side, facing the group of men. In a magnanimous gesture, Jubal offers his large chair to Kraton, saying, "Paul, please, be my guest," before he pulls one of the regular chairs from nearby and seats himself in the smaller chair.

Jubal's open hand extends to the larger seat again. Colonel Kraton, a short man ten years older than Jubal, is caught by surprise at the honoring gesture, and happily ensconces himself in the spacious chair, which overshadows his small frame. Next to him, Jubal's straight form and broad shoulders extend beyond the back cushion of the smaller seat. The comparison of the two men is unavoidable.

Several young soldiers set about the task of roaming around the room with jars of *meechi* juice—a drink made from fermented tubers. The first settlers on the plateau hadn't been here long before Genon workers discovered the plant in the jungle and used it to make this strong drink. Although making the juice has never been officially sanctioned, it's presence at occasional meetings such as this is expected.

Kraton politely declines the offer of the drink. Jubal allows a soldier to fill his own cup, then turns to his guest. "Are you sure I can't persuade you?"

"I really shouldn't," Kraton quietly responds.

Jubal looks out to the men gathered in the room and raises both his cup and his voice. "Oh come now, Paul. What are these meetings for, anyway? We give the women a chance to envy each other's gowns and arrange domestic affairs, we give our daughters the chance to catch the eye of a young soldier, and we give that young man a chance to steal a kiss in the garden. What's our role in the whole thing? I'll tell you: We have a rare opportunity to have intelligent conversation and enjoy ourselves. Well-earned I'd say!"

A chorus of "Aye!" comes from the gathering as the men raise their cups.

"Well," Kraton blushes and extends his empty cup to a soldier with a jar, "I suppose this should be a celebration, shouldn't it?"

"Aye!" exclaims Jubal, and they all drink a toast to the General and Aegea.

###

In the great hall of the house, the clusters of women at tables get down to the business of the meeting. With all the servants sent away, and the unmarried girls outside, the women can now discuss favorable mates and warn their hostess about potentially disastrous matches for Jariel.

Duana leaves her place at the head table to spend a little time with each group of guests. After all, she lives in Westland, far from the intertwined lives of people in Midtown. Although she does get to spend social time with the wives of officers stationed in the compound across the road, this isn't the same as a full social life. . . . Each of these women needs to think their input is necessary and respected. She sits down at the table where two older women and their two married daughters confer.

"What about Major Rossi's boy, Denver? He's handsome enough and he stands to inherit a good position." one daughter, Kitty, says.

Iris, the mother of the other young woman, glances around the room then gives a slight but urgent shake of the head. All the others at the table, including Duana, lean forward to hear Iris' reasoning. "It's come to my attention that he has an illness. I'm not saying anything else about where he got it or anything, but it's something he'll always have . . . and pass to his wife."

All the women at the table lean back. "*Ohhhhh*."

Iris' daughter suggests, "What about Sonny, Major Bell's son?"

The old lady shakes her head even more urgently this time. They all lean in again and she says, "I had it from my kitchen girl who got it directly from the girl of the woman who kept their house for years that . . ." she spreads her hand on

146 / Terry L. Craig

the table and points to it, "he had webbed fingers and toes when he was born."

Shocked, the others lean back momentarily then press in again when it's evident that Iris has more to say.

"They had the doctor trim him up when he was just a babe, but if you catch him with his gloves off, you can still see the scars."

The conversation stops a moment when Shaye comes to clear off some of the dishes. Once she moves on, Duana asks, "Well, do you have any suggestions?"

Iris gives a confident wink. "Major Lott's son, Gilbert— you know the one they call 'Gib'—seems a good choice. The girls all like him. He chases their skirts a bit but what young man doesn't do that? He's nearly done at the Academy and seems to have a fine career ahead of him. He's tall and not bad looking. He's the oldest child . . . and the family's home in Midtown is quite nice."

The other women nod and look at each other as they ponder this.

"What about Palmer Madison?" The other woman, Alberta, whispers.

They all try to avoid looking at his aunt at the other end of the room as Alberta continues.

"He's healthy and . . . well, as the General's great nephew, I'd think that would make him a good match for any officer's daughter."

"*Hmph*," grunts Iris before she leans in closer than ever.

All their heads nearly touch as Iris whispers, "Born on the wrong side of the sheets."

"Are you sure?" Duana asks in a low voice. "That's quite a thing to say . . ."

"Well," Iris responds, "You know they had one, possibly two shut-ins before he appeared . . . and I wouldn't declare it from the housetops or anything . . . but haven't you ever wondered why his hair is so dark?" She reaches across the table to place her hand on Duana's. "I'd want to spare you the shame of ever having a situation where people might contest the lineage of your grandchildren." With her other hand, she reaches over to Alberta, "And when our grandchildren come of age, I'd want to secure that for them, too."

Just behind the pillar nearest to the table, Shaye can hear most of the conversation and she's horrorstruck on a level she wouldn't have thought possible just weeks ago.

Alberta unexpectedly leans back and looks across the table at the other women. "You know as well as I do, Iris, that there's way too little fresh blood on this plateau after so many generations. Diseases, webbed fingers, shut-ins that are never allowed to see the light of day. . . . I say if a man's wife can't or won't give him a healthy child and a second woman living under his roof can give him one that looks like him or makes him happy in some way, why not? The wife has a child to claim as her own, the other woman has the availability of a more comfortable life, and the child has a chance at a much better life. What's with all the pretenses? How many might not know that their lineage has ties to the wrong side of a sheet? I'm not saying it's happened in *my* family, so don't you go thinking that it has. I'm just saying that I'd rather have strong, healthy grandchildren than sickly ones with pedigrees or no grandchild at all."

Duana is shocked. "I see the mixture as an abomination and I think most of the people in this room would agree with me."

Alberta shrugs. "I understand what you're saying. You have children, so you feel your heritage is secured." She nods at her daughter. "I have my children and some grandchildren already. So do you, Iris. And it's part of our nature to want to control all the aspects of life. But life isn't always as controllable as we'd like, is it? Life and love have a way of breaking free of our command no matter how hard we try to rein them in. I'm saying maybe it's not always a bad thing when they do."

Duana looks at the other women trying to ascertain whether there is any sort of undercurrent in the conversation. "Well it's certainly not anything that would be necessary or condoned in *this* house."

"I feel the same way," Iris says. "It's not anything that needs our approval. Just our awareness." Then, sensing a need to move on, she changes the subject. "What sort of girl were you thinking of for Tyrone? What sort of girl would you like him to have? He's a fine specimen to be sure—have you given much thought to it?

The ishi runs her hand over her swept back hairdo. "Oh my. No. What can any of us do with young men of his age? We're thinking Ty needs to finish his years at the Academy before he courts or marries. The man should be older than the woman, don't you think? . . . If I were pressed on the subject, I'd say Major Cam's Linsey might do nicely when the time comes. Petite, beautiful, blond hair, good teeth. They've seen each other a number of times over the years while they were growing up, and they seem like they'd be compatible . . . but, he's too young for such things just yet."

CHAPTER 22
Stratagems & Secrets

"**O**ur hearts may burn within us . . . but others should never know what gives us joy or pain. Our only means of survival is to have faces of stone, to have tongues that do not speak of fear or passion."—*Kasha, a teacher of His people in the generation after the exile*

Out in the garden in front of the house, bright torches illuminate all of the open space as the parade of the eligible elite begins. All of the young adult guests are enjoying the evening air. Several musicians stand at one end and play music. There will be no dancing, but couples who are officially courting are permitted to sit together and hold hands by the pool or walk unescorted to far corners of the garden. Chaperones keep watchful eyes on them but won't intervene unless they disappear into darker portions of the garden for more than a minute. All of the young guests are aware of what is permissible. They will enjoy the garden and have polite conversation while their parents discuss their futures.

In addition to couples, mixed groups of young men and women sit on the edge of the pool or stand together, talking or watching others. Most of the adolescent girls and boys stand in separate clumps, the girls alternately laughing or becoming breathless at the thought that one of the boys might come over and actually strike up a conversation.

The whole evening is in her honor, but until this moment Jariel has had no sense of triumph. Early on, several young men approached her, paid polite compliments, then moved on to speak to other girls. But now, Major Lott's son, Gib, is more than her suitor of the moment; he is striding alongside her, giving her his undivided attention, allowing himself to be seen with her. Some of the young ladies give her jealous stares. A few of the young men are suddenly aware of Jariel—perhaps for the first time. She wants to relish every second of it. *So this is what it's like . . . to feel special.*

As they walk, less and less of the world around her matters. He's looking into her eyes, genuinely smiling . . . ignoring the other girls. They walk past a lone servant holding a tray of drinks.

"Jariel, are you thirsty?" he asks.

How melodious it sounds when he speaks her name.

He gets more specific. "May I get you something to drink?"

Jariel feels like she's dissolving into a warm puddle. She remembers that mother told her not to giggle or do anything that betrayed silly affections. *Be gracious. Be mysterious. Be . . . what was the other thing?* "Yes, Gib, I'd like that. Thank you."

"Wait here," he says, daring to touch her hand. With a dazzling flash of teeth, he adds, "I'll be right back."

Grateful she doesn't have to formulate any sort of complicated response, she nods.

Shaye tries to balance her tray as multiple people grab full goblets and deposit empty ones before they move on. During a lull, a young man trots over to her. She doesn't look directly at him, but lifts the tray a bit higher and closer to him.

With no one else nearby and Jariel a safe distance behind him, Gib cocks his head to the side and steals a long look at Shaye. "My. You're much too beautiful to be serving drinks. I'd sure rather be trekking through the ferns with you than any of these girls."

Shaye feels as if her shame is completely visible and she keeps her eyes down as he plucks up a couple of goblets.

Gib knows she's watching him in her peripheral vision. He chuckles and winks at her. "Don't worry, you're safe. It's the duty of every male guest in this garden to see that only *officer's* daughters get kissed tonight."

A girl of fourteen or fifteen approaches and shyly takes a goblet from Shaye's tray. She chances a look at Gib and it's obvious that she's entranced with him. Suddenly, Shaye is no longer the object of Gib's focus. He shoots the girl a quick smile and says, "Well now. Aren't the women on this plateau getting lovelier every year?"

Shaye controls the urge to roll her eyes or suck her teeth in disgust.

"Your name is Jenna, isn't it?" he asks. "Promise me you'll invite me to *your* planning day."

Jenna freezes as she considers the magnitude of what he said. For a moment, it looks like she might faint, then she recovers and rushes away to a small group of friends to repeat every syllable.

Gib sighs and glances in Shaye's direction again. "Must go now. Duty awaits." With that, he turns and swaggers back to the colonel's daughter. Once he's close enough to Jariel, he hands her a goblet, then slowly leans near to her ear and says in a barely audible voice, "I almost didn't come this evening, but I'm so glad I did. You look so pretty in that dress tonight."

Not far from Jariel, her brother Tyrone strolls with Major Cam's daughter, Linsey. They've seen each other on multiple occasions, so they can talk easily, without the awkwardness strangers might feel. Linsey sees Gib walking back to Jariel with drinks and says, "May I have something to drink?"

"Sure."

They walk over to where Shaye stands with a tray. With only a glance at her, Ty stops and peers down at all the empty cups on her tray before speaking to Linsey.

"Well, it seems there is only one drink left." He picks it up and hands it to her. "You take this one. I'm sure more will arrive soon."

Linsey laughs. "You're so gallant." Her blond hair is shining against a dark purple dress and beaded earrings dangle on either side of her long neck. She raises her goblet. "To my hero."

At the fountain, a hapless young man striding along the short wall around the pool loses his balance and falls in with a loud whoop and a splash. There is a mixed roar of laughter and young women's squeals as all attention turns to the pool at the center of the garden.

Everyone rushes over to watch as a servant helps him out of the water. Shaye takes the opportunity to go back to the house. The farther she gets from the crowd, the faster she walks, so by the time she reaches the edge of the garden she's almost running. After rounding a short hedge, she catches her foot on the edge of a stone in the path. The goblets and the tray fly off to one side as Shaye crashes forward. One of her knees strikes the path before she manages to catch herself with outstretched hands. It's over in a flash, but the pain in her knee and one of her wrists is searing, and her palms are skinned. All she wants to do is to get into the house, to get out of view, but she cannot get to her feet.

A young soldier not far away sees her sprawled out on the path and calls out, "Are you hurt?"

With all her might, Shaye tries to crawl away, but she collapses back onto the ground.

"Look! That girl is hurt!" he cries out. Voices draw closer to her.

"Can you move?"

"Is anything broken?"

"What happened?"

As the distraction at the pool comes to an end, more people arrive to watch several young men help Shaye roll over and sit up. Tyrone and Gib push into the front of the crowd.

Ty kneels down and asks, "What happened? Are you okay?"

If she could will herself to die, she would do so at this moment.

Gib stoops down and offers to help her up.

"No." Tyrone says. "Let me. I'll take her inside and we'll have someone look at her to see if she's badly hurt." With that, he scoops her up and heads for the house.

Someone at the back of the crowd makes an inquiry.

By now, Jariel has worked her way forward and she replies, "No. It's just a clumsy servant who dropped a tray. Everyone is fine."

Behind the great house, in the tent erected for servants in the large space between the back of the house and the servant's dining room, the number of people swells to nearly one hundred. Few persons of importance can travel without at least two servants. Many of the servants gathered here tonight have been traded between households as political powers shift and those with status make adjustments to their holdings. As the servants mingle, old friendships and grudges are renewed, new ones are formed, and the continuing conversation about the plateau and all who live on it works its way through the group. Of course, none of the colonel's servants are partaking of the food at this point—they are all working in and around the house.

The servants in the tent are mindful of what they say about their masters (after all, soldiers are nearby). Nearly everyone in the tent is of direct Genon descent, or was born "on the wrong side of the sheets"—someone who wasn't lucky enough to look like a ranking parent. All of them were "born to serve" as those inside the great house would say.

The evening wears on and different topics bubble up here and there among them. While there is a wide range of opinion as to how or when it will happen, nearly all of the servants believe the structure of society on the plateau must change. None of them were alive during the rebellion of the Second Generation, but the event has been hammered into their collective consciousness as one they wouldn't want to see repeated. Has it stopped them from longing to be valued . . . to be able to rise to whatever level work and talent could take them? No.

A debate among all the people on the Plateau revolves around Sergeant Shocky who is the first full-blooded Genon to have successfully climbed over the barrier. People of rank ask themselves if he should be "allowed" to do such a thing. Genon ask if he should "settle" for getting the small measure the military doles out. Should he use his position as a platform? Is he a token, a compromiser, or a hero? It's a conversation that is growing—especially among some of the young people in ranking families—and no one knows yet how or when the conversation will conclude.

###

Servants for the men's dinner have been sent out of the room and all of the young soldiers are in the garden, so only officers remain. Some of the oil lamps in the room have burned out and the tone of the conversation is confidential. Colonel Kraton is slumped in his chair, sleeping it off, but everyone else in the room is listening.

". . . I'm telling you these are some serious situations," Jubal says.

"And, if those weren't enough, we may be facing a situation in the Poison Forest one day," Major Forsyth interjects quietly.

The room falls completely silent. All of them have heard the tales about possible offspring of survivors from the exile in the second generation. Could these people still be out there and plotting some sort of revenge? The general eluded to it in top-level meetings before he fell ill.

Jubal readjusts his position in his chair as he studies Forsyth—a man well past his prime. A man who will finish out his years as a Major. *Would he have gotten that far if he'd had to earn his rank? No.* Certainly, he isn't speaking from any first-hand knowledge of the forest. The man has never been off the plateau, never worked with gatherers. Jubal's brow furrows while he alternately moves each shoulder up and down, as if he's weighing some imaginary object. He chooses his words carefully.

"I know those tales pop up every few years, but I get constant reports from gatherers and trackers who actually spend time down there. There is no evidence that some of the Exiles survived in the forest." He has spoken a misleading truth, but even those who dislike him wouldn't be able to prove this. As far as Jubal knows, none of the men here have the contacts or the experience he has when it comes to gatherers and the Poison Forest, and he will let them draw their own conclusions about the general and his recent fears.

Jubal looks around at the men in the room before continuing. "There is no evidence that any of them lived— much less had children and grandchildren—in that festering jungle. There's no proof that anyone survived there." The Colonel rolls up his sleeve, revealing several long, jagged scars running up his forearm, then points to the hide of the giant creature on the wall behind him. "I was right there, in the Poison Forest, the day we killed this animal. And I've encountered *worse* things living there. Trust me, if anybody tried to stay in the forest—if the plants, insects, and diseases of the jungle didn't kill them, one of its many beasts surely would have."

His eyes survey the men in the room. "Personally, I think the rumors that continually float around about the Exiles are a ruse of some of our more unsavory citizens to take the eyes of leadership off what's happening right here on the plateau. What concerns me are the things happening up here on the plateau: brazen criminal activity, corruption among those who are responsible for public safety, lax training, failure to enforce our laws, and secret meetings to foment unrest. If I have my way, there will be grave consequences for such things."

Most of the men present solemnly nod.

Jubal takes a sip of some of his banji before it grows cold. "We've been in a season of prosperity. All the lands of the plateau are now available to farm, we have the aqueduct, and we've had some record years. We've completed a good road that makes the whole of Aegea and all of its produce accessible—but we all know how a fracture in our society, or a blight on our crops, or some small insect from the forest could bring us to ruin. It's up to us to stay strong and alert, to keep our minds sharp."

A chorus of "Ay" echoes through the room. Colonel Kraton momentarily stirs in his seat before dozing off again.

"Are there any plans to renew the push to another plateau?" a captain asks.

Jubal gives a sly smile. "Well, let's just say that I think we should have a plan. We'd be stupid not to think about where our great grandchildren will live or what they might eat. The previous attempt was made when resources were too scarce and we lacked the engineering skill we needed. No one has considered it in many years, but I think it may be time to think about it again. You just came over the fine road we completed this past year. It's as straight and smooth as anybody could want. It shows we have the manpower—and I'm certain we now have the skills we'd need to meet the added challenges of jungle and mountain slopes. . . . And a grand project to tackle might bring all Aegea together again."

Several officers say, "Aye!" before there is an interruption at the back of the room. Someone is at the door with a request. Could the doctor who was transferred here yesterday come and look at an injured servant?

Major Voss, the newest resident of the officer's quarters on the other side of the road, looks at Jubal, who nods in approval. The major excuses himself and is led out of the room.

Once the door is shut, Major Lasky decides to broach a new topic. "The draft is nearly here. I don't suppose you'll tip your hand," he says, "but are you set? Anything you want to tell us about?"

A few of the men chuckle at the thought. Everyone knows Jubal is both tenacious and shrewd. They know that *eventually* he obtains whatever he wants. Between his scouts and his personal communications with troops rotating through the post here in Westland . . . Jubal probably has a greater knowledge of Aegea than anyone in the room. The general is nearly the only man who could beat Jubal in the draft, and they all know that the general is "declining."

If nothing else, some of the men here might want to know the names on the colonel's list—so they can stay out of the way. A few might enjoy jacking up the bids. Some just want to watch the competition. The draft is the most exciting thing that happens within the military. Only the games hold as much attention on the plateau—since top contenders in the games are eligible for the draft. To be a draft pick was to be made the offer of entering military life (or for a non-com, to become eligible for a slot in the academy). The whole plateau always watches the drama but since one of the original draft pics (known by the name of "Shocky") became a sergeant, interest in the games has reached a new high among the Genon. The finals of the games will take place in two months, followed by the draft. Although no one drafted from the games has ever become an officer, there are many who think *any* position the military would be better than the average life of a Genon servant.

Jubal wants to appear cooperative with the request for inside information about the games, but he has no intention of revealing any secrets. He moves his hand so that the drink in his cup swirls around and watches it for a moment before he looks around the room and says, "Oh, I'm thinking 'Rapid' Robert Hamm will be one of those who makes the draft. He's a little guy, but have any of you seen how fast he can fly down a road on a horse? I want to add a race to the games this year—from Oldtown all the way out to the end of the road."

"Like nobody knew that!" the major shoots back.

Jubal raises his cup. "To the fine men in the draft!"

The other men in the room lift their cups to the toast. "Aye!"

On the first floor of the house, Doctor Voss is shown to a small room near the kitchen where the servant was taken. He enters the room and asks for more light.

The Colonel's son and his cook hover in the hallway outside the room.

The young woman in the room is breathing rapidly and looks quite anxious. Perhaps she's never received a visit from a doctor before. After he's handed another lamp, Voss asks for a stool from the kitchen, then squeezes it into a space near the head of the cot. Once he's beside her, he looks back at the doorway. "It's okay, we don't need an audience. And you," he says, pointing at Ty, "should go back to your sister's party. I already have a hen here," he says, nodding to Mosha, "and I'm sure she'll be hovering nearby, ready to give me all the assistance I'll need . . . if I need it."

Tyrone continues to stand there looking at her. Is it pity or remorse in his eyes? He blurts out, "I'm sorry, Shaye."

After the doctor and Mosha look at him with puzzled expressions, he adds, "Everything will be fine," and leaves the house.

Now there is only Mosha. She let all the extra help go out and socialize in the workers' tent earlier, so she's manning the kitchen alone now. Voss can see she's upset, but he needs to tend to his patient. He hangs the lantern on a wall peg and says to her, "Truly, I'll call if I need you. Will you close the door?"

Mosha reluctantly closes the door between them and Voss looks down at Shaye. "What happened, child?" he asks in a kind voice.

She doesn't want to describe the whole thing. "I fell." Then she points to her wrist, "I hurt my arm." Her voice starts to wobble when she points to her left leg and says, "And my knee."

"How did *that* happen?"

Starting to shake, she averts her eyes. "Just clumsy. . . . Just clumsy."

He carefully takes hold of her arm and runs his hands along the length of her swollen wrist. She jolts but makes no sound. He looks at her scuffed hands, then he examines her knee, slowly bending and straightening it.

He peers full into her eyes, looking from one to the other. He has neither the countenance of a predator nor a superior. He has a look of genuine concern on his face. "I don't think your arm is broken . . . but is anything else wrong? You look as if something terrible is troubling you. Is there something else?"

His words are like a knife.

She tries to say, "No," but she can't manage to get it out. Her eyes burn and she tries to marshal the strength to stop any tears. "I'll be just . . . I'll." She quickly wipes at her eyes and takes several gulping breaths—as if she can swallow the swell of emotion rising inside. In the end she has to settle for grabbing the corner of her blanket and covering her face. She turns her head toward the wall and heaves giant sobs. The fact that someone is seeing this display is every bit as mortifying as her injuries, but she cannot stop. Her soul is screaming, *Oh God of our people. Please help me! I don't know what I will do.*

Voss rises and moves to the door. He cracks it open. "Hello . . ." he softly calls out to Mosha. She rushes to the door and he asks, "I need a bowl of fresh water with some clean cloth." He watches her scoop the water out of a jar and retrieve a few folded napkins. When she hands them to him he asks, "Could you ask someone to tell my aide to get my bag and bring it here?"

She hears muffled sobs and the doctor sees the panic on her face so he leans his head out of the doorway. "Not to worry. It's not so much her injuries. I think she needs a good cry as much as a bandage." He starts to close the door, then leans out again, "And I noticed she doesn't have a pillow. Can we get three pillows or rolls of cloth or something we can use to prop her into place? . . . Oh. And one more thing. Would you be so good as to make some *thooza* tea?"

Mosha is impressed. He knows the Genon name for a plant her people brought from the old time . . . they had it with them on the doomed flight of the Aegean C. It's a plant still grown and consumed to this day, though few non-Genon people know their name for it.

The major closes the door again and sits on the stool. Shaye's face is still buried in her blanket. He begins to speak quietly to her. "It's okay. You've probably had a rough day and this is a safe place to cry."

A minute later, there is a knock on the door. The major opens it, retrieves his bag from his assistant and sets it inside the door before he steps out into the hall and in a voice just above a whisper, he asks Mosha, "Why does this girl seem so familiar to me? How would I know her?"

Mosha steps back to be sure she's out of Shaye's view before she hands him the pillow from her own bed and two rolls of cloth. "You may have known her father," she whispers back. "Frank Penway. He was a captain before he married her mother. Her name was Elle, and she was a gatherer . . . the last from a line of gatherers, coming from the house of Zim."

The doctor closes his eyes. It all makes sense now. Shaye is quiet, so he leaves the door open when he steps inside.

Stepping into the doorway to catch a glimpse of her girl Mosha says, "Your tea is nearly ready." She cannot remember the last time she saw Shaye cry.

Dr. Voss places the pillow under Shaye's head, a roll of cloth under her injured leg and one near her left side where she can place her arm upon it. He seats himself on the stool again and fishes through his bag while he continues to talk to Mosha. "After you make the tea, let it steep a little while." He looks at Mosha again. "How about a piece of that good cake as well?"

She hurries away to accomplish her new mission.

While talking quietly to Shaye, Voss wraps a small splint on her arm, then cleans and bandages her knee. When he's nearly done, he says, "I knew both of your parents."

He has her full attention now.

"Your father was a good man. A brave man. No one could take that from him. And your mother . . . she had this striking sort of look . . . like a beam of sunlight at the break of day. And she was intelligent, too—I could see in a flash why he loved her. I could see why he married her. . . ." He pauses to look kindly into Shaye's eyes. "And now I see why you looked so familiar to me. You favor her greatly."

His words are like water to her parched soul. So few people have ever spoken of her parents, it's as if they were criminals . . . or worse, like they never existed at all—like she just sprang up from the ground and Mosha found her.

"They had a love . . ." he stops and searches for a way to describe it. "No matter what, they loved each other." Voss smiles as he recalls something. "I was assigned to work on the road project for several months, you know. I saw your father—it was probably just weeks before he died. He was so proud of you—he told me it was one of the best moments of his whole life when he first held you. He said the Maker had given him a treasure."

Tears brim in her eyes again, but she is smiling.

Mosha comes to hover in the doorway and Shaye quickly wipes her face when the doctor turns to speak to the old woman. "Is the tea ready? And the cake?"

It appears that he's done tending to his patient so Mosha asks, "Are you going to want yours in the kitchen or upstairs?"

"In here, thank you." he responds, and as soon as she goes to fetch it, he looks at Shaye again. "You'll need to sit up a little." He leans in and slides one arm behind her shoulders. "See if you can scooch this way a little without hurting yourself."

She pushes herself back and he readjusts her pillow so she's sitting up comfortably.

"Arms up," he tells her and she lifts her arms as he pulls her cover up to her waist. "There you go."

Mosha is back at the door with a tray containing cups, a plate, a rolled napkin, a fork, and a piece of cake. The room is too small for three people, so he stands and takes the small tray from her, then seats himself on the stool again, and rests it on his lap. "Thank you, ma'am."

After stealing another look at Shaye she retreats to the kitchen.

Voss looks down at the tray. "I've always thought that good food should be fully enjoyed, not picked into tiny crumbs with instruments . . . don't you think?"

Shaye doesn't know how to respond.

Grabbing the cake with his hands he breaks it in half. Much to her amazement, he offers her one of the halves. She takes it with her unwrapped hand and watches him.

"It should be savored. Like this," he says, before taking a big bite from his half. A hunk of the cake breaks off and bounces down the front of his uniform onto the plate. He picks it up and pops it into his mouth before smiling at Shaye, waving a hand at her, and mumbling, "Go ahead . . . doctor's orders."

She takes a bite and closes her eyes as she savors it.

"Good, eh? That woman is probably the best cook on the plateau," he says, then leans forward to add confidentially, "but don't tell the general's cook I said so." He stuffs the rest of his cake into his mouth and his focus roams up to the ceiling. "*Mmmmmmmmm*, that's so good."

He looks around the tray again. One of the cups is a simple stoneware mug, the other is a fine piece of china from the ishi's collection. He picks up the mug and takes a sip before he says, "Here," and sets the plate on her lap. "Set your cake down on the plate." Then, he hands her the other cup from the tray, saying, "That's too pretty for me. You take it."

Never before has Shaye been allowed to drink from one of the cups that are reserved for the colonel's special guests. She carefully grasps the cup and takes a sip.

"Drink it up. It'll be good for you." As he watches her, his eyebrows go up and he tilts his head back—sort of vicariously drinking with her. Then he says, "You know, I learned so much from my mother about the healing power of food and herbal teas. The Genon know how to keep the sustaining life of plants in food and drink. And they know how to enjoy it."

Shaye swallows a big gulp and searches his face. What is he telling her? Before she has time to ponder it, he takes the empty cup from her, then sets the napkin next to her on the bed.

He places a gentle hand on her shoulder before he says, "I must go now. . . . You'll be fine." He stops and gazes into her eyes before he repeats it distinctly. "You will be fine. I know it in my heart." He stands and touches two fingers to his lips then points up. "I know it."

He turns to leave just as Mosha reaches the doorway and he gives her instructions for the patient. "She'll need to rest her knee for a day or so, and that scrape will need to be bandaged every day. It's possible the bone in her arm could have cracked, but I don't think so. In any case, it will heal. Keep it splinted for a few weeks. I know you'll take good care of her and she'll be bouncing about in no time."

CHAPTER 23
Jariel & Shaye

"**B**oth love and despair change the appearance of the whole world."—*From the Tell of His people*

Jariel awakes at first light. She's barely had any sleep but she's wide awake and feels like she is floating on a cloud. She pulls a chair to the window and watches the sky brighten, filled with wonder at her elation.

Before the event, she dreaded her planning day like nothing she'd ever dreaded before . . . and yet it became the most wonderful evening of her life. The flower Gib picked for her in the garden is on her dressing table. She goes to get it and sits on her perch in the window again. She runs her fingers over the soft ivory-colored petals and inhales its intoxicating fragrance. It's beginning to turn brown around the edges, but she has set it to memory and will never smell one of these flowers again without remembering the joy she felt when he pulled her into the garden, plucked the blossom from a nearby bush, slid the stem behind her ear, and then let his lips briefly brush over hers.

She closes her eyes and smells the flower again. *How could a more perfect evening ever have existed?* She is sure none ever has.

Is this love?

Just after the sun peaks over the horizon, a chill comes into the air so she finds a shawl she made last year with all of her favorite colors in it. She wraps the shawl all the way around herself, thinking, *Mother hates this shawl. Of course. She hates anything bright. But what do I care?* Jariel closes her eyes as she brushes the flower against her cheek.

Gib said he would be back within a few weeks.

Does that mean he intends to officially court her? She doesn't know, but this feeling, even though it's frightening, is also wonderful.

###

Hours later, on the bottom floor of the house, Shaye's eyes open when Mosha knocks on the door.

"Yes?" she manages to say.

First, Mosha peaks in, then opens the door all the way and enters. "How is my girl this morning?"

It all comes rushing back. Throbbing pain in her arm, her knee . . . and her heart. They troubled her way into the night, followed by a few hours of blessed sleep. Now that she is awake, they find their way back to her like bees to a flower. She flops her head back on the pillow, and says, "I'm sore. And I made a fool of myself."

Mosha sits down on the stool the doctor placed near the bed last night. "What's to be embarrassed about? You struck your foot on a stone and dropped a tray." She rubs Shaye's shoulder. "I'm thinking in fifty years no one will care."

"I can tell you that Jariel sure enjoyed it. *She'll* remember . . . even in fifty years," Shaye says. All the while, she's thinking, *My heart is so broken right now I'll still remember it in fifty years. When he was standing there with Linsey, Ty wouldn't even look at me. He doesn't have the courage my father had in choosing my mother . . . or perhaps he only "wanted" me and doesn't have real love . . . .*

Mosha is talking and Shaye tries to refocus. ". . . now, so that's probably not true. Miss Jariel will have better things to think about."

Shaye wants the subject to change. "So . . . I'm hoping the rest of the evening went well for you. Did everyone enjoy the food? Did the ishi or the colonel or any of the guests compliment you? Have you seen . . . anyone . . . this morning?"

While Mosha studies her face, Shaye feels a rise in her heart rate.

"The colonel came through about midnight . . . he said he'd enjoyed his meal . . . and he asked if you were alright. I didn't see the ishi. Everyone was up till the wee hours—

especially the young people, laughing and carrying on. The colonel was already up again early this morning but I suppose most everyone else is taking it slow today."

It's odd to see Mosha just sitting around at this time of day, but the colonel made plans for Belina—the officer's cook from across the way—and some of the young men to fix a big breakfast for everyone over at the outdoor grill over by the tents this morning. Large trestle tables would already be up in the beautiful garden in front of the house in addition to the smaller tables in the great hall above for those who needed a quieter, setting and dimmer lighting. Mosha would have the day off—a rare respite after all her labors.

"If you're up to it I think I'd like to sit here and keep company with you for a while," Mosha says. "You can catch me up on all the news from the Outpost and from town."

There is a sound in the doorway. Shaye's eyes widen when she looks over, so Mosha turns to see who is there.

It's Ty, clean-shaven, well dressed, and wearing boots. At his feet is a large cloth bag.

"Good morning Mosha," he says without the usual grin. His focus locks onto Shaye. "Good morning."

"Good morning," she answers back with equal soberness.

"Well, you're all dressed out," Mosha says to him, trying to lighten the mood. "Where are you headed?"

"To the academy. In a matter of minutes."

Shaye says nothing.

Mosha senses the growing discomfort on both sides of the room, so she talks to fill in the void. "I thought you weren't leaving till tomorrow. Why the change of plans?"

He answers Mosha's question, but his eyes remain on Shaye. "Father decided late last night that it would be better if we went with the escorts for the guests back into town. But I wanted to say goodbye to everyone. . . . I especially wanted to check in on you, Shaye."

He stops speaking for a moment and looks to his left before his father joins him in the doorway.

"My," Mosha says, "the two of you almost look like a matched pair of spoons. All he needs is a uniform."

A brief smile lights the colonel's haggard face and then he looks at Shaye. "Are you recovering from your fall?"

Shaye nods and finds her voice again. "I think so."

"Good." After a pause, he looks at Ty and says, "The guests are fed and ready. We need to get moving before your mother and sister start wailing again."

"Goodbye Mosha," the young man says. "Goodbye Shaye. Please get well soon. I'll see you when I get my first leave."

Mosha goes to the door and hugs Ty. "I'll start wailing myself soon. Do come home as soon as you can."

"Yes. Yes I will," he says.

CHAPTER 24
A Choice for Lemon

"**A**fter a man drains a bitter cup, it seems that nothing eases the pain
of it like sharing another cup with his friends."
—*A proverb of His people*

Old Menoh offers Lemon a seat on one of the stools down
by the little pond. On a third stool is a small wooden tray with
two cups on it, which means it will be just the two of them—
though doubtless the counsel about to be offered has been
carefully discussed by Menoh and Fiona and the other
"elders" of the community in Westland. Their words aren't
law, just the considered advice of years and experience.
Whether or not Lemon accepts it is up to Lemon.

This isn't like the evening when he came with the colonel.
There have been four weeks of hard work, of life without
meechi juice, few conversations, and sleeping out-of-doors.
Lemon is as ready as he ever will be to hear the words of
Menoh.

"Fiona fetched a few of your old clothes for you," Menoh
says. "She has them in a bundle on the porch for you."

Lemon wants to know. "What of me? What will happen
to me now?" He asks.

"What do you *want* to happen to you? What *should* happen to you?"

"I want to go back to my life as it was," Lemon says looking down. He starts scrunching up his toes and pulling off the tops of the cool green grass beneath his feet. "That's what I want, but I know it won't happen. As for what *should* happen . . . I don't know. I know I made mistakes, but should that follow a man around every day for the rest of his life?"

"Mistakes?"

"Okay, well, I took wrong turns."

"Why did you take them?"

"Well my life has just been so hard . . . others have stolen the goodness from it, and I wanted to forget, to lose myself in some dim place where things didn't look so in focus all the time."

Menoh looks out over the pond. "But you still want to go back to that life—the life that was so hard and so bitter that you took wrong turns to avoid living it?"

Lemon's head slumps to his chest. "No matter. That life isn't mine to have anymore, is it? Now that the colonel is casting me off, I'll be lucky to work as a sweeper in town."

"What if there was a different choice? One you have not considered?"

Lemon looks up as the old man leans over to grab the little tray with two cups. When he straightens up, he offers the tray to Lemon. "One of these cups is water from the springhouse. One of them is a cup of *meechi*—as strong as a man can make it—and it represents your old life. You can have the cup of *meechi,* collect your clothes, and get a ride to town. The colonel has given you a reference at the academy stables, and you can work there if you stay out of trouble. But if you keep focusing on what you lack in life, doubtless you'll go back to your old ways.

"This other cup is only water . . . for a man who wants a clear head for a good day's work, clear eyes to appreciate what he has right here in Westland. You can't go back to your old position, Lemon. That's gone. But there is plenty to do out here and the colonel says he will give you the chance to work here if you want it. This cup is for a new life. Which cup do you choose?"

CHAPTER 25
Ty—Delayed

"**N**early everything I've done, I've done with the future in mind . . . the future of Aegea."—*Jubal McClaren*

"Heads up," a classmate says through an open door. "Officer on deck."

Ty dries the nib of his pen then sets it aside before he springs up and grabs one last thing to pack. But before he can open his bag, his father appears in the doorway.

Ty stands straight and salutes.

The colonel returns the gesture before stepping into the room and clasping his hands around his son's upper arms. This is the first time they've seen each other since Ty entered the academy six weeks ago. "Hello Cadet," he says with a big grin, then squeezing his son's biceps, he says, "Terrific! They've really been working you out."

Smiling and nodding, Ty answers back, "Yes. And I'm so glad you're here. Are we leaving right away?"

His father's expression turns serious. "Well, no."

"You're delayed?"

"No." Jubal looks over at the tidy bed with the packed bag on top of it. "I was thinking you should stay here during the first break."

"*What?*" All the color leaves Ty's face. "I've dreamed of this. I only have four days to go home. I've made plans . . ."

"Yes," his father says in an excited whisper, "but I've made some special plans as well!" Jubal closes the door before he continues talking. "I connected with Colonel Kraton when he was out in Westland for Jariel's day, and he agreed to give us open access to the Archives for three days during the first break for new cadets."

Ty suspects the usual plotting. "If you knew this before we left home, why did you wait until now to tell me?"

Jubal doesn't miss a beat. "I wasn't sure I could pull it all together until recently and I wanted it to be a surprise. Do you know how advantageous this is? It can give you a leg up on some of your most important studies. You can learn techniques and formulas for calculating that are all but lost to most people. It's an opportunity that few people will get—you can't pass it up, Ty. And, I've *almost* lined up a personal meet up with Dooley three days from now."

His son's mouth drops open. The archives hold little interest for the boy . . . but what young man *wouldn't* want to see Dooley? The man was a legend on the plateau. His ancestors were the tech wizards among the Firstlanders. Although much of the High Technology on the Aegean C was lost within months of the crash, a contingent of scientists, technologists, doctors, and biologists—who were neither soldiers nor Genon settlers—were also on the doomed flight. Their descendants were part of a small, elite group of non-military people who were considered equal to those of high rank. Sage Dooley was not only their progeny, he was a prodigy whose inventions boggled the mind. Considered a man of *extreme* value, he was the only civilian with body guards. According to the few accounts of him, he was an odd man who mostly associated with family, keeping strange hours, scribbling endlessly on whatever was handy. Rumor had it that recently, he'd developed a kite-like device that might actually bear a man aloft. Dooley was the stuff of boyhood dreams.

"Really?" Ty asks in a low voice.

Jubal has a twinkle in his eye. "Yes. Really."

Ty looks down at his own hand, still clutching an item he was going to pack.

"What have you got there?" his father asks.

"Just something I got the other day."

Sensing an evasion, Jubal asks, "Well, what is it?"

Ty opens his hand, exposing a small comb, made of scented wood, with delicate carving along the top. Although it might be considered "pretty" it was probably not a thing an elegant lady would select for herself. As the colonel looks at it, something about it seems familiar. It reminds him of something from many years ago. *What was it?* A small stone bird he bought for Duana comes to mind. He pries his focus off the comb and looks back into his son's face. "I'll be staying here in town for a few extra days too and I'll show you where to look in the archives, where I got the most help years ago. It could make a huge difference in your studies. You know, Dooley spends a good deal of time there. Spending some time with him will be unforgettable, won't it?"

The younger McClaren nods. Meeting Dooley would be an impressive event. . . . But he really wants to go home.

"I can tell you now," Jubal says as he sits in Ty's chair. "You ever hear about the Zoom Project?"

Ty sits on his bed, near his father. "Wasn't that another one of those disastrous projects of the general's?" he asks, chuckling.

"Not exactly," Jubal says with a sly smile. "Dooley designed a giant cable system by which men or cargo could descend straight down into the forest in a matter of minutes instead of the nearly forty minute trek down the ribbon of road that loops back and forth along the mountainside. It was nearly finished when the road project folded and the general decided to stop doing anything that wasn't right here on the plateau. . . . It languished for a number of years, but a few months ago Dooley wheedled an okay to at least test it again. And it's nearly done. You wanna go see it this week?"

"Seriously?"

"Yes. But you cannot speak of this to others, okay?"

"Yes sir."

"And . . . to top it off, I accepted an invitation for you on the last day of the break," he stops to give Ty a playful punch, "Linsey's family has invited us to a banquet at their house."

What could he say and not be accused of being soft, a homesick calf, or one not willing to keep his word and do his utmost? He looks at the comb and tosses it over onto his desk. "That would be great sir."

"That's my man," Jubal says. "Why don't you come with me and I'll take you out to my apartment for dinner?"

CHAPTER 26
Shaye—Gathering Darkness

"**P**eople will always try to find ways to disown the truth, but truth will eventually catch up with them no matter how far they wander from it."—*Aunt Pearl, a chaplain of Aegea.*

Shaye wipes the last plate, then picks up a whole stack of them and takes them to the shelf where they belong. It's been a long day. The ishi entertained officer's wives today, so there were plenty of things to do, plenty of extra dishes.

"You look so tired, my girl," Mosha says. "Go ahead and leave. I'll be done here in just a few minutes anyway."

Shaye nods and says, "Goodnight, Mum," before she steps out the back door of the house.

Mosha watches with concern. Things have happened in the house and she is powerless to undo them. She doesn't know what she can do to cheer her girl up . . . and she is worried.

Shaye steps outside the house and stands alone in the courtyard for a few moments, in the cool night air, looking at the sky to the North. She doesn't even try to talk to the Maker. *What would be the point?* she asks herself. She cannot bring herself to talk to God anymore.

Ty had gone away many times before—out to the fields or to work on projects for the colonel—sometimes for weeks. But those times, she always had a sense that he wasn't far away, that he might wander into the kitchen at any moment and ask what was for supper. Now, it's as if the whole world is between them, as if he's on the other side of a gulf she can't cross. She doesn't know if it is more that she misses him so badly or that she is so scared about what is happening to her, but most days, his return is nearly the only thing on her mind.

When the colonel went to town two months ago, everyone assumed he'd be bringing Ty home for his first "leave" from the academy. Despite her growing fears, Shaye's heart lightened when the colonel loaded up and left. But he didn't return the next day, or the next.

On the second morning after the colonel went to town, a rider arrived from town in with a communication for the ishi, but there was no hint, no word given to any of the servants about the contents of the message. The ishi stayed on the upper floor of the house for the remainder of the day.

Mosha took light meals on trays to Duana and Jariel upstairs. Before sunset, the ishi sent Raymond down to the kitchen to find Shaye. He came through the stairway door with a cloth bundle hanging from his hand.

Although he said he had a message for Shaye, he wouldn't look her in the eye when he said, "I'm to tell you that you're moving tonight. The ishi has kept a place in a room for you in the new quarters."

Mosha gasped. "*What?*"

He flinched. "Yessum. That's what she said. I'm to show Shaye her new room over in the quarters right now. She is to collect her things and bring them."

Shaye was speechless.

"I need to talk to the ishi." Mosha said, heading for the door to the stairs.

Raymond flinched again. "And she says she's not to be disturbed tonight. She says Shaye will still work in the kitchen and where needed, but she'll live in the servant's quarters."

Raymond said he would wait for her to gather her things and he would carry Shaye's cot to the new room when she was ready. Still unable to find words, she went to her room, moved her cot, and retrieved her things from her hiding place before rolling up her mat. With her heart racing, she put the mat under one arm, grabbed her bag with the other, and followed Raymond out of the house.

It was time for the evening meal in the dining room where the servants ate, so when she and Raymond stepped out of the courtyard gate, nearly every person who worked for the colonel was there to witness the event. The dining room slowly fell into silence as the people at tables looked over and saw Shaye, walking behind Raymond with her mat and her bundle. He led her around the back end of the dining room and along the walk, to her new room.

The joy of a small community is that most everyone knows you and cares about what is going on in your life. If you are sick or burdened, they can help. The horror of a small community is that everyone knows you and can find out what is going on in your life. If you are in trouble they will soon know of it.

After he dropped her off, Raymond went back into the great house and came back with her cot. He leaned it against the wall outside and knocked on the door to the room. There was no answer, so he entered. Shaye was still sitting where she had sunk to the floor just inside the door. It was dark, so he fumbled around to find a lamp among Chessie's things and lit it. Once he could see more clearly, he moved Chessie's cot to the far side of the room and set Shaye's down beside where she was sitting.

"Just one more thing, miss," he said. He leaned down and took the small bundle he'd carried out to the room on the first trip and left by the door. Shaye hadn't even noticed that he brought it until then. He untied the knot at the top of the bundle and extracted a single item. "Miss Jariel said she wanted you to have this."

Shaye looked up. The first thing she saw was the puzzled look on Raymond's face. Next, she saw what he was looking at: a pillow. The pillow was damaged in some way, for there were feathers dangling out of one seam. She didn't take it, so he set it on the cot.

Not knowing what else he could do, he wadded up the cloth from the bundle and cleared his throat. "I must be going now. Do you need anything else carried here?"

Shaye pulled her knees up close to her chest and wrapped her arms around them. She kept staring at one of the white feathers that had come to rest on the new stone floor.

After a few moments, he left and closed the door.

As it turned out, the colonel was gone for a total of six days, and when he did return, Ty didn't come with him. After he learned of Shaye's relocation, the colonel told Mosha it was probably for the best. Later that night, when Shaye and Mosha served the meal, the colonel brought up the subject of Ty at the academy.

The ishi was displeased. "I don't know why he couldn't come home for a few days." She said, "We've missed him so."

"He told us he'd come home for a visit as soon as he could," Jariel added.

"Well, he decided to hunker down while everyone was away from school and get some extra studying in. Did I tell you that we got to meet with Sage Dooley while I was in town? Ty was thrilled. Plus, he was invited to a special banquet at Colonel Kraton's house. Linsey would have been so disappointed if he hadn't come." Jubal looked at his wife, "I should think you'd be happy that he is starting to have a social life in town."

She said nothing in response.

As he took a dish from Shaye's hand, he looked straight at her before glancing around the table again. "However much you may be missing him, he's far too busy to think of home. It's best that we all get used to his absence. I'm actually very proud of the way he's taking to military life."

That was all that was said on the matter.

The days after that seemed endless. Shaye held onto the thought that sometime soon, Ty would come home. She didn't know how that could possibly solve anything, she just wanted to see his face, hear his voice.

Nearly two months have passed since the colonel's return. And now she is standing in the cold night air, staring up at stars that gleam like pieces of ice in a dark bowl.

Each day, she must endure the quiet musings of fellow servants who wonder why she's been "demoted" to the place of an ordinary servant who merely works in the kitchen of the great house.

> "Oh you poor dear, did you break something valuable of the ishi's?"
> "Did they accuse you of scheming with Lemon?"
> "I always knew that Mosha would see you as a threat one day . . ."

Not since her mother died has she felt so alone.

Although the room in the new servant's quarters is larger and a bit nicer than the little storage room she occupied in the house . . . this is the first time in years that Shaye shares living space with another person. Whether or not it was planned that way, Shaye must now live with the *other* woman being re-pegged in the eyes of the community: Chessie.

Chessie, isn't pretty or clever, and she comes from a family of gleaners—people on the lowest rung of society with no special skills. She's gotten a domestic job with the colonel, which is a step "up," but, given her family's status and her lack of desire to learn anything new, it's probably about as far up as she's likely to get—and she's likely to lose all she's gained if her conduct doesn't change. Recently, she's been slipping off alone with the construction men into the orchards or other places, and slinking back like a cat with a smile. Shaye knows that, in part, Chessie does it to irritate sour-faced women like Menoh's daughter-in-law, Monique, a woman who prides herself on her extreme work ethic and high moral standards.

Even though Chessie's liaisons are creating increasing amounts of strife, and she seems to worry about getting pregnant, she continues to scorn the advice of other women in the community, calling them "old maids," or "fat, jealous wives" to their faces. Yesterday, when a fight between two of her suitors broke out and one of them was badly injured, she treated it like some sort of triumph.

"All this talk about what I do," she said to Shaye once when they were in their room. "What's it to any of them? You know, there are women who live out in the woodlands not far from here. I've seen them. They live like they want and nobody stops them. The soldiers and the workers call them 'the wild women' but they bring them gifts and food . . . and the women don't even have to work. They do what they want and live like they want. Perhaps I'll just go and live there someday."

All Shaye knows for certain is that Chessie is well on the way to an ugly, public disgrace . . . and she wants no part in this drama. She sighs, realizing that the only reason she's still standing in the courtyard shivering is that she dreads going back to her room. With slow, weary steps, she trudges across the grassy space behind the house, through the dining area, and to her room. When she opens her door, she's startled by a man coming out. It's Bayoh, a field worker. Making no apology, he just lowers his gaze and slides by, holding his shoes.

Anger gives Shaye new vitality. She steps inside the dimly lit room and closes the door. "*What* are you doing?" she demands.

Chessie is seated on a chair and she's pulling her hair back into a knot. Shrugging, she says, "What do you think? I got tired of being lonely, of being passed over for women who have bigger breasts, or lovelier faces—or passed over for ugly women whose only appeal is that their family connections will give an advantage in the world. Why should everyone have a better chance of being loved than me? I'd rather be desired by men in general than loved by no man in particular. It's so easy for women like Monique to preach about being an 'upright woman.' I don't think they have any natural desires."

Shaye unclenches her hands and lowers her voice. "You know, I've tried to stay out of your concerns but you cannot bring men to our room. Ever."

"Or you'll do *what*?"

"I don't want to *do* anything to you. I thought we could be friends before you started acting like this. I valued your honesty and openness in the past. But don't you see what's happening to you? It's like something is devouring you, eating away at who you are inside. You are treating yourself like you're nothing—and that's what they're all starting to believe. You've scorned the friendship of nearly everyone here just so you can be about as important as a meal to the next man . . . and when they're done with the tasting party, what will happen to you? You've taken a path that has no good destination. Who will claim your children? Who will come to your aid?"

Chessie gives her a long look up and down. "Who are *you* to talk?"

Shaye's mouth falls open.

"Don't look at me like that," Chessie says, "You're the almighty Shaye who was led out the back door of the house. How many friends do you think *you* have? I hear you crying at night. I see what's going on with you. I may be the first one here to have noticed, but soon everyone will know." Before Shaye can respond, Chessie puts up a hand. "Don't deny it. And don't lecture me. You have no right."

Shaye cannot bring herself to lie, so she settles for a question. "What are you talking about?"

"Fine. It will be one of our little secrets." Her eyes sweep Shaye's figure again before saying, "But not for long." With that she saunters out of the room.

Until this moment, Shaye has continually pushed the reality of her own situation out of her thoughts. She has been this other person who numbly goes through the routines of daily life, refusing to think about what might happen next.

At first, she hoped that her mistake would just end as a regret that few would ever know about. A lesson learned.

Then, she clung to hope that she could wait until Ty returned home on leave and . . .

"And *what*?" she asks herself aloud. For the first time, she allows herself to place her hands upon her belly and consider the life she has tried so hard to ignore. As she does so, sorrow engulfs her like a landslide of boulders in a heavy rain. A tumble of thoughts rumbles into her mind.

Even if he came back, what would he do about this? He stood in my doorway the night of Jariel's party and said "I'm sorry." Sorry for what? Sorry he ever knew me? Sorry that he loved me? Sorry that he pretended to love me? He's gone and he may never come back to me.

All this, for an hour of his "devotion." Oh, if only I had listened to my heart and fled from the roof that night.

CHAPTER 27
Jubal at "the watch"

"Your perception of time changes the closer you come to running out of it."—*Gen. Fairmont of the Fourth Generation*

Colonel Jubal McClaren and fifteen other men have been waiting in the house of General Fairmont since they were summoned there in the early morning hours. Jubal isn't used to sitting for such long periods of time, and the conversations around him hold little interest. He's tired of looking at the paintings of the general's predecessors and the random trinket-ry gathered over time by Aegea's empowered sons.

His eyes scan the room until they light on a book. An actual book, printed and bound in another time or another world. It's on a wooden pedestal, protected under a bubble of clear material that isn't glass. Jubal has seen one of these bubbles before: It's a window from the Aegean C. The technology to create these clear, shatterproof windows didn't travel with the passengers of the craft, so no one here knows how to make one. Jubal wonders if General Fairmont ever unsealed the case and looked inside the book or if it's just an ornament like everything else in the room. Given that the current policy is *origin denial*, it's unlikely the General ever cared to read something from a world he claims never existed. Having it here in the private office of his home simply serves as a reminder to Fairmont that he is in charge of everything in Aegea . . . including its secrets.

Jubal stands up and moves away from the low buzz of conversations to stand by a window and gaze upon the landscaped garden surrounded by a tall stone wall.

For more than a year the general has been wasting away. His staff (and probably his wife) have been maintaining appearances and making decisions that would keep Aegea chugging along. But just barely. It will all come to a halt this morning, though, since his doctor says that today will most likely be General Fairmont's last day to live.

An assembly of top ranking officers and officials was convened here, as the law demands, in hopes of a smooth transition to a new leader—whomever that might be. Colonel Grayson Mosely, Jubal's chief rival for the top post when the general expires, is among those who have come to "the watch." General Fairmont is slipping in and out of a coma. Will he make a selection before he passes on?

When they first arrived, all the men were silent, but as the hours crept by, they began to gather in small groups and speak in low voices. The power brokering—which began earlier this year—has a new urgency.

Colonel Kraton joins Jubal by the window. "You know," he says quietly, "my wife is still bubbling about the wonderful time we had at Jariel's planning day."

Jubal glances at him and gives a nod. "Good to hear it."

The two men watch as a solitary soldier walks by on guard duty.

Kraton tries not to lean closer or alter the tone of his voice. He doesn't want to give the appearance that this is anything but bored chatter between two officers. "Mosley is trying to rally the public works and security forces to his side."

Jubal shrugs and continues to stare out the window. "Kraton will make lots of promises, but all he'll *do* is sit back and maintain things in a state of decay. The public works people know I have actual plans for improvements. The professionals like Dooley know all Mosley will ever want are things that give him a tactical edge. And as for the security forces . . . they all know Mosely shamed them by not acting before I did. He should have cleared out the bandits along the road between here and the outpost. Corrupt men might want to hide under his protection so they can hang on . . . but I'm offering a chance to regain some respect."

The double doors on the other side of the room swing open and all the conversations come to a halt. A young soldier, one bearing the insignia of Jubal's battalion, sees the colonel and moves across the room to deliver a message. Jubal tries not to wince. Duana sent word earlier that he needed to come home and tend to a problem with Shaye. He ignored it. With so much hanging in the balance, this was no time to be away from town—especially not for an issue that was probably more a product of his wife's mind than a reality. This new note is probably a scolding for not answering her first message.

The young man hands Jubal the note and says, "The rider was told it was urgent, sir."

Jubal is about to open it when the general's doctor appears in the doorway. Jubal sticks the sealed note in his pocket and says to the soldier, "Wait outside the gate. Go now. I will call for you when I need you."

The young man exits as the rest of the men in the room gather around the doctor. When they are all near enough to hear, he says, "The General is conscious now, but there is not much time. I don't know how long he will remain awake. He has made no requests, but you should all come now and watch."

When the men reach the top of the grand staircase that sweeps from the central hall of the house up to the second floor, they see General Fairmont's wife, his sister, and his daughter exiting his room. The women already have the dark appearance of those in mourning. None of them look at the men who have gathered to watch the General die. The women will retreat down the hall and wait for news of the end. It's what tradition prescribes.

Upon entering the room they see General Fairmont propped upright in a large bed. The gray tone of death is in his skin. His unwashed hair is combed away from his face and his long-nailed fingers are gripping a small pillow in front of him. If they couldn't hear him laboring for breath, Jubal would assume he was already dead.

The general's eyes scan the group. "Here," he says. He is unable to speak more than a word at a time. "Ranking. Officers. Here."

The four colonels, Paul Kraton, Grayson Mosely, William Wexler, and Jubal McClaren draw near to the bed, two on each side. The general slowly moves a hand. He's waving for them to stand further away, near the foot of the bed, so he can see all of them without moving his head. His eyes dart back and forth between the men as he draws each breath through a drooping mouth. The rest of the men in the room, move closer to the colonels so they can hear anything that is said, see all that is done.

The old man's eyes close and his head slumps forward. The doctor leans in and listens before he says, "Give him a minute. He's still breathing. Perhaps he's gathering strength."

Twenty minutes later, General Fairmont's daughter, Novelle, hears the door down the hall open and the sounds of men exiting the room. She knows this means her father has died, hopefully after making a selection. Her mother and her aunt are huddled together weeping, and she makes no attempt to communicate with them. They are already engulfed in their own world of grief. Novelle rises from her chair and silently leaves the room, closing the door behind her. The men of various rank and uniform are already moving down the stairs, so she goes to the railing of the balcony that overlooks the hall below. She knows that if her father selected someone, that man will have the complete attention of all the others.

She watches them descend in twos and threes. When they reach the bottom of the staircase, they fan out into the main hall, then gather to face one man: Jubal McClaren, the new leader of Aegea. Although grieved by her own loss, she is somewhat heartened that her father must have indicated McClaren.

The decline in her father's health this past year brought a lot of tension to the plateau—especially between colonels McClaren and Mosley. Had her father not selected one of them as a successor, things might have degenerated into violence as supporters for each man dug in for a win. She and her mother could testify that the General had always preferred McClaren, but as women, their word to an all-male military council wouldn't have carried a lot of weight. There might still be trouble, but she was hopeful that, for the sake of Aegea, McClaren could make a smooth transition.

Having just been affirmed and taken an oath, General Jubal McClaren stands in the hall of a home that is now his to occupy. Three colonels and a host of others from the ranks of officers plus the elite of Aegea's society gather around him to hear his first council as their commander.

Jubal notes that Colonel Mosely isn't one of those who stand nearby, but the man seems unruffled. Although Mosely's lack of resistance should seem a welcome surprise, it doesn't. Something isn't right. For now, it will have to remain a mystery.

Jubal looks at the expectant faces of the men and speaks in a clear voice. "My friends and fellow officers . . . this is not a time of celebration, but of mourning. It's not a time for speechmaking or policy decisions, for we have just lost the man who has ruled over Aegea for twenty years. I think we would do well in the coming days to remember the things that General Fairmont accomplished and the things that are yet to be done as we allow the people of Aegea some time to mourn his passing.

"Having said that, I am ready and able to command. My staff will serve as general staff until appointments are made. I will, of course, accept the council of the colonels as I make decisions in the coming days and consider the pool of possible replacements to the position of colonel I vacated.

"I think it's only fitting that we allow General Fairmont's family some time to remain here and mourn before the clamor of moving back to his family home. As of today, my office at the academy will serve as a command post until other arrangements are made. I will be available for any emergencies and my office will be open tomorrow before dawn." He considers if he wants to give any further instructions and decides he doesn't, so he simply says, "Dismissed."

All of the soldiers in the room salute the new General of Aegea. Many of them offer the obligatory, "If there is anything I can do . . ." to Jubal and leave condolences for the grieving family.

Before the gathering disburses, a large, black flag is hoisted on the highest tower of the general's compound, signaling the death of Aegea's leader. As soon as possible, the flag of McClaren's unit will be fetched and raised above the black flag so that all will know that succession has already taken place.

CHAPTER 28
Shaye—On the Run

"How can you bargain with the God who is over all things? What can you offer to the One who is without thirst, or hunger, or fear? What enlightenment can you offer to the One who is without darkness? What knowledge to the One who is the fountain of all wisdom? What service to the One who never tires or sleeps? For God is only interested in the deepest love of your heart. If you offer it in exchange for something, then it is not love."— *A saying of Eli, an elder of His people*

Shaye's field of focus has narrowed, and the path in front of her seems like a tunnel. A sound startles her and she darts off to the side, fearing someone will see her. She must get away. She cannot leave a message for Mosha for she cannot write, and if she told anyone else they might restrain her, or they might tell the ishi. No. She must get away and no one can help her. Anyone aiding her could suffer for it.

A thought works its way into her foggy mind: A smaller road exists on the other side of the orchards. The road is less traveled and runs parallel to the great wall. It's mostly used by workers loading up wagons at harvest time. The harvest was over weeks ago, so the road should be abandoned. She begins walking through the orchard.

As she moves between the trees she admits it: *Losing your temper with Jariel was a terrible mistake.*

In a hurry to clean Jariel's weaving room and leave it before Jariel arrived, she accidentally knocked over a rack of spun yarns. Rushing to put them all back, she put skeins of similar color together with no thought of the weight of the yarns. When Jariel arrived, she quickly inspected the room and discovered the mistake. She insisted that Shaye had done it on purpose, and from there, things rapidly escalated.

After the yelling started, Jariel shoved Shaye, who stepped back onto a wooden dowel that had fallen to the floor earlier. Shaye's foot zipped forward and she lost her balance. In a flash, she went down with a loud plop.

The sudden comedy of the look on Shaye's face as she flew through the air was too much for Jariel and she burst into laughter. But when a growl began to rise out of Shaye's throat, Jariel knew she was in deep trouble and she tried to run for the door.

Shaye jumped up and blocked her exit from the room. The two of them locked arms and struggled before Shaye worked a hand free and slapped Jariel with a fury inspired by years of torment.

It wasn't until her hand made contact with Jariel's face that Shaye realized her mistake.

Jariel stumbled back into a corner as Shaye ran out the door, down the stairs and out of the house to her room in the servant's quarters. Mosha, on a rare visit across the road at the post, saw neither the exit nor the tumult which quickly followed.

Within minutes, Raymond was sent to fetch Shaye and walk her back into the house. He led her upstairs to a small sitting room on the middle floor of the home.

The colonel was away, but Shaye knew that an infraction this serious wouldn't wait for his return. The colonel might add to her punishment whenever he arrived, but something would happen to her *today*. She expected to be questioned, lectured, and punished.

Now out of breath, Shaye stops and leans against a tree. The sound of Duana's voice is still echoing in her head.

> *"Your behavior has led me to the inescapable conclusion that we are not safe in your presence. I have sent for Nob, the butcher. He asked for a trade more than two months ago so you might be joined with his son, Korel. I see now that this would be in everyone's best interest. Go pack your things and say your goodbyes. You will not spend*

another night in this compound. You can work off the remainder of what you owe us—plus whatever damages we assess—from Nob's house."

At that point, Shaye actually got on her knees and said she was sorry. Had Jariel been there, Shaye would have begged her forgiveness.

"I'm sure you may feel sorry now that you're faced with the consequences," the ishi said. "That, however, does nothing to assure me that you aren't a danger to my household."

Duana had Raymond escort Shaye back to her room. When they arrived at her door, she begged him to let her be alone in her room for a few minutes. He looked reluctant. She swore an oath to him that she wouldn't make any attempts to get back into the house, and he finally relented.

Once she was in her room, she quickly collected her hidden items and sparse belongings, and as she did so, a panicked plan of escape formed in her mind. She went out the window on the other side of the room that opened behind the building and started running as fast as she could go.

She could only imagine what might happen to her at the butcher's house. Who could or *would* help her escape the hands of Korel? Once he discovered that someone else had beaten him to his prize, the brutality might never stop. And her child would never be safe from him.

Reaching the edge of the orchard Shaye stops to rest in a stand of large shade trees. This is probably one of the original hardwood stands that dotted the plateau when the Firstlanders came. She cradles her stomach as she sits, and catches her breath. "I'm so sorry," she whispers to her child.

Her child. There is no more denial, just a need to protect herself and the life inside her.

Before long, she realizes she must keep going, but first she listens for any sounds of people who may be nearby. It's hard to decide if it's quiet or if her ears are so full of pulsing blood she simply can't hear much right now.

She wants to wait, to calm down, to think . . . but there is no more time. Undoubtedly, the ishi has sent word to the colonel. It may be only a matter of hours before he sends Menoh's son and grandson out to track her down. Would they have pity on her? Would they let her escape? She doesn't know. It's possible that their loyalty to the colonel outweighs any obligation to help a fellow Genon. Didn't they help track down the robbers along the road a few months ago? Would her case seem any different to them? Other than Mosha, does anyone in Westland truly know her? Would anyone risk standing on her behalf?

Is this how the Exiles felt?

Having no food or water, she must make do with whatever she finds. She looks up into the trees nearby and sees no remaining fruit. Chessie's kin have done a thorough job of gleaning this section of the orchard. There is nothing edible here now. How far can she run? And on a strip of land that is only twenty-eight miles long and four miles wide . . . where can she go that the colonel won't find her? She cannot flee to the outpost where her distant relatives live. That would probably be the first place anyone would look for her. Even when she reaches town, she cannot seek shelter with Aunt Pearl. She has no doubt Pearl would help her . . . but at what cost?

I must get to town . . . and then find a way to contact Ty. Even if he no longer has love for me, perhaps he will take pity on me and help me. . . . I must keep going until I can no longer see the road. Then I will find a place to hide until daylight.

After weaving her way through the orchard as stealthily as she can, she suddenly stops and stares. To her utter amazement, dangling from a tree in front of her is a water skin hanging from a branch where a worker must have left it. She grabs it and scoots behind a tall pile of trimmed branches. There is still water inside the skin. She opens it, smells it, takes a small taste of the water, then upends the skin and drains it.

Out of breath, she must rest again, if only for a few minutes. She sits down on the leaf strewn ground near the pile of dead sticks and says, "Thank you," then wonders, *Why be thankful? Who is there to thank?*

The reality of it all comes to her and she sighs. "I know. I haven't spoken to you much lately. But I am thankful for the water. I know you are probably not listening to me anymore. I know I said I wanted to be an upright woman, walking in your truth, and I have failed. Truly, if I could go back to that night, I would run back to my room."

What's the point? she asks herself. *How many times have I thought of this?*

She pulls her legs up to her chest and wraps her arms around them before she whispers. "But I am here now, God. And so is my child." For a moment, she is caught up in a memory. It's a moment frozen in time, a moment Shaye will remember all of her life.

> *Mother is brushing her hair by the soft, warm light of an oil lamp . . . just before bedtime . . . humming a tune. Mother stops brushing, wraps her arms around Shaye, and says, "Father of all the heavens, Maker of all things. This is the child you gave me, and I say thank you. Make of her all that you will. Let her be like an arrow that is not stopped by darkness or mist or even the bright sun at midday. . . . May she be more than the daughter of Elle and Frank. May she achieve more than we could, and shine among the stars."*

Tears burn in Shaye's eyes. "I am sorry, God. I don't suppose I can ever be what my mother hoped . . . but please, help my child . . ."

She stops speaking. . . . *What's that sound?* A man's voice in the distance. It's moving closer.

"That was where they told us to meet him."

Another male voice says, "So where is he?"

"We're early, George. Calm down. Let's scout around in the trees here and see if there's anything to eat while we wait."

"What about the wagon and the box?"

"What about 'em? The road is abandoned this time of year. The box is marked with the colonel's insignia . . . who would dare bother it? Besides, right now it's just tools and junk anyway. As soon as we make the pickup we'll head down the road to the drop. Once we're done, we can go find some good food and some ladies in town."

"Hey, look over there."

Shaye freezes, her heart pounding.

The same man continues, "Is that some fruit at the top of that tree?"

"Where?"

"Come here and look down that row."

"Are you kidding? That's got to be nearly forty feet up!"

"What? You never climbed a tree when you were a kid? You're *so* soft."

"I just don't like heights."

"Fine. We'll go over there for a closer look. If those are fruit up there, I'll climb up and toss them down to you."

Their voices move away from her and it occurs to Shaye that they are headed to town. In a wagon . . . with one of the colonel's cargo boxes—she might be able to hide in it! She could be in town by nightfall! Her trail in the woods would just disappear and she'd be in town before they figured it out. Shaking with the adrenaline rush pounding through her body, she slowly rises up to look over the branches. The two soldiers are walking away from her. Before she loses her courage, she runs in the direction of the road.

When she sees the horse, she slows down. She doesn't want to spook him and have him alert the soldiers to her presence.

The horse's head jerks up and he looks at her but he makes no noise. She notes that the brake on the wagon is on before she skirts around toward the back. Stepping up onto the hub of the back wheel, she looks down at the large wooden crate in the wagon. She sees immediately that it's one of the colonel's boxes for it's got his insignia on it, and it has a hinged lid. If only it isn't locked. She clambers up into the wagon moves to the other side. There is no lock on the latch! She lifts the lid and looks inside. There are several metal tools, some wooden ones, and rough burlap sacks. A few of the bags are loosely filled with goods, but many of them are empty. She grabs one of the sacks with items in it and hurls it into the bushes before she quickly crawls into the box.

She can hear voices so she quickly closes the lid and pulls some of the cargo and the empty bags over herself, praying that they don't see the discarded bag.

The men return to the wagon and stand on the side that faces the orchard while they eat the fruit they found. One of them suggests that they give a piece to the horse.

"Go ahead."

"I'm not getting around that horse's mouth. Someone told me they bite."

"Fine. I swear, you are so soft."

"Just because I wasn't raised with dirty animals and farm trees doesn't make me soft."

"If you say so."

Shaye can hear another wagon approaching.

"Took you long enough," says the soldier who climbed the tree.

"I got here as soon as I could. So take it and I'll be on my way back to the stables before I'm missed."

The wagon creaks again and tilts to one side as someone steps into the back of it. Shaye holds her breath as the lid on the box swings open.

Has she been discovered? She hears the voice of the tree-climbing soldier saying, "Help me get this big bag out of the box."

Paralyzed with fear, Shaye doesn't move, but expects to be grabbed any second.

The soldier speaks again.

"Wait, just put one foot in each wagon and maybe we can throw it over in one move."

Nobody touches her.

"*Shewwwwwww!* What a smell!" the other soldier says.

"Just be a man, would ya? Grab your end and heave."

Quick as a flash something in a large sack drops on top of Shaye, and knocks the wind out of her. The lid slams down and a lock slides through the latch. Before Shaye can get her breath, she notices a horrible smell . . . and it's making her head spin. She cannot . . . stay awake.

CHAPTER 29
A New General

"**O**ften, a moment of victory is pierced by the deepest sense of aloneness we will ever face."—*General Fairmont, on his second day as leader of Aegea*

The general's large carriage is waiting at the gate and Jubal is expected to ride from the compound to the academy in it. The gates open and he alights into the transport.

Although he's planned for this day most of his life, his mind is spinning with all the things he needs to do. There probably won't be more than a few hours of sleep for him tonight—if any. He wonders if Ty will hear the news before the wagon reaches the academy. If anyone trained a scope on the tower at the compound (likely so), the news would be all over the campus by now.

He wonders, *What will Duana say?* Probably something like, "Finally, a general's wife." It's as if he can hear her voice in his head. It reminds him of his need to contact her. *I need to send a signal to Westland as soon as I get to the academy. She and Jariel should come to town as soon as possible. The prospect of decorating her second home should keep her happy for a while. We will now divide our time between town and Westland.*

People have already begun to line the streets that run between the general's house and the academy. They see a sober-faced General McClaren riding alone in an open carriage. Some of the people wave to him and call out his name. He doesn't want to seem giddy or disrespectful. Fairmont's body isn't even cold yet. But he also doesn't want to appear aloof. He settles for making eye contact and nodding here and there.

The carriage arrives at the gates of the academy where cadets and soldiers have run to the gate to greet him. Just inside stands Tyrone, eyes shining with pride for his father. Other cadets near the young man are clapping him on the back and congratulating him. Once the coach draws near, cadets and soldiers all stand at attention. When the horses stop, Jubal stands to disembark.

The call rings out, "Greetings General McClaren, Sir!"

He returns the salute before he leaves the carriage and rapidly closes the distance to his son.

Ty, unsure whether any sort of affection would be appropriate in this setting, offers to shake his father's hand. Jubal grabs the boy's hand and pumps it once before he pulls him in for a one-armed hug. "We will need to let your mother and sister know as soon as possible. I'll go and send them a message, and then I'll send for you later."

"Yes sir," Ty answers. "I will see you later."

The crowd parts as Jubal quickly mounts the stairs and moves through the building amidst shouts of "Congratulations, Sir!" He travels through the building to the base of the tower that the signal corps staffs night and day. A soldier stands by the door.

"Sergeant."

The young man straightens his stance. "May I say congratulations, sir?"

Jubal nods. "Thank you. I need to send a message to Westland."

"Yes sir."

The academy is McClaren's realm. Everyone here knows Colonel McClaren is fluent in every aspect of military training, including signaling. The soldier asks, "Would you like to go up in the tower or would you like me to write out the message and have it sent up?"

The general weighs the choice. Part of him would like the exercise and a few minutes to process all that's happened, but he quickly realizes he doesn't have the luxury of time. "Take the message."

The soldier opens the door and steps inside before sitting at a narrow desk and dipping a quill in some ink. "Go ahead sir."

"To Duana McClaren. 'Pack enough clothing for a week. An escort will bring you and Jariel to town, departing at the ninth hour tomorrow.'" Jubal has to resist the urge to smile as he speaks the next words of the message. "'Have much more to tell you when you arrive. Signed, General McClaren.' End of message. Read it back to me."

The soldier reads it back verbatim. "When do you want it sent, sir?"

"Send it right now."

The signal system is simple. The man in the tower here signals via flashes of light to the next tower, called Waypoint. Waypoint will acknowledge the message and pass it on to the tower that's near the outpost (where the Genon squatters built a small stopping point for travelers). The outpost tower will acknowledge the signal and send it on to the tower at Westland.

The soldier calls for a runner who will zip up the tower stairs and give the message to the signalman. Jubal watches until the runner disappears up the staircase. Satisfied that the message is now on its way up to the signalman, Jubal leaves, knowing that Duana will have the news within minutes.

By the time Jubal arrives back at his office, more than twenty men are already gathered outside the door waiting to speak to his aide. Jubal eyes the crowd, then plunges down the hall toward them. As soon as they see him, several of them rush him and start speaking at once. He stops and holds up his hands. Once there is silence, he speaks to them.

"Undoubtedly, you each have a mission of importance. Please speak to Captain Blackwell, and he will sort out priorities. The captain will either see that I speak to you personally or he will defer your case to someone who will handle it." Just as Jubal finishes speaking, he notices the young soldier who delivered the message from Duana when he was at the death watch. He taps his pocket with his right hand before he speaks to the messenger. "Stay nearby. I don't think I'll need to respond, but I'll let you know."

"Yes, sir." the young man says before he moves away in search of a chair.

Once he's in his office, Jubal takes a deep breath and exhales slowly. "It's going to be a long day and a longer night," he says to himself. He briefly reopens the door to his aide's office and calls out to him.

"Seph."

There are already three men making simultaneous queries of the captain. Familiar with Jubal's voice, even amongst the din, he looks up, "Yes, sir?"

"I need to see you in here for a moment," Jubal says before moving to his desk. He opens several drawers and moves objects around in search of something.

Captain Joseph Blackwell enters the room and closes the door. In a family that apparently had too many men named "Joseph" and "Joe," he was labeled "Seph" from an early age and only his mother still calls him Joseph.

"Congratulations, Sir."

"Thanks," Jubal says before resuming the search of his desk. "I will need a lot more paper. And ink." He looks back at his aide. "It's about to get insanely busy. Select a few extra men you can trust to help out with some of your regular tasks today and we'll try to ramp up the help over the next few days."

Seph has an armload of papers. He divides them into three stacks as he sets them on the colonel's desk. "These need your signature. These were marked 'Urgent' from the general's office yesterday . . ." They stop momentarily to exchange a knowing glance before Seph slides the stack off to the side. "And these you'll need to read as soon as possible. The one on the top looks the most important."

"That it so far?"

"Yes."

The general takes another deep breath. "Okay. I'll look at some of this. Get going. Clear the entire schedule for tomorrow—we'll need plenty of time for conferencing with the colonels and the planning meetings for General Fairmont's funeral ceremonies."

CHAPTER 30
Destination Unknown

"When your enemy seeks to do you harm, you can say, 'God is greater.'"—*Great Aunt Pearl, a chaplain who learned to love the Maker*

The wagon reaches a spot where the road runs right alongside the great wall which was built along the edge of the plateau. The cut stones of the wall are stacked into a structure so wide that another road runs along the top of it.

The man driving the wagon knows they're near to their destination. He cracks the whip over the horse, shouting, "Hey hey!"

The wagon suddenly lurches forward at a rapid pace. For ten minutes, the box in back of the wagon jumps and slides around until they reach a tower built into the wall. The driver yanks on the reigns and yells for the horse to stop, then calls out, "Let's get the box loaded and away!"

They back the wagon up to a platform at the base of the wall that's just a step higher than the bed of the wagon. Once the back gate is off the wagon, they quickly slide poles into rings on either side of the crate.

"On three," the driver says. "One. Two. Three."

They groan as they heft the box out of the wagon. Within a few yards, they set it down on a wooden floor of an open elevator and they begin working a pulley system to raise it until they arrive at the top of the wall.

"Wait," the driver says. He exits off the elevator and climbs atop a railing before he pulls a small telescope from the front of his shirt. After a few moments, he hops back down, saying, "I think we may have just gotten lucky! The black flag is up, and that means McClaren will be occupied. By the time he gets the news, we could be in town having an ale and toasting to his health!"

"I'm for that."

They lift up the crate again and carry it to a roofed area where a wide plank provides access to a wooden enclosure just like the bed of their wagon with a tailgate, bordered on three sides by a railing. However, this wagon bed is dangling from a large cable, held in place by two giant metal arms that wrap around the far side of the bed and hold it up from below. The men remove the tailgate, then move the box from the "dock" on the wall onto the bed, and set the box between four eye bolts sticking up through the floor. They secure the box with ropes through the eyebolts before replacing the tailgate and returning to the dock.

The two of them begin hauling on a large wheel at the side of the platform and the floating wagon moves away to where the drop in the cable begins. When gravity takes over, the in-line wheels attached to the arms of the vehicle begin to rotate faster. Once it's away from the station, it's in a controlled fall down the side of the mountain. They watch it fly along the cable that descends more than a mile to the jungle below.

One man thinks he hears a woman screaming as the carrier whisks away. Puzzled, he looks at his companion and says, "I thought that stuff would keep her knocked out."

The other one shrugs. "Does it matter now? Let's get going. It's only a few hours till nightfall."

"Who will pick up the crate at the other end? What'll they do with it down there?"

"Not our problem, George. C'mon, let's get to town."

CHAPTER 31
Missing . . . or Taken?

"Time shoots by like a bullet from a rifle when you are busy, but it stands still in a crisis."—*Gen. Lancaster of the Second Generation*

Two hours have slipped by. It's past midday and the crowd outside Jubal's office shows no sign of diminishing. Men leave only to be replaced by others who also have "urgent" requests to make of the new general. Each trip that Seph makes into McClaren's office, he takes more documents and messages. Once he's inside, he and Jubal exchange papers and information.

On one of his returns to his own desk, Seph looks over and sees the young soldier that the general told to wait for a possible response to a message. Amidst all this frustration and activity, this kid is the only person who looks bored. Seph makes a mental note to ask the general if the young man can be excused.

An officer pushes his way to the front of the line. "I need to speak to McClaren. Right away."

Because they share the same rank, Seph knows this man and knows he's in charge of the signal corps. It's not likely that he is here on a trivial matter. "Is it a message?"

"It's a response to a message McClaren sent earlier and I need to speak to him—personally. Right *now*."

Seph rises from his chair. "Come with me."

One of the men in the middle of the line turns to the man behind him. "I should be so lucky."

As soon as the door to McClaren's office closes, the signal captain approaches the desk. "Sir. I have received word of a situation which requires your immediate attention."

One of Jubal's brows arches upward. "Yes?"

"We sent your message via Waypoint to the outpost. Waypoint received the message and sent it on. Half an hour later, Waypoint received a message back from the outpost. The outpost was unable to get a confirmation that your message was received at Westland."

Despite an uptick in his pulse, the General appears calm and he offers information that the captain would already know, "That's not uncommon. They might not have seen the message or the man in the tower at Westland might have been distracted."

The soldier nods. "That's what everyone thought at first, so they made repeated attempts to signal and eventually sent riders from the tower at the outpost with a written message just in case." The captain offers a piece of paper to McClaren. "Less than ten minutes ago, we got this back."

Jubal takes the paper and reads it. Seph watches the general's ruddy face go completely pale before he looks up at them. "I need both of you to wait outside for a moment. Don't go far. I will call for you shortly."

The moment he is alone, Jubal snatches the note from Duana out of his pocket, rips it open and reads it twice before he rereads the message the signalman brought. By the time he's finished, he's out of breath. He stands and squeezes his head at the temples before he starts pacing.

Several minutes pass and Seph tries to look as if everything is business as usual, but he keeps an ear and eye trained on the door of Jubal's office.

The door opens a crack. "Seph! I need you in here."

As soon as he's inside the office, Jubal starts firing off orders in rapid succession. Seph sets more paper on the desk and begins jotting down notes as the general talks.

"Send someone to find my son and bring him here without delay." Jubal also starts writing while he continues. The two men are rapidly scribbling while intermittently dipping in the inkwell at the center of the desk. "There's less than half a day of daylight left. I'm making out an order that I want delivered to Captain York. He is to assemble the Special Forces unit for a drill as covertly as possible and have them ready to ride in less than two hours. Have the second order

I'm writing out delivered to the stables. They are to have twenty horses ready to ride out with full gear for a drill in less than two hours. I also want a doctor with full medical supplies ready to ride." Jubal stops as his mind ticks through the list of doctors until he remembers the name of Col. Mosely's doctor. "Make sure it's *not* Jannick. Send a secure runner to get Captain Randall at Intelligence. I want him here now. Send out a soldier to find my tracker, Kosh, and bring him back here immediately. He'll be in Oldtown," Jubal says as he places another piece of paper on his stack of orders and scribbles on it. ". . . possibly at this address. If he's not there, they will know where he is." Jubal hands the stack to his aide. "That's all for the moment. Go. And send the signal captain back in."

When the captain from the signal corps is at his desk, Jubal begins writing again. "I'm going to write out a message. I don't want anyone other than you to see it. You are to take it into the tower, and you are to personally signal it."

"Yes sir."

"Everything that has happened and everything you hear or see regarding this is officially classified. No one, I repeat *no one*—no matter their rank—is to be told of this unless they hear it directly from me."

"Yes sir."

"If I understand correctly, there is now a signalman in my compound at Westland."

"Yes sir."

Jubal starts writing again. "Once you have personally sent this message wait for the confirmation that he has received it. I want to know what has been done in the way of a search thus far—and specifically if they have used one of my trackers by the name of Tre. The name is spelled *T-R-E*. Anyone out there will know who that is. I expect to see a runner in less than half an hour saying either that you have confirmation that the message was received and any response, or that you have no confirmation."

"Yes sir."

Twenty minutes later, General Jubal McClaren's son, Tyrone is shown into his office, but the happy glow in Ty's heart begins to dim as soon as he sees the grim demeanor of his father's aide. Once he's in his father's office, he is swallowed up by concern. Jubal is standing by the window. There is a look on his face . . . as if he were standing at a grave.

"What's wrong, what's *happened*?" Ty asks.

Jubal turns and his eyes watch the door until it closes. "Ty," he begins. He has to stop and take another breath before he can say it. "Something has happened to your sister."

"Tell me! What is it?"

"Someone has taken her and no one has been able to find her."

Ty shouts, "*NO!*" before he steps closer to his father and asks, "When did this happen? Are we mounting a search? Who would *do* this?"

Jubal touches the pocket where Duana's note sat for several hours. "I'm not certain," he says, then looks directly into his son's eyes. "We have to be *very* careful not to panic or to reveal our plans. All I know for certain is that Shaye and Jariel had an altercation this morning. Shaye struck Jariel, so your mother was going to have her sent to fill out her contract with the butcher . . . and no one can locate Shaye, either."

The room seems to spin before Ty finally finds the air to say, "What?"

CHAPTER 32
Deep in the Great Forest

"**B**lood is stronger than stone or metal. The blood of your seed and the blood you shed will both testify one day—on your behalf, or against you."—*A proverb of His people*

Shaye's eyes flutter and then open.

Where am I? I was in a crate in the dark . . . with something heavy on top of me . . . and then falling . . .

The weight is gone, the lid is open . . . and her astonished gaze is traveling over a sea of green leaves above her, wafting around in a breeze, allowing winks of blue sky to appear here and there. As her conscious mind awakens, she realizes that these are not the leaves of trees that grow on the plateau. None of this adds up. Perhaps if her head didn't hurt so badly, she could figure it all out.

Am I in a dream?

Her thoughts are interrupted by a sound she's never heard before, resonating through the forest. It's a bone rattling scream. Her hands instantly cover her belly.

Something terrible is happening and she must protect the child. She cannot remain here till whatever it is comes and gets her.

She can barely move, but finally wills herself to find the strength to sit up. After a few more seconds, she crawls over the edge of the crate and drops onto the ground. She leans on the box in an effort to stand but her legs are wobbly. She looks around and realizes where she is.

Giant trees shoot straight heavenward, as if they were holding up the sky itself, and from their smooth-barked trunks emerge great roots that look like tall fins that snake their way into the leafy soil. The canopy of leaves above shades the entire world below from the brilliant light of day. Vines as thick as her leg wrap around the trees and dangle down from branches. Huge ferns dot the forest floor, and a steamy vapor rises from the thick bed of rotting vegetation.

All she can hear now is the sound of the wind in the canopy above. Although she has never been here, she knows the smell of this place. She is in the Great Forest, *the land of cloud and leaf.*

Shaye knows for certain that she isn't just at the edge of the jungle. If she were, the growth would be quite dense, studded with hundreds of sprouting trees and young plants, barely penetrable without a machete. But someone must have brought the crate much further into the jungle, for, just as her mother described it, the space between huge trees is twenty feet or more. Nearby, an old tree has fallen and its trunk has turned into a giant planter box for dark green ferns. Wherever tiny shafts of sunlight penetrate the canopy above, a tangle of plants vies for the chance to capture that light, then grow, dominate, and eventually choke out neighboring plants. She notes that the vapor rising out of the forest floor is starting to gather along the ground and between thickets of underbrush . . . and she realizes her precarious position.

I am in the forest, with no knife, no weapons, nothing but my . . . she panics as she pulls herself along the edge of the box. Before she can look into it for her bag, a movement in her peripheral vision catches her attention. Something is emerging through the mist, not thirty feet away. It's a man. A Genon man.

Even though he's not a soldier, he doesn't he look like a gatherer from the plateau, either. His skin and his beard are smeared with red mud, his long dark hair is pulled back, and his minimal clothing is made from an animal hide. He has a javelin in his hand and she sees a bow with a quiver of arrows is slung behind his shoulders. A couple of sheathed knives are on a belt at his waist.

Had she not always hoped to meet exiles out here? Had she not hoped that the stories were true and she'd find they had survived and lived on in the Great Forest? But fantasy and its realization are often quite different. She could be seconds from a violent death.

Is any of this real?

As her mother instructed her, Shaye gestures the vow of silence. She touches two fingers to her heart, to her lips, then points to the sky, then looks at him and holds her breath.

His yellow-gold eyes are wide with wonder, and he says in Genon. "Please. Speak to me."

His manner of dress and weaponry give the appearance of fierceness. His eyes and his voice convey something else entirely. Hope? . . . Loneliness? Is he the last descendant of the Exiles? He has managed to survive, but just barely judging by the look of his weight and clothing.

Her fear is only somewhat tempered by his request. She says the words to the vow slowly, in Genon. "I will . . . speak of this to no one. God bears witness."

Shaye is startled by the sudden noise of several bright green birds darting between the trees above, screeching a warning as they make haste to fly away.

He looks up at the birds before he addresses her once again. This time, his voice is urgent, his speech rapid.

Shaye realizes that he either speaks Genon more fluidly than she can, or he has a greater vocabulary than she does. She struggles to catch and digest his words yet many of them make no sense to her. She has spoken Genon all her life, but for the first time she can remember, she's aware of the limits of her abilities in her own language.

" . . . and there is no time," he says. "You [unknown words]. You must choose now. [Unknown words] woman?"

He looks intently at her and tries again. "They come. The woman [unknown words]. Decide now if she dies."

Shaye scarcely has the courage to shake her head and reply in Genon. "I don't know all of your words."

Now he seems to understand her dilemma. He speaks slowly. "His people come."

She processes the words. *His people come. . . . Perhaps there are more exiles—and they are nearby? Or maybe just Genon gatherers?* Her brow furrows with concentration, but she still not sure what he's trying to convey. She shakes her head.

He tries again. The urgency is still there, but he's using simpler words. "His people—not from Aegea—come. You understand?"

Her eyes widen and she nods. This is more than she ever could have imagined. She's still not sure she's awake.

"They come chasing the *k'mosh* and find her, not you," he points to the box. "[Unknown words]."

Shaye has heard a word similar to "*k'mosh*" before but needs a moment to put it in its proper place. The word replays in her head until it comes to her.

K'mosh . . . k'mosh. . . . The hide on the colonel keeps on the wall: a chamosh! A beast that lives in the shadows of the forest, stalking and killing even the largest of animals with long claws and teeth like a multitude of knives! Now other parts of the warrior's statement finally filter into Shaye's mind: *the woman . . . decide if she dies . . . they find her, not you.*

Another scream pierces through the forest and Shaye realizes that *this* is the sound she heard described in childhood tales: It's the scream of the *chamosh*. A creature that terrorized and killed many Firstlanders.

"What woman?" she whispers.

"Here," he says, walking around to the other side of the crate and pointing.

Shaye wobbles around to the opposite end of the box and then sees someone, bound hand and foot, and gagged.

"Jariel," she gasps.

The warrior speaks with urgency. "Think now . . . what you tell His people. You hold life or death for her. . . . God bears witness."

As Shaye kneels down at Jariel's feet, the warrior says, "They are surely coming back," before he disappears into the ferns and deep shadows.

Jariel's eyes open to see Shaye untying the ropes around her feet, then her hands. The expression on her face vacillates between terror and fury. Once her hands are loose, she pulls the gag from her mouth and then shoves Shaye with all the strength she can muster. When Shaye falls back Jariel pulls herself up, teetering, but still preparing to wage hand-to-hand combat.

"You rotten, worthless Genon. How dare you kidnap me!" she says.

In renewed fury, Shaye stands as well. "Why you ungrateful, scheming, liar. If ever there was a princess of untruth it's *you*! I didn't do a thing to you other than untie you just now! I know not how or *why* you were brought here, but if I had even a small basket of sense, I would have left you tied up!"

Even the trees seem to shake with another scream in the distance. It sounds like a woman falling from a great height.

They both shrink to the ground and crawl next to the box without another word.

Shaye grabs Jariel's arm and whispers urgently, "You will not live another hour unless you do exactly what I say. Don't raise your voice, and don't run. There is no time for stupidity. That sound you hear is a *chamosh*—like the one your father had skinned and put on his wall."

A closer scream echoes through the trees and Jariel sucks in a terrified breath before Shaye continues, "You need to know that hunters from my people have come. . . ."

Within a second, Jariel feels a sudden rush of relief. Genon workers can kill the *chamosh* and take her home! But Shaye keeps talking. Jariel tries to focus.

" . . . . *Listen to me!* They may still have knowledge of Command Dialect, so don't speak unless I ask you a question and answer only '*yes*' or '*no*'."

"What do you mean, 'they may still have knowledge of Command Dialect'? Everyone speaks Command—"

Shaye squeezes her arm. "These people are not gatherers from Aegea. Make the exact gesture I do and then stand completely still or they may cut you to pieces and leave you for the beast."

Jariel's mind is spinning. "How can someone not be *from* Aegea?"

Shaye growls in frustration and then whispers, "These people are not gatherers from Aegea! They are the descendants of the Exiles and they are coming! Your life depends on this: Watch me, make the *exact* gesture I do when they come, and then stay completely still and *don't speak.*" Shaye squeezes tighter on Jariel's arm and gives it a tug. "Do you understand me?"

Before Jariel can respond, five men encircle them with spears, stone knives, and shields covered with animal hide. Four of the men have black hair, one has brown hair, but his eyes are golden yellow. Shaye lets go of Jariel, touches two fingers to her heart, then to her lips, and then points to the sky. Terrified, Jariel watches Shaye, then haltingly does the same. The hunters are wearing more clothing and appear better fed than the man Shaye met earlier, and they aren't covered with mud.

Breaking the protocol, one of the men speaks.

Just as it was with mud man, Shaye cannot understand all the words in what should be their common language. The man with brown hair reaches over to touch the fine cloth at the hem of Jariel's dress and she pulls away from him.

"Who are you?" he asks in Genon.

She's almost hyperventilating as her terrified gaze shifts from him to Shaye.

He frowns at Shaye. "Who is this?" he asks. He goes back to inspecting Jariel with a critical eye. "Look at her feet. She has no shoes but her feet are as soft and white as flowers. Is she [unknown words] plateau?" His hand goes to the hilt of a knife stowed near his left hip. "Is she not one of His people? Why is she here? Were you going to kill her?"

Jariel is shaking.

Obviously, the "no talking" rule has changed since the Exile encounters of Shaye's mother and grandfather. And even without understanding all the words, Shaye knows what he's asking. She lowers her gaze and addresses him in their ancient language. "This girl doesn't speak our language . . ." she says, then halts. She begins again. "She is—"

An unseen man in the trees, shouts, "Brothers! *K'mosh* [unknown words] this way!"

The brown-haired hunter moves closer to Shaye and says, "Stay down. Don't leave. We will drive *k'mosh* into [unknown word]. We come back for you."

Within seconds, the men are gone, but Shaye and Jariel can hear shouts and loud noises as the hunters attempt to intimidate the creature and drive it in a specific direction. The beast screams again.

"What were you saying to them? Where are they going?" Jariel asks, breathlessly.

Shaye looks all around before she answers. "They are chasing the *chamosh*." Although Shaye wouldn't have thought it possible, Jariel's face has paled considerably. She finally adds, "They want to know who you are . . . and they're coming back."

Until now, Jariel only thought the Genon had a few forbidden phrases that servants whispered to each other like secret code words. The sound of the hunt is fading. She finally asks, "Will they take me home?"

"No! Have you not heard anything I've said?"

"You just wait! My father will find me and then he will come after you and catch you! And then he'll have you *flogged* before he sends you away from here—maybe to stay in the fort!"

Shaye rolls her eyes. "So what enticement is that for me to help you? Ohh *lah* you are a stupid girl. Just *where* do you think you are?"

Jariel gives a little more attention the trees around her before she offers, "In . . . the woods?"

"What woods? Where are these woods?"

Jariel shrugs. "You know I've never spent any time out on the farms or in the orchards since we were little."

"When was the last time someone saw a living *chamosh* on the plateau? Have you ever seen trees like these on the plateau?"

Jariel's panic is growing by the moment. "What are you saying?"

"What's the last thing you remember before you woke up here?"

"I was sitting at my loom."

"Is that all?"

Jariel squeezes her face up with the effort of trying to recall. "I picked the yellow yarn—no the green . . . and I— wait. A soldier came through the door."

"Someone you know?"

"No. One of the new men. He had small eyes and a crooked nose. He had something in his hand. That's all I can remember."

Shaye looks into Jariel's eyes. "I don't know how they got you out of your house, but I know that soldiers threw you in this box and somehow brought you down to the Great Forest—not just to the edge of it . . . but far into it. I have no idea if they had some sort of plan or if they simply intended to leave you here to die."

"Why would they do such a thing? And if you aren't part of it, why are *you* here?"

"Don't you remember you had me banned from the compound? You were going to trade me to Nob the butcher and his son—and I was running for my life! The box was sitting in a wagon when I met it. I opened the lid and hid in it. The next thing I knew, soldiers dropped something into the box on top of me. It was *you*. And then I couldn't stay awake. And then I was here and these men found us."

"Tell these people my father will be searching for me. Tell them he will pay them well if they take me back."

Shaye groans. "You still don't understand. These are the descendants of the Exiles and your people are their enemies. They won't allow *any* of your people who see them to live." The idea finally seems to be soaking in when Shaye adds, "They want to know who you are and if you are one of His own, a Genon."

Jariel leans toward Shaye and begs, "Just take me back. I'm sorry if I ever hurt you. I swear I'll never tell a soul I saw them. Take me back right now while they chase the beast."

"Even if I knew the way, they would overtake us long before we reached the edge of the forest and the road. Right now, they don't know who you are, but if we run, that will be the same as telling them you are not one of our people. If they knew who your father was . . ." As Shaye speaks angry tears begin to simmer in her eyes until they boil over and pour down her cheeks. She wipes her face with the back of her hand. "You have *ruined* my life and rejoiced in all my sorrows . . . you gladly cast me out of your house—but I must *lie* to help *you*, to save you?"

Jariel realizes it's getting difficult to breathe. The tops of the trees may be blowing, but there is no movement of air near the forest floor. Never before has she experienced air this close, hot, or musty. The smell of all the rotting leaves is almost too much for her. Her perspective of the whole world is shaken, and whether it is the shock of all these revelations or some toxin in the rising mist, or something else she doesn't know, but it feels almost as if her mind is melting away. She says, "My neck is burning," before her eyes roll back and she slumps sideways onto the forest floor.

Shaye is horrified. She quickly scoots closer and puts her face near Jariel's. *Is she still breathing? Yes.* "Oh God of all things," she whispers, "if you don't save us, we shall surely die."

Not far away, the *k'mosh* lets out a last, long scream when it is pierced by a multitude of spears. At the sound, Shaye leans over Jariel.

When silence once again engulfs the forest, Shaye sits up and tries to force her mind to think. In a matter of moments the hunters will return and she must have some plausible answers concerning Jariel and their shared predicament.

Shaye looks up when two of the Exiles return. One of them is the hostile brown-haired man.

"What happened with this woman?" he asks, pointing at Jariel.

"I do not know. She may have . . ." Shaye realizes she doesn't know a Genon word for *faint*. "Forgive me, brother, I have spoken Genon all my life, but I do not know all your words. She . . . ." Shaye wonders, *Does the Genon language even have such a word?* She tries to explain it. "The girl went to sleep—but very fast. Not real sleep. Maybe very frightened or sick. She said her neck hurt."

The darker-haired man walks over to Jariel and nudges her with his foot. He bends down and moves her hair, and then looks up at his friend as he points to Jariel's neck. "*Eh eh.* [Unknown word] met her here."

Shaye looks at the two men, not comprehending.

"*Uhhhhhhh,*" brown hair says as he searches for the memory of a word. "*Speeder*?"

He can see she doesn't understand, so he flattens out one hand and then splays out the fingers on his other hand and moves it as if it's walking on top of his palm.

Shaye's mouth falls open and she speaks in Command Dialect without thinking. "A *spider*?" There are many deadly things in the forest. "Will she die?" she asks in Genon.

"Do you *wish* this?" the man with dark hair asks. "I think you don't like this woman."

Both men are staring at her.

Shaye is stunned by their words. "The Maker gives all life, He tells us to respect *all* people, does he not? Can't you help her?"

The two men exchange glances. Dark hair looks back at Jariel and tilts his head while he considers it, then gets up. "I find [unknown]. You wait here."

Brown hair is agitated and revisits his earlier line of questioning. "Who is this woman?"

Shaye tries to think of any Genon family tree where some of the lines ended. "Her name is Jariel."

"What kind of name is this?"

"She is of the clan of Nashe, but her mother . . . was the last of her line and she became a second woman. She gave the baby to a wealthy house. They named her Jariel and she was like . . . a *pet* to them. She made good cloth for them—look at her hands, they know how to work."

Brown hair squats, lifts up one of Jariel's hands, and nods.

"She is a stupid girl," Shaye says. "She doesn't know our ways or language."

"How do you know her?"

"I knew her when she was small, but we are not friends now." Shaye's mind is gliding over ideas at the speed of light. "The people of the wealthy house died . . . and she was cast out by their other kin."

The brown-haired man scowls, then scans Jariel's bony frame. "She doesn't eat good for a long time. She has no man?"

Shaye's eyebrows fly upward. This is an unexpected turn in the conversation. "No."

"And you? You have a man?"

She looks away and shakes her head to indicate "no." She doesn't think she can manage to manufacture any more details at present and hopes the interrogation will stop soon.

"Why did they send you in the big basket down the mountain on the strong rope?"

"What basket? What rope?" At least she can be completely honest about not knowing this part of the story. She shrugs and says, "I do not know about a basket or a rope. I hid in the box to get away from the house where I was mistreated. I thought the soldiers were taking the box to town and hid in it. After I was in there, they threw *her* into the box . . . and there was a smoke or a smell that made me sleep. . . ."

She stops talking when he leans over the crate and sniffs, then pulls out a large rag and smells it before throwing it to the ground. "Medicine craft," he says. "Why did soldiers do this to her?"

A picture of the warrior who first appeared to her pops into her mind. It was as if he knew more than his fellow exiles . . . as if he knew Jariel wasn't Genon, yet was pleading for her life. Shaye decides to omit her conversation with him. She says, "I woke up in the box. Of a truth, I don't know why they put her in the box. I don't how we got down from the mountain, or how we got so far into the forest . . . but I think that if the ones who brought us here find us, they will harm us both."

"No need to think of this," the man with brown hair says, "Soldiers carry the box here but then they run from *k'mosh*.

Big mistake—*k'mosh* like to chase." He nods and smiles at Shaye before adding, "You were not here to remind the *k'mosh* that the Maker gives all life, so she killed them."

It takes her a moment to realize he finds this amusing. She doesn't know what to say.

"You know this place?" he asks.

"No. I am of the line of Zim—my grandfather was a gatherer for many years and trained my mother . . . and she told me much about the forest. I see the trees here are tall and far apart so I know we are not near the edge of the jungle."

He squints and tightens his lips as he nods.

His companion returns—not a moment too soon as far as Shaye is concerned. With him is an elderly man who wasn't one of the group she saw earlier. His hair and beard are not as white as Old Menoh's, but his beard is long. He's carrying a leaf in his left hand, the way a servant would carry a small plate away from a table. The three men have a brief, rapid-fire discussion that Shaye can only partially understand, but it revolves around discerning why Shaye and Jariel are here (and she clearly hears the names "Nashe" and "Zim"). In the conversation she also hears "dark medicine craft" when the old man smells the rag. Then brown hair points at Jariel and says "on her neck" before the elderly man walks to Jariel's side. He may be old, but she can see he's still quite limber because, when he squats down, his bottom is just above the ground and his knees are level with his ears—it's almost as if he's a leathery kin to a frog.

Certainly, she thinks, *his parents would have been among the original exiles.*

He glances over at Shaye and hands the leaf to her before he pulls a flint knife from a sheath at his right hip. After making a small cut near the bite mark on Jariel's neck, he takes the leaf from Shaye and scrapes a glob of translucent green goo from the leaf onto Jariel's neck. He seems to be studying his work, moving his head back and forth, as he smears the substance around on the bite. As a final touch, he presses the leaf on top of the goo. While he's busy, other men from the group straggle in and they watch.

"We will see," he says to Shaye. "Before night time, I think she will wake, maybe vomit, but she is stronger than she looks." He stands and says to his fellow hunters, "The *k'mosh* rids us of soldiers and gives us to two women, eh? Maybe this was her penance for what she took from us."

They all nod and say, "Just so."

Shaye doesn't know what to make of all this. She remains silent.

The old man gives instructions to one of the men in the group. "Tooth, the sun sets in two hours. You and Loash run ahead to the widow tree and make a place for us to stay the night. You two," he says pointing at Brown hair and another man, "go and make [unknown word] to carry the girl. The rest of us will bury the *k'mosh*. More soldiers may come looking for their brothers and they must think the animal still lives and hunts. They cannot know that we killed her." He glances over at Jariel and then at Shaye before he says, "We leave nothing that will bear witness of us."

Because he speaks more slowly and deliberately than the others, Shaye can understand nearly all of what he says. He leans over and looks into the crate. "It is sad but we must leave most of these things here or they might be missed. Perhaps we can take two of the long knives," he says, pointing to the machetes in the box. "But the rest is for the forest to reclaim."

"What about *us*?" Shaye asks.

He gives her a semi-toothless grin. "Do not worry. If soldiers come, they will think the *k'mosh* killed both of you. We will take you," he says, spreading his arms widely, "where His own walk free."

When freedom in the Great Forest was an imaginary quest for her, it was framed in the golden light of a girl's mind, it was an escape from bondage, a fantasy where lasting joy would be the outcome. This, on the other hand, had already involved running, hiding, sheer terror, lying, killer creatures, bloodshed . . . and bringing along the one person in the world she most wanted to leave behind. No one here requested that they tag along, it was *assumed* they would go.

All of the men peer into the crate and one of them hops over the edge and pulls out two of the machetes. Shaye's eyes sweep over the box that carried her here and her hand brushes over the insignia of the colonel on the side of it.

There is no way of shrinking back from this, no way of warning the Exiles about who will be hunting for Jariel soon—not unless she wants to be responsible for the girl's death. For the Exiles to succeed in slipping away with them, everyone who has ever known her and Jariel must think they are dead. Shaye cannot allow herself to dwell on this thought.

Surely there will be more questions. But, at least for now, they seem satisfied. "How far is your home from here?" she asks.

"Oh it is many days, daughter—even longer since today we must carry this girl. But do not worry, we alone know the way."

Within an hour, the preparations are made, evidence is erased, and the slain animal is buried in a pit beneath the compost of the forest floor to be picked clean by ants and other insects within days. The crate will be left open, the way they found it. The men have bruised the leaves of plants for Shaye to rub on herself and on Jariel to help repel flying insects.

Shaye notes that Jariel has more color in her face when they load her onto the litter and begin carrying her through the jungle. Several of the men scatter again, some to scout, some to watch behind.

When everyone is ready, Shaye gives one last look in the direction where the crate was carried through the trees before she picks up her bag and slings it over her shoulder. She is frightened and she doesn't know what the coming days may bring. She doesn't know what the future holds for her or for Jariel. Once they are walking in single file, she puts one hand on her belly then lifts the other hand upward. *Perhaps the Maker has brought me here so you can be free, my child.*

End of Book 1

Thanks for reading my book! If you enjoyed it, would you take a moment to write a review for your favorite retailer? Thanks again!
Terry L. Craig

This story will be continued in:
Through the Land of Cloud and Leaf,
Book 2 in the *Scions of the Aegean C* series

About the Author

Terry L. Craig

Born in the Southwest, Terry has lived all over the US and spent many years living in the Caribbean. She is a people-watcher and a comparative thinker who is fascinated with words, art, and ideas. She has a passion to share spiritual life in a way that allows the reader to weigh the values of different ideologies from a non-threatening perspective.

Terry is a follower of Jesus, a wife, mom, and grandma who currently resides in North Carolina with her professional pilot husband (her lifetime love) Bill. The development of true friendships and healthy community life are high on her list of life's essentials.

You can learn more about/connect with Terry L. Craig at:

www.terrylcraig.com

Or her author pages at:

Wild Flower Press, Inc.: www.wildflowerpress.biz
Amazon.com
Goodreads
Google+
Smashwords
Terry L. Craig on Facebook

Other Books by Terry L. Craig

**This is Book 1 of the series *SCIONS of the Aegean C.*
Book 2 is *Through the Land of Cloud and Leaf.***
You can check in at www.wildflowerpress.biz, on CreateSpace,
Amazon.com or other retailers for updates on the series.

She also authored the ***Fellowship of the Mystery*** trilogy,

**GATEKEEPER
SOJOURNER
SWORDSMAN**

(Terry says that nearly every month that goes by, she is
amazed to see technologies and events—written into
the Fellowship of the Mystery trilogy YEARS ago—
unfolding before her eyes.)

And an Apologetic study entitled,

What Mama Never Told You about the Afterlife

Terry's books are also available as *eBooks* through
Amazon.com, Smashwords, Apple iStore, Barnes & Noble and
many fine retailers.

Other Books by this Publisher

Wild Flower Press, Inc. also publishes

Passport for the Journey, 21 Day Challenge
by Tonya J. Brown
- A Devotional / Journal for use by individuals or groups

The *Within the Walls* trilogy
by Stephanie Bennett
- *Within the Walls,*
- *Breaking the Silence*
- *The Poet's Treasure*

    Futuristic novels chronicling the life of Emilya, a virtual travel agent in 2070

The *Fellowship of the Mystery* trilogy
by Terry L. Craig
- *GATEKEEPER*
- *SOJOURNER*
- *SWORDSMAN*

Apocalyptic fiction from an uncommon perspective

www.ingramcontent.com/pod-product-compliance
Lightning Source LLC
Chambersburg PA
CBHW060922180626
46817CB00004B/1357